I0598919

The Lark

A Novel

Dana Glossbrenner

BOLDFACE BOOKS • LUBBOCK, TEXAS

WWW.BOLDFACEBOOKS.COM

The Lark: A Novel
Copyright © 2016 Dana Glossbrenner

Published by Boldface Books, an imprint of Bookadelphia
www.BoldfaceBooks.com
www.Bookadelphia.com

This book was set in the Palatino Linotype and Ribbon typefaces for Adobe InDesign CC on the Macintosh computer.

ISBN 978-1-935619-16-1 (trade paperback)
ISBN 978-1-935619-17-8 (ebook)

www.danagloss.com
dgloss@suddenlink.net

Contents

Prologue	GOOD-TIME CHARLEY	1
1	Burned and Burning	3
2	Dog Days Memories	23
3	No Way	33
4	The Lark	51
5	Stalked?	60
6	Relations	74
7	Family Secrets	83
8	April	97
9	Belonging	105
10	New Dawning	109
11	New Impressions	115
12	Running	128
13	Black-Sheep Nephew	135
14	Goodbye to The No	139
15	Helluva Celebration	150
16	An Interrupted Picnic	170
17	All in a Name	187
18	Truth in Gossip and DNA	193
19	Face-to-Face Encounters	201
20	Summer Heat	214
21	Eastbound	220
22	Hezekiah	231
23	Finding Ann	239
24	In-Laws and Outlaws	245
25	Hawaiian Print	258
	ACKNOWLEDGMENTS	265

for my children

Prologue
Good-time Charley

CHARLEY BRISTOW PACED his small living room. Celibacy was burning a hole in his pants. The rays of late afternoon Texas sun streaming through his window overheated the apartment and heightened his awareness of the passing day. He swiped the list of contacts on his phone, watching the names scroll by. Finally, he came to one that calmed his nerves.

Wayne.

Charley stopped pacing as he heard the call go through. Over the irregular hum of the underpowered window unit, he could hear the digital ring. Once, twice, three times. He straightened the collar of his western shirt in the reflection of a framed picture on the wall and adjusted a tuft of hair. "Come on, pick up, pick up," he urged.

"Hey, buddy, what's up?" The voice answered at last.

Charley felt a little guilty at what he was about to ask. He hadn't called since his older friend had brought a trailer into town and helped him move out of the rent house, a failed experiment Charley had hoped would change his outlook on life but instead flopped miserably. He didn't have a big brother, father, or uncle—no family that could help him move—and he sure couldn't afford to pay professionals. Still, this favor was small in comparison.

"I have a win-win proposal, Wayne." Charley's relief that Wayne answered his call brought out his most enthusiastic tone.

Very persuasive, he thought.

"And what would that be?" A tinge of suspicion hovered in Wayne's voice.

"How about you get off your butt and get to town for some drinks at Hopper's? Ladies' Night. You need to get back on the pony, you know. There might be someone there who's dying to meet you."

"Why are you suddenly so interested in my love life?" Forty years old and five years out from his own last marital disaster, Wayne probably didn't consider himself in a league with Charley—but he was no monk either.

"My car quit on me, to tell the truth."

"Oh, and you need a ride. *Now* I get it. Well, I've spent the day on a dozer and I'm showered and settled in on the front porch with a cat in my lap and a glass of iced tea on the side table. Besides, I'm taking a load of cattle to auction early tomorrow, so I'd better pass."

"Oh, come on!" Charley's disappointment surged. "We don't have to stay all night. Candy's in AA now, so I wouldn't feel right asking him, and I'd call Jarod, but Sue won't let him go out on a week night. And I've pestered the ladies at work too much already."

"Why don't you go to a singles' Sunday school class?"

"Real funny, Wayne."

"Sounds to me like your loneliness meter is pegged."

"I only want to dance a few songs with someone sweet and pretty," Charley said. He figured he was about recovered from his latest divorce and deserved a break. Boredom shadowed him now, a greater threat to him than the risk of another entanglement. He grinned at his reflection and checked his teeth.

Wayne let out a sigh and seemed to relent. "I guess you need a night out, and it's my turn to provide the transportation. I'll be right over."

1

Burned and Burning

TUESDAY NIGHTS WERE SLOW at Hopper's, so to pick up the pace of business, female patrons were offered watery drinks for three dollars. That and the live band brought in a reasonable crowd, even on a weeknight when the long spring evenings of April enticed more settled types to the Little League park to dine on hot dogs, Cokes, and funnel cakes while they watched their children, grandchildren, nieces, nephews, and cousins play baseball.

As soon as they stepped inside the club, Charley saw Dick Raney wave Wayne over to the bar for a neighborly chat. Charley headed for his favorite table. No stranger at the nightclub, he nodded to the guys at the pool tables. He saw the familiar look on their faces as they concentrated on their games, their body language telling him they weren't in the mood to take a trouncing from him. He smiled as he remembered the old regulars who'd taught him to play at Hopper's and the VFW.

Mitch Teague, still haunting the tables, sat on a bar stool in a corner, arms crossed, watching a game. He lifted a hand to Charley. With a big, brushy mustache and bristly whiskers under a crooked nose that had been broken a few times, he looked rough. The scar over his left eyebrow hadn't faded over the years, either. A smashed-up straw western hat he seldom removed, broken-down western boots, raggedy jeans, and a leather vest over his T-shirt of the day completed his ensemble. Since the age of twelve, Charley had considered Mitch a mentor in the game of pool—and of life.

He nodded to his role model.

"How's yer mom these days?" Mitch asked.

"Hard to tell. You know she's not a big talker."

"I remember she used to be. Friendliest waitress in three counties."

"Yeah, she got lots of practice between working here and the VFW."

"She don't get out much now, does she?"

"Nope. Health issues, I guess." Falling back on the mention of a woman's physical condition tended to divert further questions.

"Well, I'm glad *you* still come around."

"It's good to see you, too, Mitch," Charley said, clapping him on the back. It was a good thing people had never been too rule-conscious in Sulfur Gap, so that even when he was under age, Charley had been able to go with his mother for her daytime shifts and hang around afterwards while she caught up on her own drinking. Charley had better-quality supervision at the bars, playing pool with guys like Mitch, than he would've had staying home with his mother's boyfriend of the moment.

As he turned to walk away, one of the younger pool-playing regulars—Wes Farley, sharpening his skills at being a jerk—picked the moment to be a smartass. Overhearing Charley's conversation with Mitch, he picked at a sensitive topic. "Last time I seen yer ma, she was drivin' through the Party Warehouse gettin' that van loaded with booze. I wonder how she affords that on her disability check?"

Conscious of the audience of pool players, who had frozen in disbelief at the sniping remark, Charley took a deep breath and turned slowly to stare unblinking at his tormentor. "Well, Wes, not that it's any of your business, but everyone's different on how they field life's curve balls."

Farley backpedaled. "Now, Charley, I didn't mean nothin' by that. I was just curious."

Charley gazed at him for a few seconds while the shorter man squirmed. "Forget it, Wes. Just give some thought before you talk about people's mothers."

Leaving the players behind for now and aiming his stride toward his usual table, Charley felt admiring glances from the women. He wore his best-fitting jeans with his most comfortable boots for dancing. A head taller than most of the other men, he stood out. Running his fingers through his blond thatch, he set his hat in an empty chair. As he settled down, he waved to Dorothy, owner of the salon where he'd been cutting hair since he was eighteen. She gave him a casual nod but kept her perch at the bar. They'd spent the day together at work, and she would maintain a distance, knowing that Charley was checking out the possibilities in the flock of sweet young things who might appear tonight.

Charley could give pointers on meeting women. He liked the table on the way to the women's restroom. Interesting traffic might pass by all night. The women frequenting the trail to the bathroom were usually the drunkest, and the drunkest often carried the most baggage—but, oh, how he loved to help them. They were so appreciative . . . at first.

The trickle of women coming in so far tonight had disappointed him, though. Then he spied one of his salon clients coming over to say hello.

"Hey, Charley," she said. "Look how good my haircut's holding."

Charley stood to hug her. "You're my best advertisement, Joann. Keep looking that good and I won't run out of customers."

Some guys he hadn't seen before sat a few tables over, probably some oil-field workers new to the area, judging from their heftiness and sun-baked skin. If he didn't find a steady dance partner tonight, he might hustle a pool game with them. But Charley felt honor-bound to never let his unwitting opponents lose much money. Sometimes he even let them win.

The jukebox played as the band began to check equipment and tune up. Live bands were scarce around Sulfur Gap. He still loved the jukebox oldie goldies he'd learned to dance to—Charley Pride, Ray Price, Willie Nelson, Tammy Wynette. The oldies stirred echoes of loneliness, but it was a feeling he'd become accustomed to, like a familiar ghost that hollowed him out and sent him looking for a hand to hold, if only briefly.

Charley's skill set had been honed, thanks to being a fixture at the nightclubs for a good portion of his twenty-five years. Even the old veteran Sheriff Sparks, and his son who succeeded him, hadn't objected to Charley's hanging out at Hopper's and the VFW as a teenager. Their minds rested easy, because he could be counted on to observe the law. No underage drinking, no wrecks or fights. No stumbling onto the highway and getting flattened by a speeding giant SUV. And he didn't try to bring his less reliable friends.

Wayne finished visiting with his rancher neighbor and joined Charley.

"What's up with Mr. Raney?" Charley asked.

"Oh, we're working on a deal to get some shooters out in choppers to see if they can do something about our coyote problem. They're so thick, they howl right under our windows at night and carry off our cats."

"How come there're so many?"

"After Chance Marshall died, his heirs donated his section of land to a conservation group who let it go back to nature. So now it's a den for the varmints, including bobcats and hogs. The shooters need to bag about seventy coyotes and we'll all be happy."

"Good luck with that."

"No luck needed. Only good strategy."

Wayne and Charley sipped their longnecks and looked over the gathering crowd.

"Seen anyone to bat your baby blues at yet, Charley?" Wayne teased.

"Nope."

Charley was alert, though. He felt optimistic about the odds of spotting a dance partner, especially since the odds of his mother showing up were absolutely nil. April Bristow Erwin couldn't deflate his mood with her presence, since she now weighed close to three hundred pounds and stayed in her trailer house these days, doing her best to flatten the couch. The change in his mother had been gradual, he remembered. A slow slide toward isolation. Now her best friends were her bags of potato chips, cartons of ice cream, bottles of gin, and packs of cigarettes. Charley had long ago resigned from his battle to cheer her up. Sadness crept into his thoughts for a moment, but he had learned to put her into a box in his mind and get on with the good times. And tonight would be one of those good times, if he had anything to say about it.

Charley's initial dance-partner selection required only that a girl look good in her jeans. But beyond that he used a little test that no one knew about. If his dance partner's hands were extra-dry when he held them, he knew she didn't stop to wash after peeing—this little hygienic detail turned him off. A woman who kept her hands clean must be decent in other ways, he reasoned. Damp hands from the bathroom's weak-winded hand blower meant a clean person—his only standard for screening those he selected for further dancing. He could compensate for a partner's lack of rhythm and coordination. Heck, they could learn a little and become less self-conscious by dancing a few rounds with him.

He thought back to that first dance with Vicki, wife number one. He had noted her damp hands—moist and cool in a good, just-washed way—so she earned a thousand points right there. They married within three weeks. She worked as a secretary for an oil company but was laid off two months after the impromptu wedding. After that, she lay around and shopped the QVC channel with his credit card. Empty beer cans on the end table, greasy film on countertops, fuzzy deposits on window sills, and random dirty laundry on the floor accumulated in their apartment.

One day, Charley came home after long hours of cutting hair and began picking up. As he carried a pile of dirty laundry to the bathroom hamper, he realized the boxer shorts slipping off the top of the pile and almost brushing his chin weren't his. And they sure as hell weren't Vicki's. That was the beginning of the end of a very short marriage.

Snap out of it, he told himself. This was *not* the way to ensure a fun evening.

Charley and Wayne contented themselves watching the dancers. The band lured a good crowd to the dance floor with their opener—"Take Me Out to the Dance Hall." Very fitting, Charley thought, impressed at how well this band played Pat Green. He wondered where they were from.

Despite himself, his mind wandered back to Vicki. He'd wrested a tearful confession from her. She had admitted sleeping with a neighbor who was also laid off. She said since Charley had let her down, that he wasn't everything she'd hoped he'd be, she'd looked for love elsewhere. So he bid her *adios*.

He tried to do the right thing. He paid for Vicki to stay at the Navaho Inn for two weeks and shelled out for all divorce expenses. So much for his damp-hand test, he had thought at the time. But still, a man needs some kind of standard besides the usual ones of youth and beauty assessed in the dim lights of the club.

One of the oil-field workers twirled his dance partner past the table. A nice-looking blonde. Charley had seen her make a beeline for her man when her eyes adjusted inside the club, so she was obviously already taken. Good. She reminded him of Joyce, his second and last ex-wife. With a slight shudder, he did his best to set aside thoughts of that failure for the moment, just as he finally had the intrusion of the Vicki debacle into his head.

The rat-a-tat of the drum helped bring him back to Hopper's. The band launched into "Bad Moon Risin'" as the swing dancers swept onto the floor. Wayne gave Charley a thumbs-up to let him know he had no regrets about coming out tonight. Neither of them expected this level of entertainment.

But the snare drum reminded Charley of something else. Joyce's gun. And he'd thought Vicki was hard to live with.

So tonight, twice-divorced Charley and his friend Wayne sat at Charley's favorite table along the path to the women's restroom, where he hoped to spot a chance to at least flirt with a pretty face.

The band was good and the beer was cold. The musicians looked like a bunch of old farts, except for the good-looking woman drummer. Charley again sized up the girls at the bar. All the butts on the bar stools looked familiar, as well as the faces that went with them. Everyone fell into one of two categories—girls he wouldn't touch with a ten-foot pole—and those he couldn't.

Wayne interrupted his survey. "When are you making a run to Shreveport?"

"I'd like to be playing cards right now, but without a car I'm flat grounded." Then Charley had an idea. "If I could get a ride to Abilene, I can take the bus from there. You headed that way soon?"

"Well, yeah. I need to drive up to see my accountant on Friday," Wayne said.

Charley knew Wayne was puzzled at the idea that fun and fulfillment could be found in riding a Greyhound bus for five hundred miles to spend forty-eight hours in the casinos.

"I'll wait for you to finish your business in Abilene and you and I could go from there," Charley offered. If Wayne would only try it, he'd like it, he just knew.

"I gamble enough by ranching. Not to mention, I spent the worst evening of my life over at Jarod and Sue's when they hosted that Yahtzee party that time."

"That's not a fair comparison," Charley argued.

"I know. I'm saying . . . I don't like games—holding cards and throwing dice. It goes against my grain."

"You would like the slots."

"Nope. Waste of money."

"You might get lucky and win big. Then you'd be hooked."

"No thank you," he responded emphatically. "Betting money on luck and trying to get dealt a royal flush makes about as much sense to me as trying to make water run uphill or betting that the path of a tornado stays away from the barn. It's like trying to make it rain but not hail. . . . Nope. Won't work." Wayne wouldn't budge.

Charley shook his head at Wayne and smiled, enjoying how well his friend took the bait. He knew full well what Wayne would say when he asked him to go gambling, but he always thought it was worth a try. He enjoyed the anti-vice speeches, too.

Wayne warmed to the topic. "Making deals with the luck goddess makes no sense to me," he continued. "You can pray, but why should God favor you over your next-door neighbor or the one in the next county?"

Charley tried to enlighten his less worldly companion. "I'm not as philosophical as you, Wayne. You're missing the fun. Gambling is an international sport. Poker's poker, wherever you play—Texas Hold 'Em, Flop Poker. Blackjack's a good game, too. Guess I'm your basic card player. Then if I lose too much and can't buy into a game, I go play slots and usually win enough to get back in. Before I know it, the night's gone."

Charley saw Wayne's look, indicating that his bullshit detector was fully activated. He was Wayne's most adventurous friend, and he knew his escapades always kept him entertained. Charley's simple plans became diabolically convoluted, but Wayne enjoyed hearing about them.

Charley shifted the subject. "I've got a friend named Danielle in Shreveport. I can stay with her now."

"Oh?" Wayne lifted an eyebrow.

"Yeah. Met her on my last trip out."

Charley had set his hook, so he waited while Wayne said hello to Mattie Gilstrap, another neighbor, who'd stopped by their table on her way to the john.

As she walked away, Wayne said, "She sure looks better fixed up for Ladies' Night than she does drivin' her tractor in hot weather wearin' nothing but her bra and shorts. Anyway, you were telling about Danielle."

Charley rolled his toothpick to the other side of his mouth and drew on his longneck.

"Yeah. You probably remember Jarod had to go to an old aunt's funeral in East Texas last month. I made the drive with him so we could go over the Louisiana border and put in a little time in the casinos."

"Yeah, I remember that."

"Well, I drop in at the bar to take a break and see these two honeys sitting over at a table. One of 'em is wearin' her blackjack dealer's uniform. I'm about ready to forget my no-women rule for either one."

Wayne looked incredulous. "Where was Jarod?"

"Oh, he made a run to the men's room, and I spotted the two lovely ladies."

"Looked like fair game, huh?"

"So I introduce myself and ask if I can join them. They look at each other and grin and say 'Sure enough. Pull out a chair.' So we're making inroads in the conversation. The one with the black-jack uniform, turns out she's a barber, so we have some common ground there, but the other one, Julie, is even cuter, so I'm homing in on her."

"Yeah?"

"The table service is slow, so Danielle—she's the barber—goes over to the bar for another round for us, and I see my chance. I ask Julie for her phone number, and she laughs. You know I'm not easily offended, so I say, 'What's the joke?' She's a nice person, so she gets all sweet and says, 'Sorry, but I'm taken.'"

"Since when has that ever stopped you hitting on someone?" Wayne asked.

"I'm getting to that. I say, 'How *taken* are you?' Right then, Danielle comes back with our drinks, sets the tray on the table, and plops down in her chair. She reaches over and *grabs* my nose between the knuckles of her fingers and says, 'She's taken with *me*, cowboy.'"

"What?" Wayne looked confused, but knowing soon crossed his face, and laughter overtook him. He whooped so loud, people on the dance floor turned their heads to look. He wiped the tears from his eyes and caught his breath. "So you were hitting on a couple of lesbians."

"Yes, but they were very *nice* lesbians." Charley kept a straight face.

"But she grabbed your nose! I'm expecting to hear now how she beat the crap out of you."

"No. No fighting, only nose-grabbing. I was kinda shocked.

I've been slapped, punched, kicked, and bitten, but no one ever did that. It struck me funny, so I couldn't help it. I started laughing."

Wayne pounded the table with his fist and laughed some more. He leaned forward. "But where was Jarod? Surely not on the can while all this was going on?"

"Oh, he saw us in the bar, but he thought I was cooking up one of those three-ways, like I would even consider that, so he headed back out to the casino floor. Sue would be able to tell if he came within twenty yards of a deal like that. He kept his conscience clean so she wouldn't sniff any mischief. "

"Then what?" Wayne's voice still cracked with suppressed laughter.

"Danielle and Julie decide it's funny, too, so they start laughing their asses off. I tell them I've been turned down before but never had my oxygen supply cut off. I apologize. And they both apologize, too. They say they should have told me sooner, but they were enjoying the company."

"Very considerate of them," Wayne said.

"I actually got both their numbers, and Danielle invited me to stay at their place if I needed to, so it looks like I made some friends anyway, even if my ego did take a harpooning."

"So this Danielle's a barber, too?"

"Yeah. She wants to open her own shop someday, like I do. Good business head. I could get some pointers."

"Did you tell Jarod?"

"Oh, hell no. I had to bite my tongue all the way home. Jarod would tell Sue, and then it would get back to Dorothy, and I'd never hear the end of it from that wacko bunch at the salon."

"Why don't you go to Ruidoso to gamble?" Wayne asked. "Land of Enchantment, and all that."

"Oh, I plan to someday. People I know always liked

Shreveport, so I go along with them. And now I have a standing invitation to stay at Danielle and Julie's. I guess the trip up to the New Mexico mountains would be more relaxing than joining the eighteen-wheelers on the interstate. But I won't be driving myself anywhere for a while until I find another car."

"I'll take you as far as Abilene," Wayne promised.

The band took a break. Charley stared. Was the drummer lady the new barber-and-beauty-supply rep who recently made a delivery to the shop? Hard to tell in the light of the club, with her wearing a western hat. She was a tall woman, built like a basket-ball player. She swayed toward the ladies' room, right his way. She nodded, and Charley flashed his best smile. Wayne even gave her a slight wave.

After her bathroom break, she stopped by his table.

"Hey, there," she said, nodding to both men. Then to Charley, "I know you. You're that famous hair stylist from the Wild Hare Salon."

"Yeah." The closer inspection caused Charley to lose his enthusiasm. She was too old. "How'd you know?"

"I recently moved to town and bought the barber and beauty supply business. Delivered some boxes to y'all at the salon and saw you there, cuttin' hair."

This lady was closer to his mother's age than his, he guessed — not a stretch since his mother'd had him at seventeen.

He stared. Rude. He knew he was being rude. He wouldn't admit out loud that he recognized her as well.

Wayne broke the silence. "I'm Wayne, and this here is Charley," he said, holding out his hand. She shook their hands. Charley noted that hers were damp, and he approved, but he sure hadn't come to check out the mature crowd.

"I'm Lou Trainer. Mind if I join you during the break?"

"Please, have a seat," said Wayne, half rising. Charley

frowned as Wayne reached to pull out a chair for her. This older woman could kill any chances of his meeting someone, *anyone,* should the girl of his dreams materialize tonight. Charley's fleeting concern about Wayne's love life skipped his mind.

Lou sat down and pushed her hat back, took a swig of beer, and folded long, tan forearms on the table, fencing in her bottle. The jukebox played a break-time medley of Willie Nelson songs. Willie sang about the red-headed stranger who shot the blonde woman for touching his horse.

A brand-new, petite brunette in tight jeans sauntered to the restroom. Charley steamed. The cute brunette must have been sitting at the dark end of the bar, where she'd escaped his notice. Now she would think he was with Lou. A fresh prospect down the drain, for now anyway.

Lou said, "I hope I'm not intruding."

"Not at all!" Wayne beamed at her across the table. "You're a pretty good drummer. Played long?"

"Practically all my life. My dad was professional and toured with some of the top country bands, so I learned early and kept at it. Music is only a hobby, though. I would have needed to spend my life in Nashville or out on the road if I wanted to be a Dixie Chick type."

"Must be nice to have the choice at one time," Charley commented. He forgot his resolve to stay out of the conversation. He wasn't good at giving anyone the silent treatment, even some older lady coming on to him.

At least she'd have to get back to work behind the drums sooner or later.

She grinned at him. "I'm not out of the game yet. Musicians who keep in form have lots of choices as long as they're not too ambitious. Playing for pure fun is always an option."

"Some people do have long and varied careers," Wayne observed. "Look at Johnny Cash. Even Bob Dylan still gets some play. He's the one that said to never trust anyone over thirty, but I wonder what he thinks now."

"Probably, 'Oops, I woke up and now I'm an old fart,'" Charley added, taking a swig from his bottle.

"Yeah, now most people below thirty don't know who the hell Bob Dylan is."

"Ah, but he still has choices," Lou said.

"Yeah," Charley said. "Which gold-digging, fame-seeking vixen shall I do tonight?"

"You apparently haven't kept up with his religious philosophy," Lou said. "Don't stereotype him because he's a famous musician and product of the sixties. He's not Mick Jagger."

"Whoa! I guess I better be careful what I say around you."

"Not at all," Lou said. She patted Charley's hand, and he flinched. "I'm too blunt, honey."

Charley sized her up as one of those women from the Deep South, always calling strangers "honey."

Willie Nelson sang about losing his heart all over again to his former love when he passed her on the street. Charley thought wistfully about what a powerful statement that was—to have your heart falling at someone's feet.

Lou said, "I know you from further back than seein' you at the salon last week."

"Have I cut your hair?"

"You did."

"When?"

"Three years ago—in '05—I came to Sulfur Gap on some family business and heard about you, so I stopped by—a walk-in. I'd've come back and been a regular, except I got a job working pipeline construction and repair in Alaska. Just got back." She gazed at him and took a drink as Willie sang "Can I Sleep in Your

Arms Tonight?" Charley held up his empty longneck at the waitress, then surveyed Lou with admiration in spite of himself.

"You worked pipelines? In Alaska?"

"Yeah. And I see you're looking at my arms. Driving heavy
equipment doesn't take huge muscles. It helps to be in shape, but
bench-pressing your weight isn't required."

Charley concentrated on holding his mouth shut. He and
Lou could actually wind up being friends. He wouldn't mind that
a bit, as long as she didn't get the wrong idea.

Lou went on. "There weren't any other women on my crew,
but we all got along fine once the guys got to know me. They
found out I was okay—no threat to physical safety on the job,
and I didn't stir up rivalry or play damsel in distress to get out of
work. I was engaged at the time and wasn't looking for a beau, so
that helped."

Charley wondered about living arrangements. Did they
share Quonset huts out on the job site?

Wayne said, "That must have been hard, working with all
those oil-field types."

"Not as much as it would have been ten or twenty years ago.
I think men have done more changing for the good than women
have. Men are more accommodating, and women are more de-
manding. But don't get me started on the pros and cons of sexual
politics."

"You don't look that tough," Charley said.

"I'm not. But I've never listened to people telling me I
couldn't do something because I'm female. Like being a drummer. And, with the right power tools, even *I* can get most jobs
done." She smiled.

The guitar tuning up signaled the end of the band's break.
Wayne slapped the table with an open palm. "Well, I'm going to
have to run on home. Nice to meet you, Lou. Will the band be

playing here again soon?"

"Yes, we will be. Brady Hopper wants us to play every chance he can get us, so you come back and see us."

"Great! I'll look forward to that." Wayne shook Lou's hand and turned to Charley. "You coming, Charles?"

Before Charley found time to think, Lou said, "Charley, if you want to stay here another hour or so, we'll wind up our set and I can drop you home. They close early since it's a weeknight."

Charley was well aware of Hopper's hours. He thought about how it would serve this woman right if he left with someone else before the end of the set. She *was* moving in on him, too forward, especially since she was so much older.

He should go with Wayne right now.

But he leaned toward staying. After all, a cold beer was headed his way. And he wanted to check out the little brunette, at least get a phone number.

"So, Charley, what's it gonna be, me or her?" Wayne stood up.

Charley, his mind on the brunette, blinked in confusion until he realized Wayne only wanted him to decide who was driving him home. Not a lifetime commitment. "Wish you wouldn't put it that way, but I'll stay and listen."

Wayne waved back at Lou and Charley as he pushed the door open and stepped out into the spring evening.

"You might convince some of these ladies sitting around the bar to dance or shoot some pool to pass the time," Lou suggested, as if Charley didn't know how to spend an evening in a pool-hall-dance-hall-bar. Didn't she know who she was talking to? Well, no, he guessed she didn't.

The fiddler began tuning up, so Lou made another quick trip to the ladies' room.

On the way back to the bandstand, she touched his forearm.

"Any song requests?" she asked.

"Naw, I'll take potluck." That damp hand wasn't lost on him.

The band's singer was pretty good. He did a decent rip-off of "Lonely Nights," carrying it off with as much passion as Mickey Gilley himself. Charley enjoyed the music, making his plan to move in on the brunette, but before he could act, he felt a little hand on his shoulder and turned. There she was.

"Wanna dance?" she asked.

He lost no time escorting her to the dance floor.

Her good looks convinced him to overlook a few drawbacks: her hands were dry, and dancing with her was like pushing a log around the floor. As Charley maneuvered her, he caught Lou looking his way, brushing her snare as the singer crooned. She smiled at Charley and the brunette as if a wedding date was set, with her as matron of honor. He didn't get it. The brunette was cutting in on Lou, and she smiled, not missing a beat.

Charley caught himself not being his usual charming self on the dance floor, so he started up a bit of conversation. "I'm Charley. Nice to meet you."

"I'm Darla."

"You new around here?"

"Yes and no."

"Beg pardon?"

"Yes, I moved back to stay with my parents for a while. I got a divorce."

"So you lived here before?"

"For grade school and part of middle school. Moved away. Came back for high school. Graduated three years back, moved off, got married." She looked sultry. Was that look for him, or did she always lower her lashes like that? Or was it that she had trouble talking and dancing the two-step at the same time?

Probably from a family that worked the oil field. Some of

them moved around. She was definitely cute. She had long legs for such a short person. Overall hot. Not exactly Miss Congeniality, though. Often, he'd discovered, good-looking women possessed no personality, didn't try at all, it seemed. Well, they didn't have to.

Darla swayed into him during the song's bridge, as the music rose to the lyrics about long nights and needing a friend. Her hand on the back of his neck gathered him in as he pressed her to his chest. Normally at about this point he would be thinking about whisking her out the door. The way she leaned in through a turn as the music swelled and the perfect timing of the words would be enough to convince Charley that this was the woman for him—at least for the next week or so—hygienic fault and all.

But he had no vehicle—that was an undeniable fact—and he had no idea whether or not Darla's was sitting in the parking lot. He wanted to avoid the subject of cars so he wouldn't incriminate himself. He thought about Lou giving him a ride home. He could show Lou that she didn't call the shots if he walked out with this girl. But there was that subject of cars. *Crap.*

He looked at the bandstand again. It would be a good time for Lou to be making meaningful eye contact, but instead of watching him, she was turned toward the singer, waiting for a signal to end the song. Talk about focus. Maybe she wasn't coming on to him after all. Maybe she was being nice to someone she knew, however briefly, from when she visited here before.

Between songs, Darla linked an arm in his and turned toward Charley's table, but he instead escorted her to her bar stool and said, "I see a friend over at the pool table. Think I'll go shoot some. Thanks for the dance. See you later." And off he went.

He was losing his mind, he thought, letting a great-looking girl sit the night out on a bar stool. Brady, the owner, chatted with her from behind the bar. The owner's specialty was to make people feel welcome. Darla talked with the other women around her, too. So at least she wasn't doomed to an evening of isolation.

No other temptation was evident at Hopper's tonight. What a relief after all, Charley thought. He could keep up with his vow of not getting married or anywhere near it for a while longer. His car situation had determined his fate for the evening. He played pool and stayed away from the path to the ladies' room. After a safe time, he checked the bar stool where he had parked Darla. It was empty.

After the last song, Lou left her hat on the stool of her trap set and met him at his pool table. She was pleasantly sweaty. Charley picked up a faint almond scent stirred up by the ceiling fan. Her auburn hair was gathered at the nape of her neck, but little ringlets escaped in wisps around her temples. Without the cowgirl hat, she looked softer and younger . . . or was it the several beers he'd had? Didn't they all look good at closing time?

"I don't have to load the drums up since we're playing here the rest of the week, so I'm free to go," she said.

In the parking lot, she unlocked the passenger door of her plain little red GMC pickup. It smelled of a recent waxing, the interior pristine. The same smell of almonds he'd noticed earlier was stronger inside the cab.

As they turned onto the highway, she punched on the CD player. George Strait was singing about asking a woman if he could drive her home. They looked at each other and laughed.

"I promise I didn't rig that," Lou said.

"I usually do the pickin' up of the woman, and here I am being driven home." In a mock-helpless voice, Charley added, "I'm not sure I can trust you."

"You shouldn't," she said, looking serious. Then she laughed at Charley's alarmed look.

His laugh turned into a snort. He shut his mouth and looked

straight ahead, feeling out of his league. If she wanted to come on up to his place, he wouldn't stop her, but she made him nervous.

At the Shady Arms Apartments, Lou didn't look for a place to park, but stopped next to the outside stairs. Apparently, she was going to drop him off. Charley was relieved. Then disappointed. Then relieved. Then he went numb, as he always did when confused.

"Are you coming back to Hopper's any time soon?" she asked.

"Sure, if you're not married and have no more than two kids and two prior felony convictions," Charley quipped, resorting to humor as a cover.

Her face went slack. "How did you know?" she said.

Ready to deny knowing anything about her, he saw the play in her eyes.

"Oh, so that's how it is. Well, if you can't give a straight answer, neither will I." He opened the door.

"Sounds like it's someone's time to go night-night," she replied, and all he could do was hop out.

Before he closed the pickup door, she leaned across the seat. "Hey, if you come back to hear the band, I'm not going to think you're in love."

Charley smiled and waved goodbye.

She drove away while he climbed the outside stairs. At the landing, he stopped and watched her taillights disappear around the corner of the building.

2
Dog Days Memories

CHARLEY TURNED THE KEY to his second-floor apartment, flipped on the light, and opened the door to the familiar sight of his threadbare couch and slipcovered, bargain-basement arm chairs. His TV was so old it didn't interface with much of the available technology, sure. But he owned his furniture, not furnished-apartment-furniture so low to the floor he had to squat on it, with its scratchy, knobby upholstery worn down by a previous tenant. And he was proud of that.

He sat down a moment to appreciate his apartment home.

After Joyce had left for the psychiatric unit of the VA hospital, a rent house with a yard had seemed like a good move. There was a cute two-bedroom available for about the same price as his apartment.

He'd patched up Joyce's bullet hole in the bathroom so well the landlord returned his security deposit, and he didn't have to worry about another deposit at the rent house, since the landlady was a client of his who liked the idea of having Charley as a tenant.

With his security deposit refund, he shopped the garage sales in Sulfur Gap and surrounding towns and bought himself some housewarming presents . . . floor lamps, a couch and chairs, an industrial-strength coffee table, and a bedroom set that said "single man" like only fake oak grain with no embellishments can.

A couple of old oil paintings appealed to him—one of an old-fashioned water well with a red pump and bluebonnets in the background, and another of a landscape with Herefords grazing, surrounded by prickly-pear cactus and clumps of yellow flowers. He put the red pump over the couch and added some red throw pillows, and he hung his cows over his bed, covered with a green comforter that matched the prickly pear.

All these purchases fit just as well when he moved back to the apartment.

He plumped a red pillow, stood, and stretched. He needed to get a good rest, since work awaited him tomorrow. But first he had an errand to run—literally, since he had no car. Stripping down to his stretchy boxers, he threw his jeans in the pile for the steam press at the dry cleaners. In the bathroom, he stood in front of the mirror and flexed his pecs and stomach. He could build up a good six-pack if he tried. He pulled his jogging shorts from the hook behind the door and slipped into them, along with his T-shirt, socks, and running shoes. Lou had brought him more than half the distance he needed to go tonight by giving him a ride home from Hopper's. Since she'd left him at his doorstep, he could take care of some business with his mother and not have to pay her his Wednesday visit. Besides, he needed a good run. It would be a mile-and-a-half jog to the trailer park at the edge of town where she lived. Although it was late, he could make that in an easy ten minutes.

As he brushed his teeth, he thought back to his brief time of living in a real house.

His foray into the sphere of homemaking had begun simply enough. His house furnished, he decided the yard needed a dog. Growing up, he'd never had a pet. He would get a dog for companionship in case the recent memory of flying bullets failed to prevent him falling for Miss Right when the right song played.

At his weekly breakfast meet with Wayne at the Navaho, Charley had told him about his celibacy pact with himself.

After managing to swallow his coffee, Wayne laughed. "You'll last about as long as it would take a bull to trot across the pasture to visit a cow." Wayne reached over and gave him a good-natured punch on the arm. "But good luck. I admire your intentions."

Charley bristled, even though he knew Wayne had good reason to express doubt. But he hoped the rent house, the dog, and the different geography in his life would boost him past the feeling that he would dissolve into the air like a thin puff of smoke if he were alone for more than a week.

He trotted down his apartment steps and jogged toward Sunset Estates, his way lit by weak streetlights. It was almost midnight. No cars were moving about, and only a few windows glowed with the light of an insomniac or someone staring at the glow of a computer screen into the wee hours. He knew his mother would be awake. She tended to stay up to watch the late-night talk shows and lull herself to sleep in the dim light of the television with her drink and cigarettes at her side.

Jogging steadily, he thought about his lame attempt at a more conventional lifestyle. The dog idea had seemed trouble-free. The black-and-white boxer he found at a kennel in Briargrove was a bit inbred—cross-eyed and dumb. He named her Boxer after trying names like Vanessa and Vivian. Whenever she heard his car in the driveway, she went berserk and jumped at the bedroom window, scratching her toenails over the screen and down the siding, leaving claw marks and sagging screens.

He asked around for dog-training pointers. "Dorothy, how do you make a dog poop in the grass?"

His wise mentor, owner of the Wild Hare, stared at him across the break room table. "Dogs don't have to be trained for that. It's natural."

"Boxer doesn't know that. She lets loose where the urge strikes her—her dish, her bed, the dog house."

Dorothy groaned. "Oh dear, Charley. Even your dog has a screw loose."

Boxer escaped one day through the alley gate. After three days, Charley assumed she was gone for good. Someone must have stolen her, he figured. He expressed this thought to Wayne and caught him biting his lip.

"What?" Charley asked.

"I can't picture anyone stealing that dog," Wayne said.

Irritated, Charley changed the subject.

He printed out some "missing dog" flyers in Dorothy's office and posted them all over town.

When his phone rang, his hopes lifted. Caller ID showed it was Vaughn, a fellow pool player he hadn't seen in a while. He hoped Vaughn had found her.

"Hey, Charley. I saw your flyer," Vaughn said.

"Yeah? You found my dog?"

"Uh, no. But I have a great replacement for her. I'm moving to Albuquerque and thought you would like my full-blood male Cocker spaniel. Name's Tuffy. Friendly as all get-out. Shots are current. I hate to leave him, but I know he'd have a great home with you."

Charley couldn't resist sweet-talk, and he was sure Vaughn knew it.

Tuffy moved in to Charley's empty back yard. Within the hour, his phone rang again.

"Charley? This is Miz Lawless. That dog you're looking for?"

His heart sank. "Yes, ma'am?"

"She's in my front yard eating grass. I'm giving her a drink. She's pretty thirsty."

Charley walked down to Mrs. Lawless's with a leash and deposited the dehydrated Boxer back at home. Now he owned two dogs.

The memory made him groan aloud as he dodged a pothole in the street. In hindsight, his mistakes were neon signs. Tuffy had chewed up several of the old pine fence slats, so Charley bought a stack of replacements and kept them in the garage. He figured that before long, he would build the landlady a new fence by replacing a slat at a time.

Tuffy compounded Charley's problems by doing what male dogs do—he screwed the other pooch. Boxer was pregnant.

Jarod had said, "Get at least one dog fixed or you'll have puppies. Spay Boxer, since she gets out."

Charley resisted. "I'd have to leave the dog at the vet's until she can get to it. It's too pricey for me right now."

"Puppies are pricey, too."

At least the complications were keeping him occupied—leaving him no time to find a quick replacement for Joyce.

Charley called Wayne for advice on birthing puppies.

"Leave her alone," he said. "Dogs know what to do."

Charley wasn't so sure about that.

He watched Boxer deliver a litter of eleven pups. Finally, after two months of picking up puppy poop—he had to be fast or Boxer would eat it—he put an ad in the paper to sell the puppies for fifteen dollars apiece.

A few sold, and the remainder went into a big laundry basket with a sign that read, "Free Puppies! ½ registered Cocker, ½ registered Boxer!" He spent a Sunday afternoon standing around the Wal-Mart parking lot, but he managed to go home puppy-free.

The same day, he found a home for Tuffy. Beside the basket of puppies, Charley had posted a picture of the handsome parents.

A little girl and her father stopped to look. At the sight of Tuffy's picture, she stamped her feet. "I want THAT doggie!" she pointed at Tuffy, tongue lolling for the camera.

Before she wound up to a full-scale tantrum, Charley said, "I can let you have him. He needs children to play with."

He managed to look noble and keep the smile off his face as he wrote down his address and told the father he could drop by and take the Cocker spaniel.

The moonlit route to his mother's place tonight took him up a familiar alleyway, passing between fences and rousing barking dogs. The shortcut would be worth the disturbance, he hoped, feeling guilty for bothering the sleeping residents of Sulfur Gap, even as he chuckled at the quagmire he'd gotten into while trying to be a pet owner.

He remembered that when he finally had Boxer spayed, she took only three days after she came home from the vet to escape through some loose fence slats Tuffy had left behind.

He learned the sad news when his phone rang while he was in the middle of a haircut.

It was Patsy from Animal Control. "Sorry, Charley. Your boxer dog was run over. Killed on the spot."

"Holy shit. What happened?"

"The ice cream man stopped for some kids on their way home from school. She must have been following them and lay in front of his tire when he stopped to serve ice cream. When he put his truck in gear, it lurched over a strange bump."

Charley wondered how many kids were traumatized by the sight. "Now what?" he asked. He wondered if there was a fine for letting your dog out to be run over by the ice cream man in front of a bunch of kids.

"You can come by and get her if you come today. Or we'll cremate her and you can get her collar."

THE LARK

Charley had never before been forced to make decisions like this. His client waited while he talked to Dorothy.

"Do what you feel like is the right thing, or you'll regret it," she said.

He finished with his client and called Joann, his landlady. She agreed that Boxer needed a decent burial. The back yard would be fine, if he made the grave deep enough.

As he jogged through the entrance to the Sunset Estates, he ran past a split-rail fence that was more split than rail, and down the lane another quarter of a mile, past rows of trailer houses to his mother's, situated near the back of the lot. The old mulberry tree that once offered shade over the small front porch and gravel drive hadn't begun to bud, even though it was well into spring. Charley suspected it was dead. It should be cut down, but April would resist. Change upset her. To further grace the entrance to April's home, a BEWARE OF DOG sign was nailed to the short banister leading up to the porch. His mother didn't have a dog.

He stood on the narrow walkway and rapped loudly enough to eclipse the blaring television and waited while the familiar, shadowy movements he could see through the thin curtain indicated she had heaved herself from her chair and was lumbering to the door. He heard the unmistakable sound of a bullet being chambered in a 9mm pistol.

Opening the door a crack, she said, "That you, Charley?"

Who else would it be? The Schwann's man? "Yeah, Mom, it's me."

"You want to come in? I wasn't expecting you until tomorrow. Tomorrow's Wednesday, isn't it?" She opened the door further. Her voice was hoarse from cigarettes and the silence of her day. He heard the soft but distinctive sound of the hammer being released on the pistol hidden in the pocket of her voluminous bathrobe. It took all of his self-control not to run from the porch.

He didn't care to be this close to being shot at. With good reason, he was incredibly jumpy about women wielding guns.

"No. I just got out for a run and thought I'd bring that cash you needed from the bank." He handed her the folded bills. "Do you have a grocery list for me? I can probably go for you Sunday." Wayne would give him a ride and help deliver April's groceries. Wayne was familiar with her lifestyle, and, unlike some others, didn't judge his younger friend for his mother's choices. Charley always paid for as many of her essentials as he could, a fact unknown to such observers as Wes Farley. He feared she would go without necessities to pay for liquor and cigarettes.

"Sure, Charley. Let me see what I did with that list."

He regretted asking. It would take her another five minutes to trudge to wherever she had laid the list and back to the door, while he stood in this realm of solitude on her porch. But she found the slip on the lopsided table beside the door.

Putting the scrap of paper in his shorts pocket, he turned to leave as she reached for his arm. He stood still, his skin crawling a little at her touch. He felt guilty about his mixed-up feelings. He didn't know what to do but help out as much as he could in his own way while avoiding his mother as much as possible.

She gave his forearm a little squeeze. "Thank you, Charley."

He waved and jogged away, grateful that he had escaped before she asked him why he hadn't driven instead of running at that hour of the night. He wanted to avoid a discussion about his lack of transportation. He didn't want sympathy from anyone, especially not from April. Headed home at a faster pace than he had traveled to his mother's, he picked up the thread of memories.

After retrieving Boxer's body from the animal shelter, he wrapped her in an old blanket. The dog's body lay inert on the back seat of his Jetta while he drove by the site of the accident. A couple of boys stood on the corner. They waved to Charley, so he stopped.

"Hey, guys." He stood with one foot on the pavement to talk to them over the roof of the car.

"Hey, Charley. Sorry about your dog."

"Thanks. You guys see it happen?"

"Yeah!" The boys were almost enthusiastic as they looked at each other.

"Y'all know anything about dog funerals? I want to do something like that."

The boys ran away to find their sisters and other friends.

In the backyard, Charley used a pickax when he reached a layer of hard caliche, but he kept at it until he had carved out a grave. He had to stop twice to wipe sweat and tears from his face with his bandana. The grave was ready when the kids came. They brought dandelion flowers and verbena, bright mementos of spring, to throw on Boxer. While the girls gave brief eulogies about what a pretty dog she was, the boys took turns filling the grave with shovelfuls of dirt. Charley wiped a tear from his eye and swallowed hard. He didn't break down until the kids left and he was alone with the fresh grave.

He fell to his knees and sobbed. He couldn't remember crying like that since he was a small boy. He didn't know he had been so attached to Boxer. It was more than Boxer, though—it was Vicki, Joyce, and loneliness, all wadded up in a place that ached in his chest.

Turning again into his alley shortcut, Charley thought about his apartment bedroom. He wished it was more cozy, a place to look forward to coming home and being alone. Even his co-workers couldn't tell how much pain he carried around. He could probably go online and get advice from *Better Homes and Gardens*.

"It's probably for the best," Dorothy had commiserated the day after he buried Boxer. "Something was wrong with that dog, and maybe she'll get to come back as a higher form of life—or at least a smarter dog. She won't be adding any more stupidity to the gene pool at least."

"You're right," Charley said. The dog saga of his life spanned a few months and cost him a couple thousand dollars. Not nearly as bad as his marital decisions, but bad enough.

He wasn't ready for a house, he had decided. The backyard felt too empty, with only a dog's grave inhabiting it.

He fixed the fence and the torn window screen, patched and painted the claw marks on the window trim and siding so not a hint of the damage remained. He even scooped the poop. Charley, true to his reputation, fixed his mess.

He declared his house-dwelling venture a glorious flop and called the manager of the Shady Arms, who still appreciated Charley's repair job on the bullet hole that Joyce made. The old place was available. Wayne came to town with a trailer and moved him in a matter of hours.

Charley reached his apartment stairs for the second time that night, huffing from the run. He bounded up the stairs and let himself in, heading straight for the shower.

Scrubbed to what felt like a shine, he folded back his cactus-green comforter and picked up a magazine from the stack on his bedside table. He tried to read to wind down from the evening at Hopper's and the run to his mother's. Finally, he turned off the lamp and drifted toward sleep, conscious of the empty space in the bed. The fleeting notion struck him that with no one to balance the other side of the bed, it would dump him on the floor. He scooted toward the middle. At least his trip to Shreveport was on the horizon.

3
No Way

CASINO WINNINGS WEIGHED in Charley's wallet. He'd had a good weekend playing blackjack and working the slots. The westbound Greyhound made a late lunch stop at the Hiss Pit Bar-b-que Hut close to Tyler, and when Charley stepped out to stretch, the multicolored flags of a used-car lot beckoned.

He went to investigate. As he drew closer, he spotted a gleaming blue compact car with chrome accents and European lines. He stepped over the low chain fence to take a closer look. A sign taped to the windshield read, $925, AS IS.

"Need a car?" A voice called from across the lot.

"This thing run?"

A short man in slacks and a dress shirt with rolled-up sleeves hurried toward him.

"Sure!" he said, pushing a lank strand of hair off his forehead.

"What is it?"

"A 1986 Renault. It's a classic."

"The price is mighty low."

"We've had it on the lot a while. It's the kind of car that won't appeal to just anybody, so we're trying to move it. But it's a good car. They don't make 'em like they used to."

The salesman went to get the keys while Charley kicked the tires.

The engine whirred to life and idled smoothly. He drove up

the service road a ways. The brakes worked. Drive, reverse, neutral, park—the gears all worked.

"Want to look under the hood?"

"Sure."

Charley bent over the clean engine compartment. He didn't see any loose wires or hoses about to blow. After revving the engine a few more times, he signed the papers and waved at his fellow bus passengers as he drove away, his wallet empty and his heart full.

He ignored the rhythmic plinking under the hood as he nosed onto the interstate. He called Wayne's voicemail to say he wouldn't need to pick him up at the bus station in Abilene. Now he had miles to go with his own thoughts for company. He'd been trying for days to push aside thoughts of Joyce—and focus more on the brunette he'd met at Hopper's Tuesday night. What an idiot he'd been—he hadn't even gotten her last name, much less her phone number. He had no trouble recalling that cute face. But somehow it was the earlier memories that won out.

He had met his second wife at a club in Lubbock. Dorothy had asked him to make a run to the barber and beauty supply outlet rather than wait on Sulfur Gap's disorganized distributor at the time. He'd found a room at the Days Inn close to the Texas Tech campus, donned his leather jacket, ostrich boots, newest crispy pair of Wranglers, and best-fitting shirt accessorized with his Justin Time horseshoe-and-star watch. With a satisfied last look in the mirror, he had headed out to the Blue Bonnet.

He recalled how the excitement had surged through him as he paid his cover charge in the lobby. He could hear the familiar echoes of the night scene. The DJ filled the joint with sound, accompanied by the clicking of balls from rows of billiard tables and the clink of glasses and bottles from the bar. The club was so large it boasted three restrooms, so he could rotate where he sat.

But he didn't have to.

Joyce showed up before he was ready to sit down and enjoy the view.

He'd started a game of pool with one of the college boys. A group gathered to watch. As he took aim with his cue stick, a flat little stomach decorated with a king-sized belt buckle sparkled at him. Above that the arc of some very nice curves was accentuated by a clingy, low-cut neckline. And the face wasn't bad, either. He winked and smiled. She cheered on the remainder of his winning pool game and then led him onto the dance floor with a sense of entitlement.

Even as he remembered his best times with Joyce, he couldn't help but notice as he neared Dallas that the cold air streaming from the vents was beginning to warm. Outside Fort Worth, hot air wafted heavily. But it was springtime, so he drove on toward home with the windows rolled down and the afternoon sun glaring in his eyes.

Joyce had clasped Charley's shoulders, his hands at her waist, as they waltzed to "Old-Fashioned Broken Heart." She was a smooth dancer, following his turns. They stepped into the new rhythm of "I'm Not Strong Enough to Say No." Between songs, Charley hadn't wanted to take his hands off her.

He thought, *Vicki was practice. Here's the woman for me.* He soon learned that, after a stint in the Army, Joyce had settled down in Lubbock to work for the postal service.

She moved against him, song after song, until he said, "Let's go."

She said, "I thought you'd never ask."

Joyce spent the night at the Days Inn with Charley and followed his Jetta back to Sulfur Gap in her Crossfire. They married at the courthouse the following weekend.

As he tried to pass an eighteen-wheeler struggling up a

slope, he sighed. He realized he wouldn't be able to get around the truck in the anemic Renault with any more likelihood than he could have stayed married to Joyce.

One night soon after the courthouse wedding, a punch in the nose had awakened him. His wife's angry eyes hovered inches from his in the dim light.

"Who's Vicki?" she yelled.

Charley held his nose and stumbled to the bathroom to check for blood.

"Who's Vicki?" Joyce shrieked.

He heard a thump on the floor of the next-door apartment. His neighbor was up, a long-haul truck driver who didn't spend very many nights there, but when he did, he liked his sleep. Now, *he* probably wanted to punch somebody.

"Who's Vicki?" His bride's voice grew shriller.

Finally, Charley gathered his senses and established that his nose was intact but that he would have to sneeze any second. Facing her, he held up his free hand to stay the banshee in his bedroom.

"Vicki was married to me before you. You know about her."

Joyce slapped his ear. Now Charley held his ear with one hand and his nose with the other. Instinct made him turn sideways and crouch a little to protect his groin, since his hands were busy.

"You kept saying her name!" Joyce lowered the volume to a shout. Animosity burned in her eyes.

"I'm sorry! I didn't mean to!"

"What's the big idea? You're married to me—you should be saying *my* name, you two-timing son-of-a-bitch."

By now Charley was awake enough to pursue the logic. He grabbed Joyce's shoulders and shook her a little. "Are you awake? Do you know what you're saying?"

Her expression cleared. "I guess that's dumb, huh?"

"Doesn't make much sense to me."

"I know Vicki was your ex, and you were muttering about her in your sleep."

"Probably a nightmare."

"I was jealous, waking up to your saying something about Vicki. You sure you're over her?"

"Yes, more than over."

He spent several minutes talking Joyce down but slept lightly for quite a few nights after. Joyce had an illogical streak, to put it mildly. He wondered whether her cache of pills helped her, or scrambled her even more. She couldn't stand it that he'd been married before, couldn't get past it. During sex, she even made comparisons between herself and Vicki. Tended to ruin the moment and challenge his youthful stamina. She also became obsessed with his working alongside so many women. Good grief. Dorothy was like a mother to him, and the other females at the salon were married or otherwise involved.

Close to Abilene, the rumble of a Harley-Davidson brought Charley back to the interstate. A man with a long ponytail streaming in the wind pulled along beside him. The biker waved dismissively at the Renault and twisted the throttle with a heavily tattooed arm. The hog surged ahead as if the Renault were standing still, the engine rumble sounding too reminiscent of gunfire—and Joyce's pistol.

When Joyce had bought the handgun and put it in the bedside stand, Charley couldn't sleep at all anymore. The last thing he needed was a bullet in the face if he happened to mutter during the wrong dream. He decided to find a good time to break the news to Joyce that his wedding vows didn't include sticking around to be shot. Dorothy gave him some advice, and he came home with a plan.

Dorothy had said, "Get her in a public place so there'll be witnesses. Then you very firmly tell her it's over. Do it, Charley. It'll save your life. Believe me, please."

He thought he would take Joyce to dinner at the Navaho Restaurant. She couldn't make much of a scene there, and surely she wouldn't be packing.

Joyce wasn't at the apartment when he got home, so he decided to shower. He hooked his little radio over the shower curtain rod and tuned to one of the few stations it would pick up—a country FM with a husky-voiced female DJ. He shampooed, scrubbed, and rinsed, while singing to his favorite tunes. He warbled with Lee Ann Womack in his best shower falsetto. The throaty DJ blended her own voice into the last few notes of the song and laughed. She was beginning a sentence with "What a naughty girl" when the radio exploded as a loud bang burst from the other side of the bathroom door. Pieces of tile rained from the wall behind him. Charley stood confused and shocked, still naked.

Then Joyce yelled, "Who's in there with you, Charley?"

As he assumed the child's pose yoga move on the floor of the tub, he heard her kick the door open. He trembled in the fetal position as she yanked back the shower curtain.

"Please don't shoot, Joyce," he pleaded.

She dropped the .38 onto the bath mat and knelt beside the tub. She picked up the remnant of radio that lay beside him as realization crept across her face.

"I'm so sorry, so sorry, Charley. I came in with groceries and heard that slutty-sounding voice singing along with you and thought you were with someone in here."

It took an hour for Charley's heart to stop banging. He said as few words as possible. Joyce alternated between "I'm sorry" and more chipper comments. "I guess they'll award me the Drama

Queen prize of the year," she said with a wry smile. "It's good I'm a lousy shot."

They assessed the damage and decided Charley could fix the door and the tile. They could make a run out to Wal-Mart and get a new shower curtain and radio and put all this behind them.

Obviously, dinner at the Navaho was off, so he waited until they were together in the middle of Wal-Mart, with plenty of witnesses and no firearm, at least not one that wasn't locked up behind a counter.

In front of the video game case, he looked into her eyes and said, "Joyce, I'm scared of you."

"Why?" Joyce stared in surprise.

"You punched me in my sleep, and you're jealous way out of reason, and now you've shot at me."

"I'm not going to shoot *you*."

"Promise?"

The split-second hesitation made the truth apparent. It was a truth that passed between them with the firing of a single synapse.

"Yes. I promise."

But it was too late. They both knew she couldn't keep any kind of promise about anything. Truth overwhelmed and reached around them. Charley's compassion showed in his eyes, and he could see her register the pity he felt for her. She began shaking, then cried and sobbed and crumpled to the floor. Concerned shoppers gathered around as he sat on his haunches beside her, wondering what to do next. The next thing he knew, Sheriff Larry Bob Sparks, the go-to guy in Sulfur Gap when someone needed a ride to the funny farm, was patting Charley on the shoulder.

Larry Bob took his place kneeling beside Joyce, talking quietly while she nodded.

Charley drove home alone, feeling like part of his heart had just been wrenched from his chest. He was grateful to the sheriff for handling the scene so well. It could have been much more humiliating for him, and especially for Joyce, if someone less tactful had been called. He knew Wayne didn't like L.B., something about a misunderstanding over a woman a long time ago, but as far as Charley was concerned, the sheriff deserved some credit for his dedication to a difficult job.

In the days that followed, he went through his work routine, spending evenings immersed in television and his latest best-seller. He counted his blessings. Joyce never came back to the apartment. She agreed to a trip to a psychiatric facility, so he didn't have to screw up the courage to have her committed. What a relief.

Ending a marriage involved far too much drama. His own "stepfathers" had simply faded out of sight. Women were definitely . . . different.

Charley packed up Joyce's belongings, having her clothes all freshly laundered and dry-cleaned. He delivered them to a storage facility in Big Spring and left the key for his wife at the Veterans Hospital.

After a month of therapy at the VA, Joyce called. "They say I've got PTSD," she said. That made perfect sense to Charley. He wanted to point out that she had passed it along to him, but he kept that quip to himself.

"I'm not able to be a decent wife. I'm gonna need lots of recovery time."

Charley thought, *Me, too.*

The divorce was amicable. He had dodged one more bullet — a real one. He had decided he would stay single. For a while at least. When his body ached for Joyce's curves, he replayed the day a bullet whizzed past him in the shower. That stopped him from hankering after a quick fix for loneliness.

He'd been thinking so much about Joyce on his drive back to

Sulfur Gap, he hadn't even tried the Renault's radio. Music would be good, he thought. He moved to switch on the radio. But the knob pulled free in his hand. Where are my needle-nose pliers when I need them? he thought.

Despair crept up as the Renault limped down the interstate. Several sweaty hours later, Charley rolled into the lot of the Shady Arms. Just as he pulled to a halt a red CHECK ENGINE light flashed on. He surrendered to a bitter tide of disappointment as he opened his apartment door. He still hoped all the problems could be fixed.

He thought again of his winnings from Shreveport as he looked sadly around his small living room. He could have replaced his old television and bought a Blu-Ray player. And, oh yeah, he could have made a down payment on a decent little pickup or sporty car.

He'd take the Renault to Jarod's repair shop, where he would be subjected to good-natured torment about the stupidity of his spur-of-the-moment purchase. Then Jarod would give him a decent deal on repairs. Fair enough.

* * *

He slept that night under a cloud of recurring nightmares. In one of them, he was running through a trailer house neighborhood looking for a lost cat. The cat morphed into a dog or a good-looking woman in tight jeans or a saleslady running away with an antique punch bowl that he wanted, but he kept the chase going, pursuing lost treasure. He woke up with his heart squishing in his chest like a swollen sponge.

He was glad to face the day, even if it meant letting Jarod see how little he knew about cars. Well, come to think of it, this would be nothing new to Jarod. Nor would it be news to Jarod that Charley made some dumb moves when feeling lonely on a bus trip home from Shreveport with a thousand dollars in his pocket. Jarod knew all this from his long friendship with Charley, but in true West Texas manly fashion, Jarod wouldn't make a sound about it. Not seriously, not without a good-ol'-boy backslapping, the whole kidding-around vibe.

Charley created his spiky, mussy-hair look with extra mousse and ran his clipper over his beard stubble at the ideal length to fit the part of a macho hair stylist. Wranglers, flip-flops, and a snap-button shirt gave him a look that he hoped shouted, "Don't assume I'm gay because I cut hair in a salon called the Wild Hare."

Jarod would poke fun at him, but Charley would find out about salvaging the situation before calling auto salvage. The warning light could indicate that the gas cap was simply loose— but that only applied to newer model cars, he remembered. It could mean a loose wire or a blown fuse. But in reality, he knew it meant worse. He was pretty certain he had turned a golden opportunity into a leaden turd.

Charley shook off the feeling as he jogged down the outside stairs to the parking lot. He stopped in front of the Renault.

Something looked different.

"Well, shit," he said, and stood looking at his investment. Through the early morning film of mist on the windshield, he saw that overnight the roof liner had collapsed onto the car's dashboard. He about-faced and took the steps three at a time back to his kitchen, where he rummaged through a drawer for his tube of fabric glue. The stuff had worked wonders when some of the trim on his leather jacket started letting go last fall. He soon secured the roof fabric in the Renault so that he could see out the windshield, but the lining still drooped, much like his spirits.

At least the cobalt blue and bright chrome Renault didn't *look* too bad as it tappeta-tapped to Jarod's shop. Charley had thrown his running shoes, shorts, and shirt into a backpack. He might as well turn the prospect of a breakdown into an opportunity to get in a run. Turning off the street, he was crowded by a three-quarter-ton pickup equipped with a cow-catcher grille bearing down on his rear bumper. That's when he noticed his turn signal didn't work. The truck nearly ran him over but turned when Charley did, right into the other stall of Jarod's garage.

Jarod spotted Charley pulling into the bay and smiled as he stepped out of his office, wiping his hands on a red rag.

The Renault coughed and dieseled as Charley turned off the ignition.

"Hey, Charley. So is this what you won in Shreveport?"

"Sort of," Charley said, levering himself out of the Renault.

The driver of the cow-catcher truck walked toward them, eyeing the Renault like it was a hairball the cat hocked up.

"Hey, Bo. Be right with you." Jarod turned to Charley. Bo leaned against the wall and smoothed his neatly-trimmed salt-and-pepper beard with a strong, well-manicured hand. Charley would rather not have an audience, especially a guy driving a sixty-thousand-dollar truck, but neither he nor Jarod could very well ask Bo to step outside or into the tiny office.

Jarod lifted the Renault's hood as Charley joined him to peer at the engine.

"So whatcha think?" asked Charley. He looked, unseeing, at the crankcase, where oil now seeped around its gaskets.

"This engine was steam-cleaned in case someone checked under the hood before buying. Didn't you look?"

"Of course I did," Charley said, "but I thought a clean engine was a good sign, not a red flag."

The man named Bo snorted but then cleared his throat to tamp down a derisive laugh.

Jarod continued his examination of the ailing car. "This thing needs some work. I'd say for starters, we'll need to put four hundred into the engine. You wouldn't have noticed any noise at first from worn-out belts because they've been treated with belt dressing. New belts will be another couple hundred."

Charley stepped back and whistled a low tone. "Don't shit me now."

"I shit you not, Charley. Where'd you find this heap?"

"Oh, never mind. Can I leave it pulled over here out of the way until I get the money next month to get you to work on it? And in the meantime, if someone else wants to buy it, I'll let them have it for $900."

"You paid that much?" Jarod whistled through his teeth, marveling at Charley's stupidity. "I can put a sign on it and park it over here. I imagine there's even sawdust in the transmission. I don't think it would ever be reliable transportation unless you take the body off and run a new chassis under it."

Finally Bo inserted himself. "I just have to say, son, you've got a damn good friend here." His voice was low and gravelly, full of manly manliness. He seemed like the kind of guy who imagined himself to have extra-large testicles. The kind of guy Charley loved to beat at pool.

"Yeah, Jarod and I go way back. He's a damn good friend as well as mechanic. . . . I mean, good mechanic, too."

"I get it," Bo gave him a warm whap on the shoulder and smiled. The smile was friendly enough, but laughter lurked behind it. At Charley's expense.

"Bo, this is Charley Bristow. Charley, Bo Buchanan." Jarod spoke over his shoulder as he wiggled the plug wires.

"You live around here? I don't remember meeting you before," Charley said.

"Naw. I live over in Big Spring. I have a tire business and keep Jarod supplied."

Bo's dress and bearing suggested prosperity and a membership in a small country club. Expensive shirt and jeans, big belt buckle—personalized with "BB," Charley noticed—nice boots, heavy gold wedding band. Perfect teeth that could be a gift from God, or bought. A man who made a lot of money, but not at a desk. His voice and bearing could be intimidating to some people, Charley thought, but not his height. Charley could look down on the top of his head.

"I'm with Jarod. This is an eye-catching jalopy that won't get you far down the road," Bo said, hands on his hips, looking like a junior high football coach on the sidelines shaking his head at yet another fumble.

"At least I made it from Tyler."

"Wow! You must have a good luck charm!"

Bo was just being friendly, but Charley didn't relish the attention.

"Okay. Well, thanks. Guess there's no point throwing good money after bad." Charley shrugged and sat in a flimsy plastic chair to change into his sneakers while Jarod and Bo discussed the tire inventory. Bo's regular salesman was out with his wife, having a baby, and good old Bo-boss was filling in.

Without saying good-bye, Charley jogged away, his backpack bouncing. He could hear Bo still marveling at the stupidity of his car. "Ooooo-weeee! Some car salesman sure found his mark!" Chuckle, chuckle. At least he didn't hear Jarod laughing along with him. Charley quickly covered the four remaining blocks through historic downtown Sulfur Gap to the Wild Hare Salon on Main Street. As he passed the native limestone buildings, preserved from the town's heyday as a main stop on the railroad line, he chided himself. He was the poster boy for throwing good money after bad. He knew it but never realized he was doing it until it was too late. So often, a well-timed expenditure, sometimes for himself, but usually for someone else, seemed like the perfect thing to do. He thought he could perk things up and put a whole new glow on life.

He strode through the courtyard in the middle of the small horseshoe of adjoining shops, past the fountain with its statue of a mermaid balanced on her tail and holding a jug on her shoulder from which the water poured endlessly into the bowl below. Tucked behind the mermaid was the entrance to the Wild Hare.

The smells of perms, tanning lotions, and nail acrylics greeted him with a variegated mix of familiarity, bringing a vague comfort. His co-workers ministered to people of all ages, sizes, and volume levels. The buzz blended voices, gushing water, and blowing hair dryers. It was like entering a familiar hive, rubbing legs with resident bees, then going about your business.

Charley's client was waiting. Eloise smiled as he ushered her to his booth after changing back to his flip-flops.

"Okay, Miss Eloise. What'll it be today? Same style? Do you like this length or should we take more off for summer weather?"

Charlie draped Eloise and led her to a shampoo bowl. As he massaged in her conditioner, Dorothy caught his eye.

"How was your weekend?" she mouthed across the room, leaning around her manicure client.

Charley grinned. "Great," he lip-synced. He knew that sooner or later his co-workers would learn about the Renault. If he didn't tell about it himself, Sue would come in making comments, having heard from Jarod about Charley's heap that he'd brought in for repairs, and before long a whole conversation would form around his impulsive purchase. Everyone would cluck at his foolishness, and someone would have to say that at least it wasn't a woman getting him in hock this time.

He'd smile and act as though all of the unspoken innuendo were not hanging over him like a cheap chandelier from eBay. He would try to give as little information as possible, but, being a helpful person, would soon find himself giving it all up so they could fill in the blanks in their own lives by watching the play-by-play of his plight that provided so much speculation and armchair quarterbacking about how they would have handled the whole game differently.

They made the usual excuses for him, tutting over his rough childhood. Trailer park classic—mostly-drunk mother, a father who probably wasn't the real one, and a noisy life filled with volatility like a high-powered electric fence charging the air. Sharp objects flew, launched by crazy anger. People flew, too. A kid learned to look out and duck. This assessment by his friends let him off the hook for his life's mistakes.

They'd say Charley had turned out good, considering. *And he does cut a mean head of hair. And he's fun. But when it comes to women to love, his "picker" was broke.* Sometimes Jarod intentionally slipped and said "pecker."

He finished his first haircut, another client waited, and so went another typical day. One cut after another. Tips ran high. Good, he needed the money. Also, he didn't have to occupy any down time in the salon with his coworkers, who would quiz him about the details of his weekend.

He often wished he could shake his good-ol'-boy approach, but he had decided he was just born that way. Sometimes being good-natured was a drawback, but it saved his bacon at times, too.

He would begin a conversation with every intention of being politely reserved, but before he knew it, he spouted information that kept listeners wide-eyed. He wanted everyone to be pleasantly entertained. And usually they were. He studiously avoided referring to anyone local, since you never knew who was related by blood or marriage. His string of "lady" friends and what they did or didn't do for a living, where they came from, their health problems, and his financial troubles—all the details kept a conversation from lagging. He kept the patter entertaining and informational, and he spun the story so that any judgment to be passed landed on him like bird droppings. He liked to joke that now when he met someone in a bar, his first question was how many handguns did she carry. If more than two, she struck out. Har-de-har.

During a pause for lunch, he had swallowed the last bite of his quesadilla from the taco stand next door when Dorothy plunked into the chair across the small break room table. Charley knew that her interest in his life was, in part, a diversion from the disasters of her own. But she also carried a genuine affection for him.

"So, how was it, really?" Dorothy held his gaze with a motherly intent that said, *You can't keep your secrets from me. I care. I really care. And I know you're gonna tell me.* "How's your girlfriend in Shreveport?" she asked aloud, pressing for specifics.

"She's fine. She likes Louisiana. So far, she's enjoying the Cajun influences—the food, the dancing, people's accents. I think she'll get homesick before too much longer, though. She's never lived outside Texas before."

"So, did you win big?" Dorothy smiled hopefully.

"Yeah, sort of. I started out with a couple hundred to gamble with and managed to more than triple it. And then I added to that."

"Wow! What're you gonna treat yourself to?"

"Well, I already did it," said Charley. His confession began— he couldn't stop it. "I saw this vintage Renault in the car lot next to the bus stop in Tyler. Got it cheap. I drove it the rest of the way home."

"What's a Renault?"

"Oh, you remember. They look like a small Mercedes. Classy.

French. I'm not sure when they stopped making them, or if they did."

"For all I know, it's a minibike. Can they get parts around here? I mean, what if it breaks? How will you fix it?"

"Well, to be honest, I haven't thought about that. I dropped it by Jarod's this morning and jogged on over here to the shop. It's going to need some tweaking."

"Jeez, Charley. Hope you didn't get screwed."

"By the way, Dorothy, do you know a guy, name of Bo Buchanan? I met him at Jarod's, and it feels like I should know him."

Dorothy tapped her temple with the end of an emery board. "No, I think I've heard of him but haven't met him. He owns a big tire dealership that has outlets in Big Spring and Lubbock."

"Okay. He probably thinks I'm an idiot, but if he's not around town much, I don't have to be reminded of the money I blew on that damn car. Oh well, it's only money," he said. "Easy come, easy go. I was prepared to lose the gambling stake anyway, so I'm no worse off. Hey—I think I'll call my car 'The No,'" he said.

"Why's that?" Dorothy asked.

"Short for Re-*nault*. As in *no* air conditioner, *no* headliner, *no* blinkers, and *no* go. 'The No.'" Charley waited for Dorothy to laugh, but instead, she looked thoughtful.

"Hmm. . . ." He could tell she was biting her tongue so as not to give her opinion on her confirmed diagnosis that he was a moron. Then she moved to a more favored topic. "Well, did you see any cute women? Do you think your friend—Danielle?—and you will fire something up?"

"Nope and nope." This was the truth. Charley didn't have time to fall into the trap of confessing that Danielle was a nice lesbian, that hanging out with her was like being with another guy, that she let him sleep on her couch in Shreveport in the apartment she shared with a partner, and that she cooked a mean jalapeño cornbread.

His next client came in.

"Well, that's good," Dorothy continued. "You could have complicated your weekend even more if you'd hooked up with someone on top of buying a *vintage* car." Her tone of voice put the quotation marks on "vintage."

"Maybe." Charley stared into the bottom of his coffee mug, thinking of "vintage" as another word for "worthless pile of crap."

* * *

After his final haircut of the day, Charley walked to Jarod's with the hope that the day's end brought happier news on The No. He held onto the pipe dream that it wasn't as bad as it seemed this morning and nurtured the fantasy that the car would be up and running. But instead, he found the hood up and a litter of tools strewn around it. Jarod met him coming into the shop and shook his head as he wiped his hands with a greasy rag.

"Now it won't start, Charley. You're lucky you didn't have to hitchhike home. I can't begin to tell you what all's wrong with that car. You probably put the last several hundred miles of its life on it, driving it out here."

Charley still held on to the possibility that all was not lost. "Do you think somebody will buy it for parts?"

"Don't count on it, but I'll put a sign on it. You never know."

He changed into his jogging clothes in the men's room for the longer run home.

4
The Lark

CHARLEY WAS GETTING his fill of embarrassing situations.

The next day at work, while still blushing from his foolishness in buying the Renault, he thought nothing of it when the red truck with a magnetized sign that read "Scissors n' Such Barber and Beauty Supply" on its door pulled into the parking lot. But it startled him when Dorothy pointed Lou Trainer to his booth—pretty brassy of her to pursue him in the salon, at his job.

He was about to say, "Missing me already?" with a spin of sarcasm when she dropped a box on the counter with a bill taped to it.

"Here's those new precision scissors you ordered," she said, all business. "Cash or credit card?"

Charley was flummoxed. Let's see, he realized he was maxed out on his American Express. He would have the cash by the end of the day and could cover a check if he went straight to the bank.

"Can I mail it to you?"

After a second's hesitation, she said, "Sure. I know where you live." She winked and walked to the door.

Charley was always amazed at how the chatter, hair dryers, and buzzing of clippers muted simultaneously when anything remotely newsworthy might be happening within the realm of the Wild Hare Salon. Not a word of Lou's exchange with Charley had been lost on his co-workers or their clients, who pricked their ears, hoping to carry out with them some morsel of scuttlebutt.

After Charley once again watched Lou drive off in her little red truck, Dorothy said, "Okay, Charley, what's the new secret?"

Her question projected across the room from her manicure table and encompassed all listeners. It was like a pause in the loud music of a nightclub, when someone keeps yelling in a voice tuned to being heard above several decibels, saying something untactful, like ". . . and you can kiss my ass," propelled into the sudden silence. As if by a conspiracy, no water ran, and even the Christian radio music paused. Everyone turned his way, magically choreographed to maximize the last possible atom of mortification that could be squeezed into the moment.

Charley reddened. "Nothin'."

Dorothy kept quiet. She eyed him over her client's shoulder as she plied her nail file, but she said nothing, a record for her.

He explained no further. A record for him.

* * *

By the next week, affordable transportation still an issue, Charley jogged to and from the Wild Hare with his backpack flopping, Dorothy made his deposits at the bank for him, and friends drove him other places. Running to work required that he take a hooker's bath at the salon's bathroom sink so that he wouldn't run off his clients with a whiff of his armpit as he reached past delicate noses for clippers or mousse. He skipped the Tuesday night ladies' promo at Hopper's, unwilling to ask Wayne for another lift. Jarod spent weeknights home with Sue. Billy worked on a ranch out in the middle of nowhere with no cell reception. Candelario still attended AA. And he certainly didn't want Lou to think he was coming because her band was there.

Rather than put in his usual Saturday night at Hopper's, he watched movies at Jarod and Sue's. As Charley handed Sue his hostess gift of a six-pack of longnecks—his contribution to the dinner menu—she asked, "What's up, Charley? Don't tell me you're swearing off pool for my cooking."

"Sure I am," he said, hoping he didn't look the way he felt—like a fish out of his aquarium.

A wiser car purchase would lessen the embarrassment of the Renault, which still sat beside Jarod's shop, Charley decided. Fast-growing weeds sprouted around the wheels. Sometimes Jarod leaned a crowbar or jack handle against its bumper while he worked on another project. And there it sat—idle, extraneous, a shell of a reminder of what he thought it was when he'd first spotted it in the used car lot next to the Hiss Pit Bar-b-que Stop near Tyler, Texas.

* * *

On Thursday, his schedule opened up, and even though he could easily fill the time with walk-ins, he called Wayne for a ride to the car lot over in Briargrove.

The lot was bordered with the usual multicolored plastic flags that flapped in the wind in sync with the car-buying butterflies flapping in his stomach. Coy Baker, the owner, had sold Charley his old VW Jetta. The VW's odometer had showed ninety thousand miles, but Coy assured him it would go at least a hundred thousand more. It did, and then some. It had been Charley's first personal car purchase, and it lasted him seven years. It was a rather yuppie-looking car for an old trailer-park boy from Sulfur Gap to be driving. He liked the lines. His eye for lines made him a good hair stylist but caused trouble when it came to picking women and cars. He tended to focus too much on the surface and not worry too much about what lay under the hood or in the heart.

Now he looked around the lot at the rows of SUVs and minivans traded in during the last gas price hike. He saw no small pickups like Lou's, which was what he preferred. Or something red and sporty. A red Jeep would be nice.

The glass door of the little office building at the back of the lot swung open, and a stout, middle-aged woman in jeans and Dr. Scholl's sandals walked toward Charley and Wayne.

"Where's Coy?" Charley looked behind the woman to make sure Coy wasn't coming.

"Coy retired last week," she said. "My name's Irma Bridges. I'm the new owner." She held out her hand.

Charley still leaned to one side, looking behind Irma, searching for Coy.

Wayne stepped into the gap and took Irma's hand.

"Hello, Ms. Bridges. I'm Wayne Cheadham, and this is my friend, Charley Bristow."

Charley came to and shook hands.

"So, this was pretty sudden, Coy retiring."

"Yeah, the word's not out yet. Coy kept it quiet because he didn't want a lot of hoo-haw made over his retirement. Of course everyone in Briargrove knew anyway. Y'all aren't from here, are you?"

"No ma'am," Charley replied. "We've come from Sulfur Gap." He was about to say "Nice to meet you" and leave. Not finding Coy there threw him off.

"So, how can I help you?" Irma asked.

"It depends on what you have that I can afford." Charley guessed he was stuck now. He looked around the lot. There was no red Jeep, though there was a 1995 yellow Mustang that looked perfect. The purple lettering on the windshield read $16,499. Charley knew he couldn't make payments on that amount but juggled figures in his head anyway.

Irma seemed to make some intuitive leaps of her own and

pointed to a white 1998 Buick Skylark sedan, sticker price $5,399.

Charley took one look and imagined the old-lady perfume smell of the interior.

"It's the best deal for the price on my lot. We can put it on two-year financing," Irma said. "It's pretty fuel-efficient, too. Low odometer reading for being so old. Belonged to the Methodist preacher's mother."

Charley balked at the idea of buying a dead woman's car, but Irma read his mind.

"At least I don't have to say she only drove it to church on Sunday, because she doesn't go to church a lot. She and her son don't always gee and haw. Anyway, she drove it to her job over in Matilda at the prison, so every day it got highway miles. She bought a new Regal in Abilene. If I'm still in the car business in ten years, I'm sure I'll get to sell that one to someone who comes in at the right moment looking for a good deal, too. She's the type that changes the oil every three months, religiously."

Charley's standing joke about his approach to car maintenance was that he changed his oil every seventeen thousand miles, whether it needed it or not.

Irma said its whiteness wouldn't show dirt, not the kind of dirt in this part of the country. White, bland, but it wouldn't show caliche dirt or wind-blown dust. The gray interior would not get too hot, so it wouldn't fry you during the triple-digit summer heat.

Charley's imagination ran on ahead. You wouldn't be a fried egg, you'd be *driving* an egg, he thought. He could hang a big bunny face on the grill for Easter, a snowman face at Christmas. . . . If it were a bigger model, he could call it Moby Buick. He could have a bumper sticker: "Son of Moby." Probably no one would get it. Or "Humpty Dumpty." But that would be bad luck. After all, Humpty Dumpty was broken and couldn't be fixed, an idea that reminded him of The No sitting in front of Jarod's with a forlorn tire tool and monkey wrench leaning against the bumper.

"That's the best deal you're going to get anywhere," Wayne said.

Irma nodded agreement. "I used to work at the Ford house in Abilene, and I know you won't get a better deal there," she said. "You know, they discontinued Skylarks in '98. This is the last year-model. It'll be a classic in a few years."

He doubted it. It was too conventional, too compromising — neither boxy nor swoopy. Nothing about a Skylark provoked a romantic appeal. It was the kind of used car that people drove for basic transportation when they couldn't afford anything else.

Charley's eyes swept longingly over the lot, searching for a two-door coupe of any kind that might have materialized while they were discussing the Buick. He couldn't pick up women in the Skylark — they would think he was driving his mother's car or a stolen ride, or that he was a serial killer — it was too much of a disconnect with the image he wanted to project.

Wayne saw Charley wavering and said, "Don't ask me to come car hunting with you if you don't listen. At least take it for a test drive."

Finally, he let Irma and Wayne talk him into taking the car to get Jarod's expert opinion.

Wayne and Charley drove back to Sulfur Gap in the Skylark and pulled into Jarod's shop. The No still stood, abandoned, with its For Sale for Parts sign still going begging. Charley made a mental note to himself that Dorothy had bought herself a new refrigerator before his Shreveport trip and was looking for a buyer for the old one. Dorothy should give it to him to throw in with The No. He pictured another sign: Bonus! Free Refrigerator to Highest Bidder. Fridge runs.

* * *

"Now that's a sensible ride for you, Charley," Jarod said, leaning across the engine as he jiggled the belts and squeezed the hoses. "You could even keep driving it a while after it's paid off, if you bring it in for regular maintenance."

Regular maintenance did not sound exciting. It sounded geriatric, like old people talking about "being regular." Charley had a mental image of adding Metamucil to the gas tank. "Yeah, it'll do zero to sixty in half a minute!" he sulked.

"Well," Jarod said, "it's a practical choice. For the price, I don't think you're going to find another car that's as well-maintained and has the low mileage. And guys like Bo won't be able to say anything. You'll be using your head and not your sense for . . . *style*."

"Oh, sure. It'll be handy when I go to pick up the grandkids. I can get two car seats in the back. And I don't give a shit what Bo thinks. I'll probably never see him again."

Charley drove the Skylark back to Briargrove to sign papers with Irma and drop Wayne off at his truck, not completely reassured by Jarod's vote of confidence. He'd just committed himself to making payments on this boring set of wheels for the next two years. He wondered if he could resell it to one of the old ladies coming in to the Wild Hare. Even a teenage girl wouldn't mind the Skylark for hauling her friends around.

Before he drove away, Irma knocked on the driver's window. He rolled the glass down.

She handed him a manila envelope and said, "I almost forgot. The lady that sold me the car? She wants the new owner to have this. It has a song on it, I think."

Great, Charley thought, opening the flap to find a homemade cassette tape that just happened to be suitable for the car's pre-CD sound system. That'll be fun to listen to, he grumbled to himself. At least it wasn't an eight-track. But then, leaving a song for the new owner of your old car must mean you were attached to the car in some way. It probably meant the old tape player worked, too, something Charley forgot to check. The car had no doubt been loved in a way that only cars can be loved.

"Thanks," said Charley, and he pitched the envelope into the glove compartment.

Old-lady car or no, this weekend he could make it to Hopper's without having to ask Wayne or anybody else for a ride.

* * *

Dorothy admired Charley's new car when he drove into the parking lot on Friday morning.

"You'll come to appreciate how comfortable this is," she said from behind the steering wheel as she rubbed her hands over the velour seat covers. The car did seem to fit Dorothy nicely. But despite the steps—and the dust—it had saved Charley on the ride to work, he still didn't feel at one with the machine.

Later, Lou Trainer made a delivery. She waved at Charley from across the salon. He remained cordial, acknowledging her with a nod as she headed out the door. But the desire for another opinion suddenly overtook him. "Wait!" he called out to her.

Charley abandoned his caped client and followed Lou to the parking lot, ignoring the speculation he generated in his wake. "Want to see what I was talked into buying?"

Lou's glance went straight at the Skylark.

"How'd you know?"

"Haven't seen it in the employee parking spaces before, and you seem a little sheepish. I can connect the dots."

"Now I feel like a real dumbass," Charley said.

"Only for being embarrassed are you a dumbass. I like it. I hereby dub it The Lark. A fitting nickname! Now have some fun with it."

"I'll trade you for your little pickup."

"No way. I'm a delivery person, and I need it for business. You don't need a pickup. You need a smooth ride, good gas mileage, and probably low payments. It's a nice little car. I like it. The Lark. To replace The No."

He winced but decided to ignore the term for his other car that she'd probably learned from the Dorothy grapevine. "So you like this vanilla pile of crap I'm saddled with payments on for the next two years?"

"Yeah. It's reliable, attractive transportation. It should suit your needs. It's used, but none the worse for the wear."

Charley had half a mind to say "Like you?" But he sealed the snarky remark in his thoughts before it could pass his lips.

In the nanosecond he'd paused to listen to his better self, Lou added, "Yeah, it's like you . . . used but still in pretty good shape. Reliable."

Charley's little flat-mouthed, holding-it-in smile vanished. This conversation was over. Anyway, his client was waiting. "Glad you like it," he said to Lou unceremoniously. "Be seein' you around." He hurried back into the shop before the redness spread up his neck all the way to his hairline.

Lou shook her head and climbed back into her truck.

When he drove the Skylark home from work later in the afternoon, Charley admitted to himself how smoothly it managed Sulfur Gap's potholed streets. And now he could get himself to Hopper's for a Friday night of fun.

5

Stalked?

CHARLEY HAD PROMISED Jarod a game of pool, so he headed straight for the tables at Hopper's. After he slapped Mitch on the back and nodded blandly at Wes, he took his Falcon cue stick from its case and began assembling it. It had been a gift from Joyce, in the earliest, happy days of their short marriage. It truly was the nicest present anyone had ever given him, and tonight, he again reveled in the black Canadian maple, the perfection of its grip, and the balance he sensed as he sighted the cue ball. The blue engraved design on the handle was a bonus. Charley took some warmup shots as he waited for his buddy. Jarod, already a good player, wanted to polish his game, so he didn't mind Charley beating him. Charley was looking forward to being himself tonight.

At first he was alarmed to see his friend Candy standing around the tables—he was supposed to be in AA. But Charley was relieved to note that he was holding a diet Coke instead of a longneck or something stronger. Candy was on thin ice. If he didn't stay clean, he could be put on probation or possibly go to prison, and Charley knew Candy was a decent sort deep down. He didn't belong behind bars—at least not if he stayed sober.

"Hey, Candy, you're stickin' to Coke, I hope."

"Yeah, man. Thanks for the concern." Candy smiled at Charley. "I'm far enough along that I'm allowed to put in a little time at Hopper's."

"You making it to lots of those meetings?" Charley was a bit curious—maybe someday his mother would go. He'd have to talk to her about it if he ever sensed an opening to bring up the subject.

"Yeah. Makes me feel young. Some of those old geezers tote their own oxygen into the meetings. But at least they've gotten to grow old, stayin' sober, *un dia de vez*." The guys laughed appreciatively. Many were relieved that it was Candy, and not them, who had to give up a good beer with their pool game.

Jarod arrived fifteen minutes late. "Sorry, Charley," he said. "Sue wanted me to fix the commode before I could come. Figured if I fixed the shitter, she couldn't give me any shit." More guffawing erupted from the group.

As the two friends battled it out, Charley advised Jarod on which shots to take and how to line them up. The other guys were attentive, picking up some advice for their own games.

Charley hoped no one noticed that he kept looking toward the bar. He wished that cute little brunette, Darla, would make an appearance so that he could get her number and dance to a few songs after he was through at the pool table. Lou's band wasn't playing tonight, but while this different group—some guys from Abilene—got the dance crowd warmed up, Charley did his best to concentrate on his game while occasionally scanning the club for Darla. After the second break, there was still no sign of her. Charley was glad Lou wasn't there. He wanted to feel available if Darla showed, and Lou's presence would cloud his mind with options.

But she never appeared, so he drove home looking forward to Saturday night. If Darla was absent on Saturday, he would begin making inquiries. Sulfur Gap wasn't so big that he wouldn't be able to find her.

* * *

After the final haircut on Saturday, Hopper's beckoned again.

From home, Charley made a quick run toward the center of town, circled the Sandstone County courthouse, and jogged through the small municipal park, waving at the families swinging kids and staking out picnic tables. After a shower and a BLT sandwich, he was ready to go.

Lou's Crew was playing. The band had started out simply playing together—good enough to jam in public—and within a few weeks' time became the regular band, except for the times when a band had been previously booked. They never named themselves, but everyone referred to them as "Lou's Crew" until the name stuck. According to reports of Hopper's regulars, the band already knew all the old standards, and they began throwing in some newer songs as they'd found time to rehearse a bit here and there.

Charley parked on the far edge of the lot. Inside, the band was already playing a waltz. The older couples loved to swirl around the floor to waltzes, while the young crowd sat at their tables or played pool. Most of them didn't know how to waltz.

Lou's Crew was bringing in the crowd. Charley took a seat at the bar and faced the bandstand. Lou eventually saw him and waved a drumstick at him without missing a beat. Pretty impressive, he thought. A microphone angled over her. Whoa! Was Lou a singer, too?

He was mulling over this possibility when he felt a little fist ramming into the small of his back. When he turned around, Darla was smiling up at him. Biggest smile he'd seen her stir up. The last time he'd seen her, her hair hung straight, but now it bounced around her head in springy little spirals, not a style he would have recommended. He could shape her hair so it would hang real nice if she would come in to the Wild Hare . . . . Well, good to have someone glad to see you anyhow. And now he could learn more about her.

She held his hand up over her head and twirled herself so that he could get a good look. Her sequin-trimmed tank top and tight jeans with matching sequins on the back pockets showed off her gym-workout shoulders and other curves. He did ponder briefly that the sequins looked like teeth, as she flashed her quick smile.

"My, you're lookin' good," he said.

"Thanks. Oh, I want to give you my number before I forget." Wasting no time, she dragged a napkin from across the bar and waved to Brady Hopper to toss her a pencil. Catching it deftly in the air, she scribbled on the napkin and handed it to Charley. Well, that was settled. He didn't even have to ask. *She's a mind reader*, he thought.

The band was starting a new song, so Charley held out his hand to Darla. The singer—Charley remembered his name was Wylie—was crooning the lyrics to "She Let Herself Go" . . . to Vegas, Honolulu, New York City, and on a blind date. Her boy-friend dumped her, and she let herself go. Good for her.

With a chuckle, he looked at Darla. "Is that what you did?"

"Is what what I did?"

"Did you let yourself go after your divorce?"

Darla frowned. "What do you mean?"

"Oh, never mind. I was kidding." She probably wasn't listen-ing to the lyrics.

Darla seemed satisfied, and they danced on. She was lighter on her feet than when they'd first danced. More relaxed. Charley parked her on a bar stool as soon as he could. While he appreci-ated Darla's attractions and didn't want to be rude, he also didn't want to get involved while he was exploring his options with Lou. He had Darla's number, and he'd spend more time with her later, if she didn't take off, but he didn't want to rush. He joined a group around a pool table and waited to get a game going.

Charley held his pool cue and watched as the band prepared to ramp up the sound. Wylie bent over an amplifier and turned some knobs, creating an ear-piercing squeal. Lou settled onto her stool, ready to put muscle into the next song. When Wylie got the sound balanced, he positioned his guitar and mic, the fiddler took his stance, and the rhythm guitar player nodded to the bass player. Wylie counted the intro, and the players jumped together into a new song. Most of the crowd recognized "Get Drunk and Be Somebody" from the first few notes. Everything stopped—pool players left their games, barflies stopped gossiping, and waitresses froze with trays of drinks in midair. Mad excitement invaded Hopper's. No one ever expected a Toby Keith hit to be played with so much assurance by a local band in this burg. Not until it was a few decades old, anyway. The delirium caught on.

The crowd rushed to the front of the bandstand to hold their drinks in the air and join in with the chorus. Some of the women climbed on the shoulders of their dates or stood on chairs. A few of the bigger guys planted themselves protectively in front of the pool tables to prevent the green felt from becoming a celebration platform for some of the revelers gone wild. It was pandemonium as never before seen at Hopper's.

Lou tapped the rhythm and harmonized at the same time. A performer who could keep a beat and sing harmony like that was a true talent, to Charley's way of thinking. He couldn't hear her well because of the yee-hawing going on, but he, too, was caught up in the fun. He held up his beer with the rest of the crowd and admired Lou without any reservation.

The band played several standards. At some point, Darla sidled over to Charley and bumped against him with plain purpose. He looked down at her admiring face and succumbed to more dancing.

He wanted to find Lou during the break and tell her how much he liked the new songs the band had introduced, but Darla seemed stuck to him. He wondered what was happening to him. Any other time, he would have been engulfed with gratitude for a beautiful woman's attention and left the dance with her by now. At the least, he would have wrapped a possessive arm around Darla's shoulders as he peered around the crowd looking for Lou. But now, if she should appear, he didn't want her to think he was seriously hooking up, so he kept his arm to himself. Finally, he spotted Lou coming out of the bathroom and started to walk toward her, but felt Darla's finger hooked into his belt loop. This was awkward.

When he looked back at Darla, she reminded him of one of those puppies he'd taken to the Wal-Mart in need of a home. Something throbbed in his chest, so he said, "Let's go get our next beer." That line sealed the rest of the evening at Hopper's, he thought, but surely he could escape later.

Charley scoped out the crowd at the bar. He waved to Jarod and Sue, nodded to other familiar faces. Darla kept him anchored by the belt loop as he bought her next beer.

Lou waved to Wylie and worked her way through the crowd to him. He held the exit door open, and they disappeared into the parking lot. Charley felt a bubble of disappointment rise in his chest and resonate through his rib cage. A musical bond existed between Lou and Wylie, but the guy had to be pushing sixty—surely too old for Lou. Well, it was none of his business anyway, Charley reminded himself. And they could have been going out to the truck to look over some sheet music—who knew?

He glanced around for a way out, but his back was pressed against the bar, Darla standing close in front of him. So he eased onto a stool, and she perched on the one beside him. The break music played Toby Keith's "A Little Too Late" over the speakers.

Charley decided to make the best of the situation for now. He deployed all his practice in the art of polite conversation.

"So, how's the job search going?"

"Fine." Darla put her hand on his knee.

"I imagine the pickings are limited in Sulfur Gap."

"Yeah." Her hand advanced up his thigh. Charley's eyes swept his surroundings as much as possible while keeping his head still. No one seemed to be taking note of Darla and him.

"What kind of work do you do?"

"Oh, a little of this and that." She moved her hand toward his inner thigh.

"I've heard Wal-Mart is a good place to start. Have you looked there?"

"Put in an application last week." She was too close to his crotch, and with strong pressure for such little hands.

"Hey, I'm gonna need a bathroom break." Charley took her wrist and gently removed her hand. He was acting like a virgin who wasn't sure about his sexual orientation.

"Me too."

As Charley stood up, Darla slid off her stool and this time put two fingers in his belt loop.

When Charley came out of the bathroom, she was leaning against the wall of the small hallway. She reattached herself. The band started, and they were back on the dance floor, scooting along to Wylie crooning "Nobody But Me." Charley steered Darla away from the bandstand, but Hopper's wasn't large enough for him to escape the feeling that Lou would be looking on disapprovingly, even though she hadn't given the smallest hint that she gave a rat's hat about his love life.

He was in a quandary. He couldn't go, because Darla would see it as eagerness to get away with her into the night, and he couldn't stay, because Lou would see him incapable of resisting Darla as they danced the night away and Charley missed his regular pool challenges. He didn't want to hurt Darla's feelings, and being honest, he admitted to himself that he was about as hard-pressed as any normal guy would be to fend off such attention.

Oh my, she was cute. He liked her smell—a light floral fragrance. Her firm little body reminded him of ripe fruit and made him think of the pants teenage girls were wearing that said "Juicy" across their forbidden bottoms. So Charley danced on. Occasionally, she would have trouble matching his stride and would bounce off of his chest. Every bump was a jolt that went straight to his groin.

The best solution for now was a few shots of tequila. Darla kept right up with him as the evening wore on into a haze of dancing and drinking.

Wylie announced the final number. "Here's our own Lou Trainer, singing Sarah Evans's recent hit, 'Cheatin.' And if it wasn't for us other band members and our playin', you'd think you were listening to the original recording."

Wylie was right. The song was a good dance number, so the crowd pressed onto the floor. Lou's mellow contralto wafted over the dancers. Charley was blown away. He could not believe she hadn't gone pro. But then he knew he wasn't a prime critic and didn't have a notion of what it took to make it big.

Lou was toning in on the lines about a lonesome cheater eating pork and beans and deserving every bite. She looked at Charley and winked. Charley smiled at her and lengthened his dance stride as much as he could while maneuvering Darla, so that he could scoot on past the bandstand. They were moving down the side of the dance floor closest to the exit when he heard her singing that she'd take the two-timer back when she "stopped breathin'." And as she sang on about the cheater, he pulled Darla toward the exit.

The cool night air hit him in the face, and a tiny bell of caution went off in his brain. He was way too drunk to be driving. Sheriff Larry Bob would be out cruising, no doubt. Larry Bob would probably just follow him to make sure he arrived home safely, but he didn't want to take Darla home with him. She might decide to stay.

"Well, where's your car?" Darla leaned against him as she gazed across the lot.

"It's over here. Just bought it this past week."

Following his line of sight, Darla headed toward a new silver Dodge Ram crew cab. Charley felt sorry for her.

"Keep goin', sis. Sorry to disappoint you, but that isn't my ride."

She looked beyond the big pickup at the white sedan in the shadow cast by the amber glow of the parking lot lights. Seedy oak blossoms gathered around its windshield wipers.

"Don't you own the Wild Hare?" Too late to reel back the question, she clapped her hand over her mouth and giggled.

"Not hardly. I'm a poor working stiff, and right now, I'm stiff." He steered her to the car. He was surprised when Darla laughed at his quip, even though it was obvious. As he reached to open her door, she leaned her back against it and put her arms around his neck. She looked up at him with eyes of trust—or maybe just lightheadedness—he couldn't say which. She pulled him to her and kissed him. *God help me*, he thought, *she's the best kisser I ever laid a lip on.* They needed to get out of this parking lot. "Buckle up, darlin'," he said, and closed her into the Lark. When he slid behind the wheel, she was waiting to glue herself against him—seat belt be damned.

Charley made a last-minute decision and drove—ever so carefully—the opposite direction from home. He kept driving until he reached the turnoff to Wayne's place.

"Where we going?" Darla was mildly concerned as she lifted her head from Charley's shoulder.

"I can't take you to my place. I've got an ex that's still doing drive-bys and if she saw us going in my apartment at this hour, we'd have some trouble." Joyce was long gone, but the lie came easy.

"Oh . . . so where're we going?" She started loosening his belt and jeans.

"How about right here?" Charley took the small dirt road that led to Wayne's old windmill. The slightly rutted track around it told of the times through the years when Wayne—and other young friends—used it as a meeting spot for parking and partying. It served as a turnaround, a landmark, and a symbol of long ago, before electrical pumps brought up the well water.

"Okay," she said, with a tinge of resignation. Then, as if encouraging herself, she said, "I haven't been parking since high school." Charley again felt sorry for her at the disappointment he heard in her voice. She was getting a cheap deal. Treated like a cheap date and there wasn't even a date.

"First I have to make a call."

"Checking in with your mom?" Now she was getting edgy. But she was still working on getting his jeans open and loosened up.

"Not hardly." Charley thought about the pun he'd made, but skipped on. He figured it would be wasted on Darla. "I'm callin' the game warden."

This caused Darla to pause as she pulled his T-shirt free with her deft little hand.

"Am I that much of a wild catch?" she giggled.

"He's probably out prowling tonight. If he saw us, he'd be bustin' up our party, thinkin' we were trespassers or poachers.

And he'd probably call and wake up my friend. I've got the warden's number stored here. . . ."

While Darla unsnapped his shirt, Charley punched his speed dial.

"Hey, J.J. . . . I wanted to let you know I'm pulled up at Wayne's windmill, driving a white Buick, so don't be thinking Wayne's got a poacher or meth dealer out here if you're patrolling out this way. . . . Yeah, gonna hang out here in the moonlight a while. . . . Thanks, buddy."

Darla was nibbling his ear and kissing his neck now. Charley pitched his phone on the dash and turned his full attention to her. He could have kissed her for hours. She made it clear that she liked kissing him, with low purring sounds from deep in her throat. They opened the front doors for leg room and ventilation. Charley found the switch to turn off the dome light, and they tangled and slid over into the back seat. They opened both back doors. Now *this* was Charley's idea of how to break in a new used car.

Darla kicked off her boots and peeled down her jeans. She swept her tank top over her head and stood beside the car in her thong and pushup bra to jerk his jeans the rest of the way off. Once she had him stripped down, she pinned his shoulders with both arms and straddled him. Kissing him hard, she reached back to unhook her bra.

With what thought he could muster, Charley noted her ability to multitask. She could find more positions to get into in the back seat of a car than he ever dreamed possible. When he flipped her over, she slid into the perfect place for her legs. He didn't care where his legs were. A cow mooed, a distant coyote yipped, and the crickets sawed a rhythm as he fell in love again.

* * *

Her springy curls tickling his nostrils woke him up. That, and her little bit of weight on him making it hard to breathe easily in his sleep. He was sobering up. Thank God he hadn't been too plastered to remember. This would be one for the precious memories songbook, if he lived that long. He pulled one curl out and let it spring back, pushed the hair from Darla's face, and tickled her back. It was still dark.

On the way back to town, she didn't say much except to give him directions to her parents' house.

"I guess we skipped the part about being properly introduced," he said.

"Yeah. We rushed it a bit."

"So do I know your folks?"

"My mom's Janet Barta," she said.

Charley stopped in the middle of the street and looked at Darla.

"Really? Mrs. Barta's your mom? She was my second grade teacher. She gave me the first book I ever owned." The happy memory faded when he thought about all the scoop Darla's mother could tell her about his upbringing. That made him anxious. Second grade was the year Dawson became his new temporary stepdad. The bruises and a black eye he saw on his mother when he came home from school one day had encouraged him to play sick a lot. Dawson eyed him resentfully but didn't pick as many fights with his mother when Charley stayed home.

Other than that, Dawson had been all right. He worked maintenance at the prison, with plenty of night hours, so he was gone most of the time. He even took Charley fishing on the lake shore a couple of times. He showed him how to put a worm on a hook and cast his floater out to the deep water. Then one day he was gone. Charley's mother wouldn't discuss it.

"So your whole name is Darla Barta?" The rhyme scheme

was odd.

"Yewww, no!" Darla said. "My last name is Buchanan. Ed Barta's my stepdad."

"Is your bio dad in the picture?"

"Oh, sure. He lives in Big Spring. Runs a tire dealership.

Charley's stomach did an extra flip-flop. The same Bo Buchanan who had witnessed the height of his stupidity with The No? Oh, well. Thinking of cars, he asked, "What about your car? Did you leave it at Hopper's?"

"No, I rode over with Wylie. He's a friend of my stepdad's. I gave him the sign that we were leaving while he was on the bandstand."

Uh-oh.

There were too many connections all of a sudden. Charley didn't know this girl's stepfather, hadn't recognized Wylie as someone from around town, and had recently limped through an awkward moment with her father, but now he was sure all of their paths had probably crossed. Sulfur Gap was too small for him not to have met either Wylie or the stepdad. Well, you couldn't control the small-town gossip. Knowing that someone he knew, knew that he was screwing someone they knew, probably wouldn't have changed this night's outcome. Not even knowing she was related to good ol' Bo would have diverted him from the passion that had overtaken them both.

Charley had weathered far more embarrassing situations than this—like Joyce's Wal-Mart meltdown. And bullets flying in his bathroom. And his mother. Shame was a cloak he wore lightly. He'd learned to shrug it away, pretend it wasn't there.

So Wylie knew that Darla left the dance with Charley, and Lou would know for sure. Well, big whoop, he decided. Darla had girlfriend potential. In fact, he was smitten. She'd compensated for her lack in the conversational department with her gift for getting around the back seat of a car. Surely some serious romances had blossomed in the back seat of a car. You wouldn't know, because it wasn't exactly dinner conversation.

In front of her house, he gave her a deep, long kiss of true appreciation.

"Call me?" she said.

"Absolutely, but wait a minute."

He swiveled out and trotted around the car as fast as his hung-over legs would carry him. Opening her door, he pulled her to him. She teetered a bit but returned his bear hug.

"Oh, my. I'm never doing tequila shots again."

Good idea, Charley thought, watching her run toward the house before she threw up in the shrubs.

He would have to call her for coffee or lunch. At least he didn't have to figure out how to get her out of his apartment. They could even date a while. What a concept. And he was definitely up for more windmill excursions. If he could hold back. . . . His mind teetered on the edge of deep obsession.

6
Relations

CHARLEY SLEPT LATE SUNDAY. He rolled over and looked at the clock at ten and thought about how he could make an appearance at some church and surprise the congregation. He wanted to go give thanks for the memory of last night, a memory that still made him shudder. But he dismissed the idea. It was whimsical and hypocritical. The best way to celebrate would be to go back to sleep and dream about his luck in getting together with Darla.

Hunger finally woke him. Stumbling into his little kitchen, he fished a carton of milk from the refrigerator and gulped it dry. He was out of coffee. Damn. He'd have to make a grocery run.

In the parking lot of the United Supermarket, he saw Lou's little truck and braced himself to run into her inside the store. Sure enough, she was pushing her full cart out the door as he was going in.

"Hey, Charley!" Lou seemed glad to see him. Well, she must not know about him and Darla yet, he figured.

"Hey, Lou. Did you leave anything in the store for the rest of us?"

"Oh, shut up. Didn't we all have fun last night?"

Charley blushed. How could she know?

"Well, I think the band is getting pretty tight, don't you?" Lou filled in the uncomfortable pause.

Oh, right, the music, the dancing. He recovered. "Yeah, you

guys had us hoppin' at Hopper's. And, lady, you can sure sing. How come you didn't tell me you could sing like that?"

"Thanks, Charley. I didn't tell you because it never seemed to fit in the conversation for me to start bragging about my singing. Well, I better skedaddle and get my frozen stuff put up."

"Where are you living, by the way?"

"I'm renting with an option to buy. The old Middleton place right outside town. The Raneys own it now. Renting gives me time to decide if I want to stay here. Gotta run. See you." She waved over her shoulder and hustled her cart away.

Charley realized how little he knew about Lou Trainer. But she intrigued him more every day.

Later that evening, he thought about calling Darla Buchanan, but decided he should put it off. He gazed at her number in his cell phone. Be disciplined, he told himself. He began to think of getting to know Darla as a project like cutting a head of unruly hair. He would have to examine the turf carefully and work in sections with an overall goal of a tame, blended outcome. It wouldn't be as simple as cutting hair, but at least he knew that he was looking at "unruly" when it came to him and his urge to dive in head first.

He didn't know how he was going to spend his day off on Monday, but he didn't think he should fill it right away with Darla plans. Seeing Lou made him want to hold off on that. He fell asleep reading the latest *National Geographic* he had wahooed from the salon.

Charley woke up to the whir of his vibrating cell phone. It was Lou. How had she gotten his number? Oh, yeah, it was on his business cards, available for all prospective clients at Dorothy's front desk.

"Get up, Charley," she said.

"I am up," he said, the sleep obviously still in his voice.

"You are not."

"Get up and get dressed."

"Why?" Where did she get off, bossing him around?

"I have a plan for you." Charley groaned, but Lou went on. "You need to try The Lark out on the highway, and I need to run up to Lubbock for some supplies. Your trunk is big enough for my purposes."

Charley sat up. His day was unplanned so far, but Wayne had mentioned that he could come out to the ranch and help him clean out an old tack room in the barn, an idea which un-thrilled Charley no end. In the middle of the night, persistent desire had woken him up to think about Darla. He was leaning toward calling her. "This is my day off."

"Yeah, so get off your butt and be ready in thirty minutes. We can make a day of it. Or you can go to Wayne's and get filthy dirty. He told me ya'll had talked about working at his place to-day."

A surge of jealousy whipped Charley wider awake. Wayne talked to Lou! When did they exchange numbers? Were they seeing each other already? Wayne was a serious contender, unlike Wylie. They had been talking sometime—over dinner? Lou was the kind of woman that could bring Wayne back from the dead. Suspicion rose in his mind. Was she playing games? Pretty pushy of her to tell him how to spend his day. Maybe she knew about him and Darla and was trying to head it off.

Then he thought of driving up to Lubbock, up the caprock escarpment, beside the open vistas on the way up the Panhandle, with Lou or not, started to sound like an appealing idea. It would be an easygoing trip. She was comfortable to be with, but he didn't want to lead her on. He couldn't see her as anything more than a friend, especially now that he had stepped through the door with Darla, and he didn't want to give Lou the wrong idea.

But he wasn't sure. Well, he'd have to make it clear when the timing seemed right. Still, he didn't want Wayne or Wylie moving in on her. Part of him wanted to focus on Darla, but another part wanted to keep his options open with Lou. *What a slut I am,* he thought. At least Lou wasn't mad at him for leaving the dance with Darla. This could help him pass another full day before he called Darla. Would Darla be wondering about him? Was he a jerk? Yes. He felt a throb in his groin that confused him all the more.

He decided he was thinking too much.

Before long, Lou knocked at his door. Charley stepped outside and shut the door behind him before she could see inside.

On the way out of town, Lou explored the Skylark's interior.

"Mind if I check the glove box?"

"Help yerself," Charley said.

She pulled the manila envelope out of the glove box.

"What's in this?"

Charley had forgotten about the gift from the car's previous owner.

"Oh, a tape of an old song. Check it out."

Lou pulled out the cassette. She glanced at the hand-written label. "How clever! It's a recording of Hoagy Carmichael singing 'Skylark.'"

"Who's Hoagy Carmichael? He must've been before *my* time."

"He's before *my* time, too, smartass. I think the song came out in the early 1940s. I like the lady that owned this car before you. She adopted a theme song for her *car*."

"Too bad it's not Woody Guthrie singin' 'I'll Take You Ridin' in My Car.'" Charley imitated the hokey engine sounds of the old song. "It would fit this jalopy better."

Lou ignored him. "Let's see how your player works." She

popped the cassette into its slot and turned up the volume. The sound was clear and textured. A few lone piano notes introduced a man's voice asking a question and calling a name in one word— *Skylark*. The gentle rhythm of the old jazz standard settled in as Carmichael fell into the lyrics about looking for his lover in misty meadows. The car floated along the highway, propelled by the gentle rhythm and grace of the music as Carmichael called on the skylark to reveal a valley green with spring and full of the beauty of blossoms leading his searching heart to its goal.

Romance and longing trickled an ache into Charley's heart. The words took on a playful tone and staggered rhythm that sang of music as faint as a will-o'-the-wisp. Whatever the hell a will-o'-the-wisp was, he didn't care. The lilt of easy saxophone filled several bars of the song and heightened his longing. A muted trumpet played with the hovering skylark.

He wanted to hear the song again, but his wish was anticipated. As he reached to hit the rewind button, the song started again and played through, and again. The song repeated itself like a meditation. His cynicism was caught off guard.

Charley was so filled with the words of the song, he wasn't seeing the road. The highway rose up out of the small town of Post, up the ear-popping rise of the escarpment, and he pulled over at the scenic lookout at the edge of the caprock. He and Lou listened as Carmichael sang to the skylark. A silent thread of tape spooled through and clicked to a stop. The embarrassing intimacy of their sharing the song made Charley want to dive out of the car, but he couldn't move. All he could do was stare straight ahead and try to swallow with as small a sound as possible. Tears were pushing behind his eyes, and he concentrated on damming them up.

After a minute with only the sound of the wind and an occasional car whipping by on the highway behind them, Lou said,

"Let's get out and enjoy the view."

Charley moved, trancelike, on spongy legs to the railing of the scenic overlook. Lou stood beside him as their eyes reached a hundred miles across the distant, flat land. Mid-morning sun angled the lowland shadows toward them.

"Amazing how far you can see," she said.

He nodded. He was glad that she was standing close but far enough away to respect his space. If she touched his arm, he would crumble. They stood for several minutes. Charley's breathing grew easier as he unclenched his jaw and fists. He shifted his weight and cleared his throat.

Lou said, "Now seems like the time to explain something, Charley."

He folded his arms and nodded without looking at her, poised to endure the sight of the emptiness below. He couldn't yet risk opening his mouth—his voice would come out in a sob. The song had soaked into him and left him hanging with nothing to do but look out on the open vista of the flat land spreading into the distance.

"Charley, you remember I told you I came in for a haircut three years ago?" Lou examined his profile. He was quiet, listening.

"I was in town to see your mother."

Charley raised an eyebrow. Now he was coming back to reality. Mention his mother, and he came back to full alert, force shield engaged.

"She told me you were cutting hair, so I came by to see you at the Wild Hare. You worked me into your schedule. Great haircut. You're good. You're real good." She touched his arm. "I've thought about you for the last three years."

Uh-oh. Amazing how fast the mood could change.

She went on. "Let's just say that your mother, April, and I are close in a way."

April. It felt odd to hear Lou say his mother's name, and the idea of their being close in any sort of way didn't drop into a logical pocket in his mind. His mother's name—April—was especially laced with irony coming from Lou's mouth. April. What a name for a woman who stayed in the dark and drank all day in front of the television. April was far too light and airy for a woman of his mother's girth. April. The month of wildflowers for a few weeks in West Texas. The time that it might rain and settle the smell of blown dust. It was his favorite month, when windows could be left open and rooms aired out. But April, his mother, was a source of grief to him. He felt sorry for her, but he wanted to shake her senseless sometimes. He also mourned the lumbering mass of sadness she had become. What an un-funny joke her name was. The un-April April.

Lou was talking. "I know you had it rough growing up. And seeing you and how you can cut hair and be so good with people—you have a sweetness about you—I was awed by how well you've turned out."

Charley looked down at the gravel between his feet.

"I want us to be friends. I want you to know I appreciate you."

Finally, Charley spoke up.

"You know I kinda started something with Darla Saturday night."

"So?"

"Well, with what you're telling me, I'd think you'd be put off."

"Listen, Buster." Lou's tone changed. "I'm not trying to get you in the sack. Not every female that pays attention to you is trying to seduce you. Do you think Dorothy is trying to sleep with you?"

"Ah, hell no. She's like a mother."

"Well, think of me that way."

"Okay. So you're not pissed at me if I go with Darla?"

"Of course not. And you certainly don't need my permission. I do think you need a little unsolicited advice—every pretty girl that you like doesn't have to move in with you."

"So you've heard?"

"What kind of town do you think we live in? Everybody knows everyone's business, and they find a way of telling you the tidbits while trying to sound like they're not gossiping."

Charley turned to look her in the eye. "Any warnings about me?"

"Of course not. Everyone loves you, Charley."

Then why did he feel so lonely?

Lou went on. "The people who've commented to me about your romantic escapades and your spending habits are convinced you need the right woman. But I disagree. I think looking for the right woman is what gets you in trouble. Anyway, she might be out there, but she shouldn't be the one you expect to fix you."

"And that right woman—there's no way that's you?"

"Oh, God no, Charley." Lou put a hand to her forehead and closed her eyes for a moment before squaring off in front of Charley. She grabbed his shoulders. "I'm going to tell you one more time. I don't want to date you. I want to be your friend. You don't know all about me, and I'll tell you what you need to know in good time, but in the meantime, get this straight. You and I are never going to be a couple."

"I have to admit, your singing does turn me on. Did you swear off men? You turn gay?" Now he was grinning. He knew a way to pester her.

Lou punched his arm. "You cannot get your mind off sex for a minute, can you?"

"Well, I am a twenty-five-year-old red-blooded male, and you couldn't be much over forty."

"I'm turning forty this year, butt-wipe. And I like men. Men who have some life experiences. Men I can converse with. I don't necessarily want to sleep with all of them. You, for instance. You're too young in so many ways. If you had learned how to be friends with a woman before you jump her bones, you might not have two ex-wives and a string of ex-girlfriends."

"So I can jump your bones after we've been friends?" This was going to be fun.

"Oh, you are making this so hard. Okay, Charley. Here it is. I'm still unraveling things. There's plenty of good reasons for us *not* to get involved, but there's the big one."

"What's that?" Charley's tone was cocky.

Lou took a breath and blew it out. She leaned in close. Like the queen in a game of chess, moving in for the kill when it's time to end the match.

"Charley, we are *related*."

Checkmate.

He took a step back and slumped against the historical marker.

7
Family Secrets

ANOTHER CAR PULLED UP beside the Skylark, and three little girls jumped out of the backseat, jabbering the whole way. "Why are we stopping here? What's the big deal about this view? Look, there's a ground squirrel. Let's see if it'll eat a potato chip. I need to go to the bathroom. I'm not going in a Porta-Potty!"

Charley and Lou got back into the Skylark.

"Okay, Lou-see," Charley began, "you've got some 'splainin' to do." Charley was covering his shock in the usual way—with quippiness.

"It's a long story. I found out when my father died four years ago that I'm your mother's half-sister. Then when I found your mother, I found out about you. That makes me your half-aunt. I didn't even know I had a half-sister until the reading of Pop's will."

Charley worked to concentrate and process this information while avoiding getting crushed by an eighteen-wheeler as he pulled back onto the highway. "Well, why didn't you tell me sooner?"

"I wanted to find the right time. I didn't want to walk up and introduce myself as your long-lost Auntie Lou."

As they drove across the plains, Lou began doling out the story. "My father was Darrell Trainer. He's your grandfather. Your mother never knew he was her father, so you wouldn't have heard of him."

Charley drove on a few miles before he responded. "Up until now, I thought my only family was Mom. She told me she went into a girls' home when she was sixteen. There was a bad domestic disturbance of some kind, and she landed in an emergency shelter, and went from there to a girls' home. After she had me, she married a man named Eldon Erwin. Her parents had disappeared, probably to avoid the law. That's all she told me. It made her sad, so I quit asking."

Charley kept his eyes on the road ahead as Lou continued. "I knew it hadn't been easy for her," she said. "No one lives like she does unless they've been through some hard times. It's been hard on you, too."

"Some do better, some do worse," Charley said.

"When I went to see her for the first time, I showed her the will and the letter my father left with it before she would believe who I was. She wasn't trusting, understandably. I think she's still trying to get her head around the idea of me being her half-sister and that she has two half-brothers, too. While I was away in Alaska, they got in touch with April and came to see her."

"Oh, have I cut their hair, too?" Charley's irritation came on a wave of snide. He was amazed at the traffic he had missed going in and out of the trailer-hood. "Who are they?"

"Ronnie lives in Houston. He's a petroleum engineer. He's been spending a lot of time in China lately."

"Wow, he must be smart."

"We're all smart, Chippie."

"Chippie?"

"Yeah, I'm christening you Chippie to remind you that you're smart, too. You're a chip off the old block, and you need to stop selling yourself short."

"Okay, Lou. But this Ronnie came to see Mom?"

"Yes. About a year after I was here. He was on his way to

China, but he managed a stop in San Angelo. He picked up a rent car and drove up to meet April."

"I bet he was impressed." Charley went to his sarcastic mode again.

"He knew that life was hard on her, and he wasn't exactly expecting her to be a member of the Junior League. They met and talked, and Ronnie's impression was that she couldn't take it all in. She didn't want them to see her. She was embarrassed."

"What about your other brother?"

"He was recovering from surgery and didn't make it from New Orleans until about a year ago. We didn't want to put the rush on April, anyway. His name is Dwight."

"What's he do?"

"He's an actuary for an insurance company."

"So why wasn't I included in any of this?"

"April begged us not to tell you yet. It was all a big shock. And, we all three were in the midst of some upheavals in our own lives. I went to Alaska and wound up doing my own personal regrouping and, while I was at it, trying to find Ann's trail."

"Ann?"

"Your grandmother, April's mother. Anyway, I couldn't find out a thing about Ann. Her maiden name was Smith. That's the worst name in the world to look for, besides maybe Martinez. And her middle name was Martin, which was probably a family name. Sometimes she hyphenated it, according to my father."

"Needle in a haystack, huh?" Charley thought about Lou's special effort, a favor she had done for him and his mother, trying to find traces of Ann in Alaska.

"Look, more will fall into place when you read Pop's letter," she said.

"I'm not surprised Mom didn't want any connections. I'm practically the only person she'll talk to. She gets out as little as possible, and has her own miserable little rut. I don't think it was too bad when I was little. Mom and Eldon's place looked better than the others in the 'trailer-hood.' That's not sayin' much, but you've gotta be proud of something."

Charley fiddled with the car radio to dial in his favorite Lubbock country station. He set the volume on low to continue his childhood saga for Lou. "Our mobile home was a double-wide that Eldon put some underpinning on and added a covered porch. Sometimes they fought like wolverines, because Mom worked off and on at the Navaho Restaurant. Her tips were good, mostly because of her good looks, which she still had then, and she and Eldon would get into it because he was convinced that she cheated on him or was intending to."

"You got to listen to all that?"

"I thought that was normal. Since then, I've seen better examples, like Wayne's parents and Jarod and Sue. Anyway, I put it together later that Eldon wasn't my father, because when I started school, the secretary looked at my birth certificate and called me Charles Bristow. I knew that Bristow was my mother's name before she married Eldon. And I called him Daddy Eldon, like there was someone before him who was a dad."

"What happened to Eldon? All April said was that he died."

"He stepped on a nail and got gangrene in his foot. He waited too long to go to the doctor and died of sepsis. I remember sitting in the corner of a hospital room wondering what would become of us. That was the last time Mom held me in her lap. I remember feeling her tears trickling through my hair. Then she set me aside. Totally."

Lou put her hand on his shoulder. Now that Charley knew she wasn't coming on to him, he didn't flinch. And he didn't feel like he would fall apart at a sympathetic touch. What he was telling Lou now was a familiar grief, one he'd confided in Jarod and

Wayne. Telling it to his good friends lightened the load so that he didn't feel as much like he was strung together with cheap twine that would frazzle and allow him to disintegrate.

When his mother became too much heartache, he could sit at Jarod and Sue's kitchen table with the warm smell of coffee lingering around them, and he could talk about it. He could sit on Wayne's front porch and watch a sunset and talk.

His friends instinctively knew that he didn't want advice, like "You'll miss her when she's gone, so you better love her now." They listened and acknowledged that people with stable families didn't know how lucky they were. Without his friends, his life with April the last twenty years would have crushed him in the dirt.

"Anyway, everybody's got a story," he said.

They were pulling into Lubbock, and he would have to pay more attention to the traffic. He was relieved to have an excuse to quit talking about the past.

They finished their business at the barber and beauty supply. Boxes stowed in the trunk, they found the nearest Denny's and settled into a booth.

Lou pulled an envelope out of her shoulder bag.

"This is a copy of my father's letter that explains everything. You can read it whenever you're ready. But tell me what happened to you and your mother after Eldon died."

Charley thought back. He'd developed good radar as a kid, so he noticed things and listened for information that would impact him. He was aware of much more than the adults around him gave him credit for. Now, he picked up the story and felt better about telling it. His legs were back under him, emotions tucked away. He talked as if everything had happened to someone else. Heck, it did feel like it happened to someone else. That was the way his personal history affected him.

"Eldon's insurance money ran out, and she went back to work at the Navaho," he explained. "One day she brought Dawson home. After Dawson left, there were two or three others—Kenneth, Emiliano . . . I do remember those guys' names, and not because of fond memories. To raise some extra cash, she traded down from the double-wide to a single-wide with fewer amenities.

"We never had the money to blow, but she became a regular at Hopper's and the VFW, sitting and drinking with what little she had. They must have let her run a tab or donated her drinks—I don't know. They let me come, too, because they knew I'd be home alone or with Kenneth or somebody if they didn't let me. Some of those guys that hung out there back then taught me to play pool."

Charley straightened his back and squared his shoulders with pride. "I got to where I could beat all of them by the time I was fifteen."

"And what about school? How was that?"

His laugh was bitter. "School was hard because of what they called my 'spotty attendance.' I got myself up and dressed most mornings and met the school bus when it came by the trailer park. None of my teachers had high hopes for me. They acted like they were waiting for the news that I'd landed in juvie lockup. I might have, except I wanted to stay out of trouble and see after Mom.

"There were other kids in my shoes, kids where the parents weren't much good. Friends at school kept me going. Some of their mothers and some of my teachers were nice and invited me over a lot. My second grade teacher gave me my first book. It was about Indians. Other teachers gave me books, and I have my own little library now that I've added to. People don't take me for a reader, but I do read. Few people know that I have shelving challenges because of all the books I hang on to."

"That doesn't surprise me, Chippie." Lou said. "Anyone can tell you're smart and have a few reference points outside the confines of Sandstone County. But go on, you were telling me about your school days."

"I had a friend whose granddad worked on the Cheadham ranch. Billy and I would hang out with Wayne. He was like an older brother or an uncle. He used to saddle up the gentler horses and let us ride. That's how Wayne and I got to be friends."

Charley caught the waitress's attention for a coffee refill.

"Anyway, I never rode the short bus to school, but they didn't put me on the college-bound track either. There was a program called 'at-risk' for kids like me, which meant mainly that teachers and counselors filled out forms and checked the boxes about all the factors that applied to me that could cause me to drop out of school—low-income family, crappy home life, skimpy attendance. It made my permanent file a lot thicker than a 'normal' kid's. But my high school guidance counselor was all right. She knew I was good in art and came up with the idea for me to go to barber's school. It made sense to me. Cuttin' hair *is* an art. Turned out that all my problems that made me a potential dropout also got me some grants to go to school for my license, so that was that. It's worked out pretty good. At least I never have to live in the trailer-hood again. Crummy apartment, but no housing involving cinder blocks for a foundation. No tie-downs for when the wind blows."

Charley bit into a french fry. "Okay, Lou, so let's see the letter. Or why don't you read it to me? You knew him and probably sound like him."

"Okay." She set her cup down and pulled the letter out of its envelope. Her eyes clouded as she began. "Pop died suddenly of a heart attack. He and Mom were both retired and starting to enjoy being together more, so it was sad and shocking. For a drummer, he sure had bad timing. This letter proves it, too. At least he put his affairs in order—being on the road so much, I guess he felt like he needed to."

As Charley sipped his coffee, Lou read. The voice of a grandfather he had never known began to play in his head, alongside Lou's voice.

Dear Family,

I know you're surprised that in my will I've named a beneficiary that you've never heard of. I want to explain why I'm leaving $20,000 to April Bristow, last known address, Weatherford, Texas. Lou, I hope you can find her. She is my daughter, and a half-sister to the three of you children. If you can't find her, I want the money to go to the Concho Valley Home for Girls in San Angelo, Texas.

I didn't know I had a daughter named April until she was fourteen years old. But I should start this story at its beginning. . . .

As Lou read the pages, Charley imagined a young boy addicted to the radio and his collection of records, a boy who listened to everything from Count Basie to Buddy Holly and who instinctively drummed along. The boy Charley pictured dreams of playing drums or bass guitar with a group of talented musicians, regardless of their musical style.

In Charley's mind, a young Darrell falls into an exciting but strenuous life, playing venues in Las Vegas and Nashville. But war is brewing in a little-known place called Vietnam, and the draft board hovers. Before he signs up for a tour of duty, he argues with his parents against their idea of his going to college for the student deferment. In Vietnam, he stays in hot jungle barracks on the other side of the world and helps build roads that will supposedly form part of a network of defense against the spread of Communism. After the Army, the G.I. Bill makes college a no-brainer. With a degree in music, Darrell will become a teacher.

Lou stopped reading to sip her coffee. "This letter has value to the family because it not only tells us about April, it's kind of an autobiography. Ever notice how people's autobiographies center on either their biggest success or their biggest regret? This whole thing is inspired by Dad's loss of April."

Charley thought, This is *my grandfather*—a man who served in the military, formed strong family bonds, and followed career plans. When other people used to talk about their grandparents, Charley only pretended to listen. Grandparents didn't mean a thing to him. But now, a grandfather's voice reached out to him.

Lou cleared her throat and picked up the letter. As she read, Charley pictured Darrell, now a seasoned veteran and professional musician, entering a college lecture hall filled with bored students, many of them still in their teens. It's the first day of a class in music appreciation. Charley chuckled at the thought of Darrell being required to take music appreciation as a freshman music major. Charley imagined a shaft of sunlight piercing through a transom window, lighting up the long, yellow-blonde hair of a beautiful girl leaning forward in her chair. Darrell discovers that the seat next to hers is vacant, and he loses no time working his way to sit beside her.

Lou stopped reading and leaned back in the booth as the waitress refilled her coffee cup. She turned a page in the handwritten stack and marked her place with her finger. "Let's see. Okay . . . her name was Ann Smith."

Charley learns of the blossoming romance between his grandmother and grandfather. He imagines Darrell telling Ann he's a drummer and bass player looking for a day job, and she throws her head back to laugh, revealing even, white teeth. They sit together through the semester, comparing notes. They study in the library, their shoulders touching. Darrell finally gives in and reaches out to brush his hand over her silky hair. She leans toward him. Their lips meet. Neither notices the angry librarian swooping down from her desk to give them the boot.

Ann, an artist, understands Darrell's obsession with music. All she wants to do is paint, but her parents have insisted she prepare to teach so that she will have a fall-back profession.

Lou read on. "I never could figure out how to tell any of you about Ann. I loved her very much, but after we both moved on, I didn't want any of you, especially Helen, to feel like that part of my past made me love you any less."

Darrell realizes he will die a slow death from a thousand sour notes as a high school band director. The road is calling. Ann says, 'Don't sign on to a career that will press the life out of you.' One night, he's playing for fun and extra money at a Lubbock honky-tonk, when country music star Wynn Stewart, passing through, hears the band. Ann says, 'Go. Go on tour. Four months will pass fast, and I'll be here.' He signs on.

Charley focused on Lou's reading of Darrell's story. "I called from phone booths and hotel rooms to talk to Ann. I wrote letters and mailed them every few days. But the last two weeks before returning, her phone rang and rang. The sound of that ringing phone was an empty echo. When I got back to Lubbock, her friends and neighbors told me they thought she went to Alaska to work on landscape painting. I never learned what happened to my letters."

Lou kept reading, as Charley heard the words of his grandfather. "I didn't know Ann was pregnant when I left, so I concluded that she had gone pretty far to say goodbye. I decided the most dignified thing I could do was to move on. Touring finally brought me to the Nashville concert where I spotted my Helen in the audience."

Lou paused to pat tears from her eyes with her napkin. "Dad was great," she said, "even though he was on the road so much. Mom decided to keep her roots in Tulsa and raise the family—me and my brothers—while she kept up her teaching career. She was such a good teacher. Teaching would've killed Dad, but Mama thrived on it."

Charley wanted to play air violin and whistle a sarcastic tune of melodrama. Jealousy and sadness stirred in him. A grandfather like Darrell Trainer would have certainly boosted his spirits. It was the deal of the cards, he supposed. But it pissed him off anyway. He would try not to hold that against Lou. But people from happy families did piss him off.

"So, how did Darrell find out about *my* mother? And how come he didn't help her any?" he asked.

"That's what comes next." Lou continued reading.

I learned about April in 1980. I was playing in Vegas. Ann, her husband, and my daughter April found me there. Ann called the club and left a message for me to call her at a hotel on the Strip. The message said I would remember her from college, Ann Martin Smith. It was like a bomb dropped when I read that name on the message. I was anxious to find out how the years had treated Ann, gain some insight into why she left without telling me anything. I called her. I told her I tried to find her when I came off the tour. She didn't explain anything, but she did tell me about April. I was overwhelmed to find out I had a daughter. I couldn't wait to meet her. Ann asked me to wait before I told her I was her real father. April thought Frank Bristow, Ann's husband, was her father. A daughter. I could barely make it through the show that night. I had another daughter. Four children, not three.

The next day, we met in the lobby of their hotel. It was hard to hold back—I wanted to grab April and take her home with me. I had so many questions for Ann. We all walked down the Strip together while I played the part of a guide to the backstage Vegas scene. We sat crowded in the band's tight little dressing room and kept the conversation safe.

The Bristow fellow didn't say much, kept his arm around April like he thought I was going to steal her away. Ann was so different from the college girl I had known—all tied up in knots—tense. They lived close to Fort Worth. Bristow was some kind of preacher, but we didn't get into the details. I figured April and I would have time to get acquainted later. I lay awake all that night thinking about how to introduce everyone and how I could get April to spend some of her school holidays with us. She was a sweet girl. She said less than ten words the whole time, and I hoped we'd be able to talk more.

Lou looked up at Charley. "This is frustrating to read. I can't imagine what it put my father through."

We made a plan to meet the next day, but when I went to their hotel, they weren't there. I called at least fifty more hotels to see if they were registered. Then I called information for all the small towns on the map around Fort Worth, but no luck. I finally got a friend in Fort Worth to call the schools. He found out that an April Bristow had been registered in Weatherford. But she had checked out, supposedly to move to Comanche, but that was a dead end.

Frank was probably a con man who realized that I wasn't a big star and wouldn't be much of a gold mine. He wanted to keep his little family to himself, and bringing me into the picture wasn't worth the risk. It has been the greatest sadness of my life that I had a daughter and never knew it until it was too late. It was hard when Ann disappeared while I was on the road back in college, but her coming back with my daughter fourteen years later and then disappearing again was a pain I can't describe.

I decided I would feel better for now if I set aside a little money for April, in case I die unexpectedly. I think Frank was crazy, and Ann didn't know how to get away, so if you don't find April, I want the money to go to a place that helps out girls who don't have the gift of a good home.

I hope you can find her.

Love, Pop.

After a pause, Charley asked, "How'd you find Mom? She hasn't gone by the Bristow name since she married Eldon."

"I hired a detective. It took him about a day."

"And why did you take off to Alaska? Why didn't you tell me what was going on three years ago?"

"April wanted to handle telling you. I was planning to marry a guy who wanted us to settle in Anchorage. That didn't work out, but I did get to earn some good money. And I thought it would be an opportunity to find out if Ann Smith had been there. I still have some lines in the water, but so far, nothing has surfaced. Could be she never made it to Alaska. All the time I was up there, I kept thinking I would like it in Sulfur Gap. Never had tried a small

town. So I came back and decided to tell you about me—our family—rather than leave it up to April. I suspected she might not tell
you."

"So what happened to the money?"

"I brought your mother a cashier's check," Lou said. "That's
all I know."

"Probably paid off credit cards so she could start fresh with
the shopping channel. She wouldn't've told me about the money
because she doesn't trust anyone. I guess she trusts me, but she
knows I might tell someone something, so she keeps a lot to herself. But why wouldn't she let me know we have family? She has
a half-sister and two half-brothers, for gosh sakes. If she wasn't so
damn fat, she'd be clicking her heels, you'd think."

"You'll have to ask her that yourself, Charley," Lou said.

While they drank coffee and took turns going to the bathroom, a whole new shift of wait staff had come on the job. Charley
paid the new waiter a twenty to leave them alone. Booth rental, he
called it.

When they left the restaurant, the sun was dropping toward
the flat western plains, stirring up a sunset that would both dazzle
and torment them as they headed back south to Sulfur Gap.

The day had disappeared, and Charley's insides were roiling
with all the information he had taken in. He thought this should
all redefine him, but he still felt the same—handsome, charming,
lonely, goofy Charley. Goofy enough to make a pass at his own
aunt.

Well, he hadn't known.

8

April

CHARLEY DROPPED LOU OFF at her red truck and headed straight for his mother's. He turned into the Sunset Estates housing division, past the split-rail fence. As usual, he knocked loud enough to overpower the sound from the television. "It's Charley," he called. "We need to talk."

He waited on the porch for an eternity, knowing it would take time for her to heave herself out of her chair to let him in. He heard her groan as she hauled herself up and plodded to the door in her run-over house shoes. The two deadbolts slid free and the security chain rattled loose. She glanced past him but didn't remark on the Skylark parked in her drive behind her ancient van. Finally, Charley was in, smelling the stale cigarette smoke mixed with the fresh, and last week's garbage that needed to be taken out.

"I sure wasn't expecting you until Wednesday. You're early."

Her voice was hoarse, as usual, and as usual, it was probably the first time she had spoken to anyone for days. She patted his shoulder.

She turned and lumbered back to her chair. She lowered the television volume with the remote and looked at him. Her eyes were still blue but dulled and filmy in her pouched face. With her prematurely gray hair, she looked much older than a woman in her early forties. She had broken out a tropical print muumuu for the warmer weather. After a moment, a knowing look crept over her face.

"You've been talking to Lou, haven't you? That's the only reason you'd be all lathered up and paying me a surprise visit like this. . . . I figured when she came back in town, it'd only be a matter of time."

Charley took the plunge. He was seething. Time to get this over with. "Yes, Mom. I've been talking to Lou. I would like to've known that we've got a family. They're *my* family, too."

She reached for the off button on the remote and looked wistful as the image vanished from the TV screen. "I didn't want you gettin' all excited about havin' a family and then them turnin' out not to care. I didn't want you to be disappointed."

"Yeah, and I bet you didn't want any competition. If I kept thinkin' you were my only family, I'd have to stick around here."

"That's not true." Of course she would deny it. "Sit down, Charley."

He sat in the wobbly, beat-up captain's chair, a former member of an Early American dining room set, probably left on the driveway when someone vacated a rental trailer. "What *is* true, Mom?"

"I always figured you'd want to know more someday. For a while, I was hoping I would die first. I don't know how to do this." Of course she would play the martyr.

"Well, here we are. Both alive," he said. Part of him wanted to say "Never mind," to ease her pain at facing the truth. He could say "Never mind" and walk away and stay ignorant. Heck, there was probably a country-western song there. "Never mind, I don't need to know, since tellin' the truth seems to hurt you so." He could hear the steel guitar and the dogs howling in the background. But, he thought, there's another way for this to play. He would stick it out.

She straightened herself in the chair, smoothed her muu-muu, and lit a cigarette. She gazed into the empty screen as if it were a teleprompter for a rehearsed speech. He waited. She finally spoke.

For the first time, his mother told him about her life. She started slowly, like a trickle of water finding its way over a dam that finally starts to crumble until a flow breaks over.

Exhaling smoke, she said slowly, "Frank Bristow, the man I believed to be my father, was married to my mother from my earliest memory. He was a self-proclaimed preacher. We moved from one little town to another. Frank started new churches with words like 'covenant' and 'gospel' in the names he made up for them.

"I remember Frank swinging me on a screened-in porch that had a little swing suspended from the rafters. Don't know where that was." She paused to sip her drink. "There were times he could be like a real dad, back when I was little, but he started getting a lot scarier by the time I was eight, with more and more frequent temper fits, like he had some disease of the soul that got worse and worse. The itchier his anger got, the more religious he got. I can see it now, but as a kid, it was like being picked up and dropped back down by a tornado, over and over. But whatever bug he had eating away at him wasn't anything to make you feel sorry for him. Not when you were the one bearing the brunt of it."

As April flicked the ashes off her cigarette, she shook her head at the memories. Charley heard the irony in her voice, as well as the anger, sadness, and regret.

"Once, we traveled all the way to Las Vegas to start a 'mission' for addicted gamblers. Frank said they could be cured if they just had Jesus—and I'm sure he also thought, the special ministry of Frank Bristow. That's when I met Darrell Trainer. Frank and my mother never told me who he was—only that this drummer was going to show us the sinful city so that they would gain knowledge of what they were up against in fighting the satanic forces at work there."

Cigarette smoke hovering over her head, April picked up the glass beside her. Ice cubes rattled. "Hand me that pitcher over on the breakfast bar, Charley."

He stood and reached for the plastic container, hoping she would finish the story. She filled her glass.

"Bring me a couple of ice cubes from the freezer. I don't mind your fingers."

Probably not, he thought, stepping into the kitchen. Alcohol kills germs.

Her drink replenished, April seemed to think a moment, then tapped her cigarette into the overflowing ashtray and continued. "That evening, we all knelt for hours, praying for God to lead people away from the Sodom and Gomorrah, the Sin City. Early the next morning, they woke me up. We were leaving. I didn't understand. I thought we were meeting Darrell Trainer again. I knew it didn't matter to Frank if I understood or not. My job—and Mama's, too—was to be obedient and not ask questions. Frank had a whole new plan that took us back to Texas."

She shrugged. "Oh, well. I missed the chance to find out who my real father was. Too bad." She lit another cigarette and sat thinking. Charley jiggled his leg and waited. She finally picked up the thread of her story.

"I used to have calluses on my knees from all the praying we did—marathon praying. My daddy—Frank, that is—would lose his temper and we'd pray about it for hours after he broke a bunch of dishes and lamps. He would decide it was time to move, and we'd pray for hours about that. Regular times, it wasn't for so long. Then in church services and visiting people in hospitals and places, we prayed. That is, Frank prayed and we listened."

"Damn," Charley said, "no wonder you always hated church."

"It was crazy. I wanted to never have anything to do with church and churchy people."

"Did you love them?"

"Who?"

"Your parents, Mom."

"Yes. I loved them, or my mother, at least. I was too afraid of Frank to feel any love. I couldn't wait to get away from him. I always knew my mother loved me, but I couldn't understand how Frank could love me and act the way he did. I didn't understand how God could love me, either. He pretty much left me and my mom high and dry."

"How did you get away?"

"After we moved from Weatherford, they never put me back in school. Frank was afraid people would corrupt me, he said. He distrusted boys so much, it got my curiosity going. They told me we were home-schooling, and Mama and I would read books and do art projects, but after Weatherford I never got any official schooling until I got to the girls' home."

"So how did you wind up there?"

"My dad—Frank—was trying to get another church started, and we moved into a motel room on the edge of Briargrove."

April stared at the television, spaced out. "Anyway," she said, coming back to the present, "Frank told the motel owner he would do handyman work until we raised the money to pay for our room. Mama got a job doing filing in a law office for the time being. One of the lawyers saw her bruises after Frank indulged in one of his temper tantrums, and he figured out that Frank was crazy. By the time we got to Briargrove, the only reason Frank let Mama get a job away from him was because we were pretty desperate for the money. The rest of the time, he didn't want her out of his sight. So the lawyer called the sheriff's office, and, after a bunch of questions Frank had to answer politely while he was choking with rage, he lost it.

"He knew the lawyer called the sheriff on him. He had this old baseball bat, and he used to make us stand still while he swung it close to our heads. It was supposed to teach us some lesson about trust. He never hit us with it, he used fists or the flat of his hand or a belt for that. But this lawyer—Frank got the bat and went to the lawyer's house and beat him senseless on his front lawn. He would have murdered him, but there were witnesses—neighbors and the lawyer's wife."

April shifted in her chair, frowning and puffing with the effort. "Then Frank came back to the motel and started smashing up the room and threatening me and Mama before the deputies got there. Looks like he would've used the extra time to make a run for it, but I guess he thought he was cornered. Frank was arrested, but Mama wouldn't tell the cops what happened. One thing led to another. I got put in the shelter, Mama posted Frank's bail with some money she'd hid—she came to see me and said they would be back, but something happened. They disappeared. I know my mother loved me, so something happened. I think—I think Frank killed her. It's been over twenty-five years, and I would have heard from her if she were alive."

April drew a ragged breath. "I'm not sure I want to know what happened. But I've always wondered what the hell she was thinking, posting his bail. If she hadn't, she was probably afraid he'd get out and come after her." She shrugged and looked out at the dark through the dirty windows. "Sometimes I even wish he'd killed that lawyer. Then he wouldn't've gotten out on bail. Then Mama would be alive and no telling how life would've turned out. But I shouldn't wish bad on someone else so I can have it easy."

Charley sat stunned by the flood of information. For a moment, he saw the child his mother had been. All the potential down the drain. For now, while she was in a talking mood, he wanted to press on.

"So then who is my father? I know he wasn't Eldon because in school I always went by Bristow." Charley stopped. His brain locked gears. No. This can't be. Please don't let Frank Bristow be my father, he thought. Charley put his face in his hands at the terrible idea that he was a product of incest and that his mother could have thought the same thing until three years ago, when she learned about Darrell Trainer.

April's eyes widened. "Oh, Charley, I see what you think. No, no, no! Frank Bristow wasn't your father. He was meaner and crazier than hell and all twisted up inside, but he didn't bother me that way. I don't think he was able for some reason. He and my mother never had any children, thank goodness."

What a relief.

April stopped to light another cigarette. As smoke sighed past her lips, she said, "I've been changing his name in my mind when I think of him. Since Lou came and told me my real daddy was a decent man, I've stopped thinking of Frank as 'Daddy.' He's just this freak named Frank who shanghaied the first part of my life. It helps to think of him that way."

"And my father?"

"A boy I met in high school after I went to the girls' home. We were in some classes together. He asked me out. We dated a while, but then he told me his parents didn't want him going with someone from the girls' home."

"You mean my father was from Briargrove? Right up the road? Does he still live there?"

"Yes, now he does, I've heard. He's only been back for a year or so. He doesn't know about you. His mother and I crossed paths a few times at school—she was in P.T.A. and volunteered in the library—before I realized I was pregnant, and from talking to her, I could tell his parents didn't break us up. It was him. He wanted to break up, and he lied to me and let me think his parents thought bad of me because I was in a girls' home. But I didn't blame them. His mom saw me at the clinic when I went to get checked, and she was friendly."

April looked down at her swollen ankles. "Guess they were right if they were the ones to break us up. Anyway, I got involved with another boy for a short time, I was so lonely, so I wasn't sure who your father was for a while, not until you got bigger. You look just like him." She looked at Charley for the first time. He thought he even saw the trace of a smile.

"So who is he?"

"He wound up becoming a Methodist preacher. Eventually made it back to Briargrove. My mother and I must have been attracted to preacher types. Lucky us." She stubbed out her cigarette.

Charley's mind reeled. Not only was he discovering a grandfather he hadn't known about, an aunt he thought was coming on to him, and some keys to his mother's past, he was finding out his father was a preacher in a Methodist church up the road.

Then he remembered what Irma, the used car saleslady, said. The owner of the Skylark was the Methodist preacher's mother.

There was only one Methodist church in Briargrove.

He thought the floor was sagging underneath him, and not from the weight of April.

9
Belonging

CHARLEY DIDN'T KNOW whether to take a crowbar to the Skylark or to let it envelop him. When he put his hands on the wheel to drive home, he thought about his grandmother, right up the road, holding the wheel for the ten years that she'd owned the car. He had listened to her music and been moved to tears up on the caprock. Were his hands like hers? April had said Charley looked like his father. Had his father ever driven this car? Had he passed his father in Wal-Mart, or on the road to Abilene or San Angelo or Big Spring? Did his father know he existed? Did he ever think of April?

He gripped the wheel and twisted and pushed and pulled. Its unyielding reality mocked him. It was a solid thing, and he could not get around it.

Here he was, twenty-five, and finally finding out who his father was. His mother, only three years ago, had found out who *her* father was. She must have been pretty confused when Lou showed up with the news. For a moment, he was mad at Lou. Lou did what her father wanted, but apparently hadn't thought about what it would mean to April, how it might rattle her world. But that was pretty much offset by a check for twenty thousand dollars, he supposed. And who wouldn't want to be related to Lou? Or have a father like Darrell Trainer?

April hadn't been in doubt about who her father was, even if she had the wrong one. It was part of her identity to think of Frank

Bristow as her father. April must feel better knowing that the insane control freak she grew up with wasn't her real father. In her self-imposed isolation, how did April deal with the new knowledge? It wouldn't have been an option for her to call everyone together for a big fat family reunion. She could turn off her thoughts and feelings when she turned on the TV, and she drowned any residual with gin. He wondered if she had even cried a little. She probably felt cheated, lied to, betrayed, and used.

To his advantage, Charley had always suspected Eldon wasn't his dad. That much, at least, he'd figured out on his own. He had often wondered—when he gave himself permission to think about it. He knew it would've been like beating his head against a brick wall to try to talk to his mother about it, so he decided he didn't need to know, that his mother probably didn't even know. Now he knew the answer to this seed of doubt that pinged around in his head. Getting an answer to something he'd wondered about is better, he thought, than not realizing there was a question and then having the assumptions of a lifetime ripped away. That's what happened to April when Lou showed up with the consolation prize of twenty thousand dollars for a lifetime of not knowing a good and decent father.

But whose fault was it? No one's, really. People hadn't known the truth, and some of the truth got swept under the rug, often with the best of motives. And there were lies. A legacy of loneliness and loss pressed him down. Who could he blame? The resounding answer—no one. Except Frank Bristow. No telling where he was.

When his iron grip on the wheel loosened, he began driving away from his mother's, conscious of going slow through the trailer park, staying in the ruts.

Charley didn't want to go back to his empty apartment. He steered toward Wayne's place and the windmill. He pulled up and turned off his lights. If J.J. the game warden saw him, he would remember Charley's call from a few days ago and wouldn't pay an unexpected visit. A few days ago. It seemed like another life when he and Darla had enjoyed such fantastic, back-arching, toe-curling sex out here.

Now he felt drained. He rested his forehead on the steering wheel. The weight of so much truth forced him to stillness.

With his windows rolled down, he could hear the gentle metal clanking as the breeze pushed against the pulleys and chains of the windmill. The blades creaked and moaned as they turned in slow, partial arcs. He heard a stomp and snort and turned to find one of Wayne's horses standing and looking at him. Once acknowledged, the horse whipped his head around and walked away into the darkness.

The night was clear, and a shower of stars spangled the dark charcoal sky. Charley got out and sat on the hood. An owl hooted, close enough that he could hear its wings flapping when it lifted off. He rested back against the windshield and stared into the spaces between the stars. He had read that there was much more there than he could see. Faraway pulsars and quasars. And lights on wavelengths humans couldn't see. All of it worked together, somehow. Galaxies balanced on the gravity of other galaxies, stars and worlds spun through space, held on their course by the unseen forces of one another. Interacting, interlocking in a dance with unseen partners. People put their own music and words to it, he supposed, and they only get the tiniest pictures of the truth, but they keep trying.

The sky loomed closer. He felt lighter, and he tingled with the touch of breeze. He felt like he was dreaming, in that land of unconsciousness where control is lost, but the soft clinking of the windmill called to him that he was right here, right in this place, beside a windmill in a pasture with the night sky above. He felt weightless. No longer did the cool, hard glass of the windshield press against the back of his head. He was cushioned, surrounded by the sense that the elements of his body were being infused into the sky.

And he felt a message that said, "You belong. You always have."

10
New Dawning

CHARLEY'S WATCH ALARM woke him. He was scrunched up on the back seat of the Lark. Sometime during the night, he had crawled inside. He reached above his head and opened the car door to stretch. Slowly he unfolded. The seats were damp with light dew that had settled through the open window. The sun peeked over the horizon and would soon bring its full light as it began to warm the day.

He drove back to town to take a shower and get ready for work. A regular day awaited him at the Wild Hare.

Regular didn't seem the same, though.

* * *

Back at work in the salon, the hair dryers hummed around him and the chatter blended into the sound of a distant colony of seagulls. He felt like he was moving on the ocean floor, wearing a weighted wet suit and seeing the world through goggles. His coworkers and clients floated into his field of vision and waggled, suspended in the fluid of their comings and goings, and then skittered away.

He cut hair all day on autopilot. Conversing was easy. He found he didn't have to listen as hard as he had previously thought. There wouldn't be a test later. As long as he looked interested, that's all they cared about. If someone asked a question, he could replay the tape in his head accurately enough to give a decent answer.

His cell phone vibrated in his pocket while he was sweeping up the stray hair around his station.

It was Darla. Good. He had needed to call her and try to spend more time with her. And now that he knew what he knew, he could dispense with his hesitation.

"Hey, Charley." Her voice sounded more chipper than he had noticed when they were honky-tonking or making tequila-stoked love beside the windmill.

"Hey, Darla. How are you?"

"I'm good. I was gonna see if you or someone in the shop could do something with this hideous perm I've got. I let someone at Cute Cuts in Briargrove get a-hold of me." She was all business. No recriminations—not yet anyway—about why he hadn't got-ten around to calling her. After all, it was the third day out. Many women would be fuming if they hadn't received a call the next day.

This was the most Charley had heard her say at one time. But in the club with the loud music and crowd, then drunk, and later hung over—these were not good conditions for talking. Come to think of it, he appreciated that she didn't try to talk, like so many people in those circumstances—yelling, saying the same thing over and over, like it mattered. Then trying to fake their way through a hangover with profound observations or manufactured enthusiasm.

"Bethany can straighten the perm and recondition you. And I'll have time to give you a cut after that. Come on in about three this afternoon."

Charley's phone vibrated again while he was taking a break. This time it was Jarod, all lathered up.

"Charley!" Jarod was yelling as if he had won the trifecta at the race track. "Charley, you're not gonna believe this!"

"What?" Charley held his phone out from his head, glad he didn't have his Bluetooth stuck in his ear.

"You haven't forgotten that Renault, have you?"

"I'm trying to."

"You can forget it soon. I've got a good offer."

"You're kidding." This was practical joke territory, so Charley's guard was up.

"Well, I got to thinking that Renault fans are out there, especially in Europe. Some people like to restore them. I got to looking online, and the parts are worth a lot. Like, you could get five hundred for the steering wheel on eBay."

Now Jarod sounded real. Five hundred for a steering wheel would help to heal the ego blow Charley suffered for being so stupid. But Jarod wasn't finished talking.

"So I was thinking about how we could work a deal and both make a little money, and before I could work it out, in walks this guy who was driving through and decided to stop for a piece of pie at the Navaho. Anyway, he sees the Renault and asks me how much it's going for, and I tell him I'll have to ask the owner. You know, I sort of hem and haw to see if he'll suggest a price. So he says two thousand dollars!"

"No way!" Charley put his phone on speaker and waved Dorothy over. She would have vaulted over the table in the break room to satisfy her curiosity. But she played casual and took little steps to stand over the phone that Charley was now sharing with her. Jarod was still gushing the good news.

"To be honest, I tell him it don't run, got lots wrong with it. He says the body's worth it." Charley held up two fingers to Dorothy and mouthed "thousand" at her, appreciating how her eyes widened and her mouth formed a little "oh." Dorothy mouthed back, "The No?" and Charley nodded.

Jarod was saying, "So I tell him I'll check, and I act all unenthusiastic. Acted like I didn't give a flip. I tell him it sure has a lot of sentimental value. So we trade contact information. I'm thinking we can jack him up to three thousand, he can take it with him, and you've made a nice profit. If he don't call back, we can still do the eBay thing. Or Craigslist. Then he calls me back later and says he'll give *five* thousand." Jarod celebrated. "I can't wait to tell Bo Buchanan. He thought you were a fool to buy it and me a bigger one to try to sell it for you."

Charley was stunned. He was floating now, but still suspicious. Dorothy was doing little toe-jumps, her boobs bouncing. "Don't shit me now," he said.

"I shit you not."

"Cash?"

"Cashier's check. Of course, you'll sign over the title."

Dorothy's hand closed over Charley's and squeezed.

"I could pay off the Skylark," Charley said. Dorothy nodded.

Surely Jarod wouldn't keep up a joke with Charley getting his hopes up. He didn't think Jarod would pull something like those jerks that give people fake winning scratch-off lottery tickets on their birthdays and make them think they won tens of thousands of dollars. He'd seen that trick on *America's Funniest Videos* and found it not-funny—diehard cruel, mean, and manipulative.

"Yeah, I could start getting ahead for once."

"Sure could."

"I'd want to give you a commission."

"Not necessary, Bud."

"Yes it is. I will soon be driving a debt-free car. That'll let me start getting out of hock on credit cards." Charley was making plans to keep the Lark anyway, payments or not. He was getting attached to it, was even flirting with the foggy idea of taking it by to see where his grandmother lived and deciding whether he wanted to identify himself. With a little research, he could learn what her name was and then find her. Easy. That could happen in good time, when he was over this floating-in-a-fishbowl sensation. No rush.

Dorothy put her arm around his waist and squeezed. And then of course felt compelled to comment, "Don't let some woman get you back *into* hock. Or hockey."

Charley gave her a small bow. "Yes, Mum. I'll do my best." It wasn't a promise, but at least it was a stated intention.

She dropped the weekly local newspaper, the Sulfur Gap *Echo,* on the break room table as she headed to the bathroom. He grinned and rubbed his palms together as he glanced down at the newspaper.

He froze.

Above the fold, there was Darla Buchanan's picture. He already felt like a rubber band being stretched to its limit—all the new information about his family, information that made him feel that his identity was a jigsaw puzzle swept from the table, to be fitted together again. But, holy Christ on a cracker, the euphoria of Jarod's news! Five thousand dollars all at once, in one lump sum, felt like a fortune.

He floated, suspended in all the buffers that he had learned over the years to keep treading in baffling, unpredictable situations. His brain felt swaddled in gauze, and while his thoughts came in their usual random way, he observed them at a distance. It all seemed so . . . unreal.

He stared at the paper, where Darla looked out at him from the front page. Probably her old high school yearbook picture, the easiest one for the paper to come by. Underneath the image, several column inches were dedicated to a story, headlined, "Local Girl Plans Vet Internship."

He read the story in disbelief.

Darla Buchanan, daughter of Ed and Janet Barta, has
accepted an internship with Dr. Andrea Harper at the
Sulfur Gap Veterinary Clinic as part of her degree plan
with Texas A&M University. A 2005 graduate of Sulfur
Gap High School, Darla was valedictorian, National Merit
Scholar, and recipient of a Presidential Scholarship to
A&M.

Her last two-and-a-half years at the university have
been highlighted by studies abroad in Australia and New
Zealand, where she has been involved in team research
on sheep and goat breeding.

"I look forward to working with a young lady of
Darla's caliber," said Dr. Harper. "I'll learn from her, too,
this summer, and I know she'll be a great asset to the clinic."

Darla says she is anxious to expand her knowledge in
the clinical area of veterinary science. She also is happy
to spend some time at home in Sulfur Gap. "I have lots
of happy memories here," she said. "I hope I can be of
service to the community, and I'm grateful to Dr. Harper
for becoming my mentor this summer."

Sulfur Gap is proud of Darla Buchanan and fortunate
to have her.

This was certainly a day for news.

Charley scratched his head. He wondered why a girl like that
would be interested in a guy like him. She must be so smart, she
was psycho, too.

11
New Impressions

DARLA STIRRED THE USUAL anticipation that cropped up when a new girl of Charley's came in the salon. Charlene, Bethany, and Dorothy introduced themselves and pretended to be busy, but their reduced chatter signaled Charley that they had their invisible ear megaphones fully extended. After quick handshakes and smiles all around, Darla turned to Charley, giving him a light hug. He was still floating in his mental wet suit, so he didn't tense up. Bethany got right to work with quick sympathy for Darla's hair situation. After the straightening out, the conditioning, and a blow-dry, Darla sat in Charley's chair. She was shorter than he'd thought. When her boots were off, they hadn't been standing up. Most of his ideas about her were turning out to be wrong, now that he thought about it.

He worked his scissors magic and stood back to admire the crown of brunette hair that now softly framed her face. Her smile into his mirror warmed him up to ask her to dinner. And to his delight, on this day full of good surprises, she accepted.

He was finished for the day, so they strolled through Sulfur Gap's historic downtown to the Navaho.

They walked into the restaurant past the cold case with the cream pies and Slap Yo' Mama bread pudding on display. Several felt-covered card tables, outfitted with crosses and costume jewelry for sale, stood close to the front of the big, roomy eatery. Charley waved to a couple of the waiters he knew as he led Darla to a booth that afforded some privacy.

They each ordered a medium-rare sirloin and salad. He was about to tell Darla that he'd seen the story about her in the paper. When he looked up, she was grinning at him.

"What?" he asked.

"I want a re-do," she said.

"You look great. What do you mean?" How could she not be as pleased as all his other customers?

"I don't mean the hair." She raised her eyebrows and gave him a naughty look.

"Oh," he said, nearly blushing and stammering. ". . . Well, I think we can arrange that."

"Good. I'd like to be sober the next time."

"You know, you're so different, sitting here across the table. Why do I feel like you're not the same person?"

"I have a twin."

When his eyes widened, she smirked. "No, silly. It's just me."

That was a relief. Come to think of it, it would be highly unlikely that an identical twin could get as bad an identical perm. But nothing would shock him after all that happened yesterday. Just yesterday. . . . And today. . . . "Well, you do seem different. I know we didn't talk much the other night, which suited me fine. But you look even better in the daylight, and it's usually the other way around."

"Why, thank you."

"And you look happier—or something."

"I *am* happier in the daylight. I'm not all that used to honky-tonks, not with all the drinking and yelling and people acting like teenagers when they're well past it."

"You're not so old. What are you? Twenty-one? Barely old enough to buy your own beer."

"Yes, but chronological age has nothing to do with maturity."

"You sound like a psychologist."

"I'm quoting my stepfather, who *is* a psychologist."

"So you don't like the nightclub scene. That's where I've spent half the free evenings of my life since I was thirteen or so."

"I don't totally disdain it. I like peace and quiet. I love the windmill. We should go back there—sober."

Charley considered. A little scary. No alcohol buffer. But an offer he certainly would not refuse. "It'd be an honor," he said, and slid his hand across the table to hold her strong little fingers in his. They held eye contact for a longer total number of seconds than he had with both his wives combined. Her gaze was direct but unchallenging. She was simply there, and she considered eye contact part of the conversation.

Charley was the first to fidget, so he changed the subject. "I read about you in the paper."

"And?"

"I feel dumb that I was steering you toward a job at Wal-Mart."

"There's nothing wrong with working at Wal-Mart. That's what I was going to do if the internship with Andrea hadn't come through. I'm not ready to go back to the university this summer."

"You didn't talk much when we were dancing, so I didn't know you had so much on the ball."

"I don't like yelling over the music and the crowd. I tend to get quiet when I drink, too, because my shpeech is show shlurry." She crossed her eyes and laughed.

Charley reflected. Her discomfort with the club scene would explain her stiffness on the dance floor and the seeming lack of a sense of humor. That, or she did have a twin—inside her head.

Like a split personality. This was feeling weird.

He wondered why she had been so determined, hanging on to his belt loop, waiting for him beside the bathroom door. She was aiming to snag him, that's why. Lou had made him wary, but he should have exercised even more caution with Darla. Smarter and more achievement-oriented than he thought, she still might have a hidden alien fang waiting to pop out from God knows where. He could make a quick getaway in the Lark.

"Could be you stuck with me all night at the dance to keep some of the old geezers in there from hitting on you."

"Partly. I was pretty uncomfortable. It was good to see a familiar face."

"Well, I'm not that familiar."

"Oh, I've known who you were since I was five."

"How did you know me when you were five? I was three or four grades ahead of you, and then you moved off for a while."

"You remember my mother was your second grade teacher?"

"Yeah."

"She put pictures of all her students under the glass top on her desk at home. You know—the school mug shots?"

"Yeah."

"Well, I used to look at your picture all the time. Your bushy blond hair, big blue eyes, big smile. You were my childhood crush, and when I thought about growing up and marrying, I pictured you all grown up and waiting in front of the altar as I came down the aisle."

"Oh, no."

"Don't look so scared."

"I'm feeling like a marked man." Now he was getting images from the old movie *Fatal Attraction*—pet rabbits boiling on the stove, a crazed Darla leaping from behind a shower curtain with a butcher knife—misgivings he hadn't bothered to consider before marrying Vicki or Joyce.

"Oh, bullshit." She broke into his nightmare reverie. "You're taking this too seriously. Anyway, I always kept an eye on you. I used to watch you play football when you were in high school. There were other cute boys, but you were the cutest. Schoolgirl crush."

He'd played his freshman year and was looking forward to a promising career as a running back for the team, but he had to keep up his summer lawn-mowing jobs if he expected to have new clothes for school, and then raking leaves on the same lawns in the fall kept his ancient Kawasaki motocross bike running and gassed up. No work, no transportation. So, no football.

Darla remembered his few glory days on the gridiron—how complimentary. Still, he had to stifle the impulse to run out the doors of the Navaho as fast as possible and jump in the Lark and keep driving, never looking back.

He thought of something else. "Did you really think I owned the Wild Hare?"

"No. That was a lame attempt at a joke when your car turned out to be the little Buick instead of the testosterone truck beside it. I'm not funny when I'm drunk."

Darla seemed oblivious to his growing sense of alarm. Well, he did have a good poker face, if he did say so.

"Why'd you even go to Ladies' Night?" he asked. He hoped she didn't get defensive. Wouldn't blame her, though, with all these questions. But his biggest mistakes in the past had come when he denied himself the luxury of politely asking a few questions about things he had a right to know.

Darla didn't seem offended. "When I got back home from college, I hung around and read and watched television and helped my mom, but I finally decided to come listen to Wylie's band at Hopper's to get out and mingle. Then I saw you, asked you to dance . . . you know the rest. I was scared to death. Pretty shy about meeting people at dance halls. Actually, a totally new experience."

Charley was having trouble swallowing his steak. Time to change the subject again. She was building the story of their relationship.

"So you're studying to be a vet?"

"Yeah. The summer internship will help me make up for this semester that I lost."

"Why'd you leave college? I thought you said you got a divorce."

"That's only part of the story. At A&M in the pre-veterinary program, I got to go to Australia with a special group to do a sustainability study on a big sheep ranch. I think they put that part in the paper. Anyway, the supervising professor and I hit it off. He was in his forties, divorced. I was awed by his Ph.D. and academic credentials, and he was awed by my . . . you know. We got married. He never could get over how dumb a nineteen-year-old is, and I never could get over how anal an old man can be. We both crashed from our pedestals pretty fast. It was hard on me, so I took the semester off to regroup. If I'd stayed in, my grades would have slipped and I would have lost my scholarship."

"So you dropped out?"

"I got permission from the financial aid committee to take a semester off and still have my scholarship waiting next fall. I was going to stay in College Station and work, but it's cheaper to stay with Mom and my stepdad. And, getting an internship set up with Andrea means I can get some credit and not be too far behind on my projected graduation date."

"What about your ex? Doesn't he get in some kind of trouble for picking on a student?"

"Yeah. Administration officials were pretty steamed up. He

had to transfer to a smaller sister college. He'll recover in a few years. He's an asset to the vet program."

"I had no idea you were so smart. But why do you need financial aid? Your dad's loaded!"

"I wanted to be as responsible for my education as I could. Ed and Mom would be great about it if they were able to pay my whole way through college, but my dad—he's overprotective—and if I were spending his money, he'd feel like he had more leverage to intrude. After what happened with that flash-in-the-pants marriage to the prof, I was really glad my dad wasn't paying the tuition. He'd have felt even more entitled to sue the college. He gave it serious thought but backed off. I had to start telling him what *my* contribution was to the whole situation—details he didn't want to hear about." Darla smiled. "It's not nice to manipulate your daddy like that, but it had to be done."

"So, you and your dad, I thought y'all had a good thing going."

"Oh, we do. Don't get me wrong. I love Dad. He's a load of fun, but the older I get, the more I wish he'd learn that he doesn't have to keep treating me like a china doll."

"I'm glad we're talking like this."

"We haven't had much of a chance to talk about anything."

"I wasn't college material."

"So? Not everyone is."

"I wouldn't think you'd be interested in me, after being married to a professor. And with a dad who's so successful in business. And an all-round educated family."

"You're like fresh air, Charley. You're easy to be with. But that doesn't mean we're going to get married." Darla reached over and patted his cheek with mock consolation. "I learned my lesson about jumping into marriage too quick. And people with big degrees can be ignorant about life. I mean, you're not an arrogant know-it-all, and you have talent oozing from your fingertips."

She pulled a strand of freshly clipped hair in front of her face and crossed her eyes to look at its precision cut. Then she shifted to dead seriousness. "All that being said, I'm watching myself. I don't want to get in a rush to start seeing you or anyone else every day. It's tempting, believe me, but I'm afraid I'm in rebound mode. I did give you the strong come-on at Hopper's, and one thing led to another. I enjoyed every minute we spent together, except for the hangover, and you weren't there for that. I have no one to blame for that but myself."

Charley hid his surprise. His experiences had involved quick courtships or none at all. Once he'd slept with someone—and that was always as soon as possible—she owned him.

"I've been on the rebound since I got old enough to do anything about it. Truth is, I've been working hard to keep from calling you these last couple of days. I'm trying to fake being a normal guy."

"Sounds like we're on the same page," she said. "We have some good reasons to slow it down."

Charley felt the tension melting from his core, and his shoulders relaxed. They'd been cramped all day from hunkering up in the the Lark to sleep. He even managed a watery smile.

In his typical mind-wandering way, he thought about his "clean hands" test. Oh, well, it was time for small talk. He remembered Darla's dry hands. He couldn't stop himself—this must be cleared up.

"You're gonna think I'm a nutcase, but I have to ask you why your hands are always dry when you come out of the john."

Darla looked puzzled. "Well, Charley, it's not like I have to hold something and aim. I don't pee on myself." Now she was the one looking toward the exit as if she were considering an escape.

"That's not what I mean. I've gotten into the habit of noticing damp hands. The damp ones make me feel good, knowing they've washed up."

"Oh, so you think I'm a germ magnet!" She rolled her eyes and flopped back in her seat. "Sheesh! You must not be aware of what they've found out about hand blowers. The vents in those suckers collect all kinds of microbes and blow them right at you—all over your hands and up your nose. That's why I'm never caught without some of this." She reached in her front pocket and pulled out a tiny tube of hand sanitizer. She dropped it on the table between their dinner plates.

"Ohhhh, I see." He felt as dumb as the steak on his plate.

"This is funny." Darla curled a little foot under her in the seat so that she could prop up and lean toward Charley. "You thinking that I, of all people, wouldn't be into hand-washing. After the microbiology courses I've had."

All this time, he thought he was making allowances for her, overlooking poor social skills, goofy hairdos, and dry hands. Seemed like she was the one making allowances now. Well, she was. She was selling herself short to be with a guy like him. He was swimming in a soup of confusion, with images of grandparents and a father he had never known. They drifted within his grasp, but when he reached for them, they dissolved and floated away. If he could get hold of these people. . . . He was trying to pigeonhole Darla, and she didn't fit anywhere. He couldn't begin to know what to expect.

He switched to another line of inquiry worth pursuing.

"So if you're going to be a vet, do you like dogs?" Charley still felt the burnout from his dog experience. Something else to beware of.

"I prefer cats, but yeah, dogs are neat. But professionally, I'm more interested in horses. And farm animals. Not necessarily pets."

"What do you know about birds?"

"Not that much. I did take a course with some emphasis on ornithology. Bird mating habits are funny and interesting. Why do you ask?"

"What do you know about skylarks?"

"Because you drive one?"

"Yeah, and there's an old, pretty song about skylarks, too."

Darla thought a moment while she sipped her iced tea. "Nature has a way of selecting which birds get to mate," she said after giving the question due consideration. "The ones with qualities best suited to the survival of the species wind up being the most attractive to the strongest females. I think skylarks are the ones that sing long songs. I mean, when you think of the attention span of a bird, a song that lasts more than three minutes is pretty long. Most people won't listen, really listen, to a song that long, much less perform it off the cuff like the larks do. The male flies high and hovers and sings, and the closer it is to mating season, the longer he hovers and sings. It shows his endurance. The ones who try to rush get rebuffed by the females. They want to be serenaded a while. You'd think it'd be the other way around, that the ones right there on the tree branch making themselves available would get to mate. I guess nature knows what it's doing."

Charley pondered. Hovering and waiting. He could try it, though he knew he'd have to skip the singing part. He had already declared his intentions to Dorothy. And to Darla. And Wayne, who didn't believe him. "So what are your plans after the summer internship?"

"Back to school, finish up in two years, start looking for a job. There's all kinds of possibilities. Government work, private practice. Andrea could use a partner."

"What are your plans for me?"

"You know what I've got planned for you, Buster." Darla's

smirk turned quickly enough into a genuine smile.

For a moment, he pictured himself, the back of his hand pressed dramatically against his forehead, moaning, "I'm so *tired* of being a boy-toy!" Instead, he said, "Sounds like a good plan to me."

Beyond that, who knew?

Charley decided he would hang around and find out. No guarantees.

When he felt lost, he would head for the windmill. It wasn't going anywhere.

* * *

Charley's mood was soaring. The world around him was beginning to take on sharper outlines for the first time today. But as if some mad puppet master said, "Time for that other shoe to drop," Bo Buchanan appeared.

Charley and Darla were walking hand in hand toward the Navaho's exit just as the door-dong announced Bo's entrance.

Bo stopped dead. His mouth dropped open, displaying those rows of perfect white teeth, as he looked from Darla to Charley, to their clasped hands, and back to Darla. Charley decided to keep his mouth shut and let Darla handle this, but he could feel the redness creeping up from his collar.

"Daddy! Hi!" Darla and Bo hugged while Bo kept his eye on Charley. "Daddy, this is my friend, Charley Bristow."

"We've met," Bo said, in a neutral tone, rich with implications.

Charley offered his hand. "Howdy, Bo. Nice to see you."

"What'd you ever do with that car?" This guy didn't waste any time getting right to the squirmy questions.

"Just found out today it sold to a classic car collector. Made a five hundred percent profit." Charley hoped he'd succeeded at sounding like it was no big deal to him. And he said a quick thank-you to that Puppet Master of the Dropping Shoes that he got to be the one to report this news to Bo. He saw the man's demeanor change a little—maybe a tinge of respect creeping in.

"You are one lucky guy. Remind me not to play cards with you."

Charley forced a small laugh. He'd have to be nice to his girlfriend's dad, even if he was Mr. Buchanan of the big belt buckle and bigger truck. And he'd have to give up the fantasy of someday dropping him in a game of pool.

Looking at his daughter, Bo said, "You look different, Sugarfoot."

"Charley just styled my hair! Doesn't it suit me?"

"Yeah, sure does, but then, you'd look good bald, darlin'." To Charley he said, "So you cut hair for a living, huh?" Charley drooped at the idea of what a low opinion Bo probably had of his daughter hanging out with a hair stylist. At least he was in a more appropriate age group than the professor. He bucked up his pride. "Sure do. At the Wild Hare, best salon in five counties."

"So, what are you doing in town?" Darla asked, taking her father by the elbow and shooing them all back outside the restaurant's foyer.

"I tried to call to see if we could have dinner but came on over, thinking I'd reach you eventually and might get to visit a while. Just thought I'd stop in here and eat while I'm waiting for you to find your phone." He sounded like a boss giving a first gentle reprimand to an employee for being incommunicado.

Undaunted, Darla hefted the small purse that hung from her shoulder. "Oh, sorry, I guess I left it in my car while Charley fixed my hair, and then we walked over here for dinner."

"Well, then," Bo said, "if you two don't have any further

plans for this evening, why don't you keep your old man company for dinner? Have another glass of tea?"

The invitation was aimed only at Darla, so Charley said quickly, "I do have some errands I can run . . . ." He'd been hoping for a much longer evening with Darla, an evening they would begin as they walked back to the salon. But it was time for him to put on his "I'm a Good Sport" T-shirt for the dear old dad. Damn it.

"But I'm flexible." Charley looked Darla carefully in the eyes to see which way she was leaning, and he wasn't surprised when she chose her father. After all, he was her father, and Charley was just a guy she was "taking it slow" with. So he kissed her on the cheek, wishing he could carry her off. Waving them good-bye, he walked alone to retrieve his car, head home, and at least lose himself in a good book.

12
Running

TIME TO CALL A WISE WOMAN, Charley decided. Actually, Lou could be a real wise*ass*, but she knew when to tone it down.

Lou had a delivery to make at the Wild Hare anyway, so she agreed to spend some break time with Charley.

"If we can't get any privacy in the break room, we'll take a stroll around the square," he explained. "But I need to get something off my chest."

He had tossed all night, succumbing to bad dreams about Bo Buchanan with devil's horns, Bo Buchanan as King Kong, hauling a kicking and screaming Darla to the top of a skyscraper. His conscious mind was doing well, he thought, but his subconscious could be a real traitor. He needed Lou's advice. Dorothy was a good shoulder to lean on, but Lou was more seasoned and less prone to gossip.

Once they were on the street—of course the break room was no place to talk—Lou said, "Tell me what's bothering you, Chippie."

"Darla and I ran into her dad last night." He told her about his history with Bo and the territorial-tinged dislike they were developing for each other. "I don't want to let Bo wreck a good thing that might be going on with me and Darla."

"And how would he do that?"

"He could . . ." Charley stopped. In the light of day, in front

of the Sandstone County courthouse with its solid columns span-
ning the two-story façade, he took into account that Bo hadn't
stopped Darla from marrying the professor. It was Darla's decision to be with Charley . . . or not. Charley had a say, too. Then he
said, "Good question. That Darla is an independent gal."

"That's how she strikes me. But you're afraid Bo might be
able to interfere somehow?"

"That. Yes. But also that I'll make an ass of myself. I can't
stand the guy."

"What can't you stand about him?"

"He's all bluster. All hat and no cattle, as they say. But, I
guess he's got hat *and* cattle. And lets everyone know it."

"So?"

"I dunno. I guess he'll disapprove of me."

"So?"

"Dammit, Lou! Quit saying 'So?'"

"Okay. I'll speak in longhand. So what if he acts confident?
That's not about you. So what if he disapproves of you? He doesn't
know you. I want you to name me somebody that hasn't liked you
once they spend a little time with you."

"Well, there were some teachers . . . and one of the instructors
at barber college."

"And how much did that affect your life?"

"I guess they didn't, but we're talking about Darla's dad
here."

"Charley. Listen to me. I think you're letting your own problems with not knowing your real dad get in the way here."

He started to interrupt. "I don't see what that could have to
do with . . ."

Lou held up her hand. "You asked me on this walk. Now you
have to listen." She went on. "You're awkward with father figures.
Okay? Admit it. I don't blame you. It's no big deal. It's like saying

you've got blue eyes or you're left-handed. Or nearsighted—since it is a weakness. But so what? If you just realize that you're awkward with father figures and maybe think of Bo as just another good ol' boy instead of Darla's father, that'll take some sting out of this deal."

"I didn't like him before I knew he was Darla's dad. I don't want to admit that to Darla."

"Don't you dare admit that to Darla! Not for a few years, at least, if y'all are still together in a few years."

"But I should be honest. . . ."

"No. You shouldn't. You keep your mouth shut about Bo and trust Darla to use her own good sense. You'll have to meet her mom, right?"

"Yeah. And stepdad." He decided to skip telling Lou for now about Darla's mom being his second-grade teacher.

"Just try to keep it between the fence posts. Don't avoid anyone, and remember to trust Darla. If it turns out she'd dump you only because of her daddy's opinion, then she's not the one for you."

Charley felt some of the weight of his concern leaving. "Okay, thanks, Lou. You're right."

They walked back to the salon, enjoying the springtime weather and the smell of Indian hawthorn in bloom.

Later, when Darla called to apologize for deserting Charley at the Navaho, he said, "That's okay. Your dad wants to see you, too." And they left it alone.

Darla said, "I sure wish we'd had more time together. I've got to go back to College Station for a final exam in a correspondence course I took this semester. While I'm there, I'll stay with my old roommate and meet with my advisors. It might take several days to schedule all the appointments. And there's a between-semester mini-course I can take that'll get me ready for my intern-ship. Anyway, I'm saying all this to tell you that I'll be gone a few weeks."

Charley's heart sank. School had interfered rather than Bo. But to someone like Darla with long-range plans, a few weeks might not be a serious absence. The thought came to him, unbid-den, of Ann, and Darrell Trainer, who'd left for four short months on the road.

"I'll miss you," he managed. "Will you call me and let me know how things're going?"

"Of course, you goose. I don't plan on *not* staying in touch with my boyfriend."

Hot dog. *Boyfriend.* He used to think that meant you moved in together. Now it just meant she was leaving for three weeks.

But he was her boyfriend.

* * *

Charley was still smiling at the thought of being a boyfriend to a vet student who was not running up his charge cards as he changed into his running gear and headed out from his apartment to take advantage of the spring weather. As summer neared, he'd have to change his schedule to running just before sunrise, when the low 80's nighttime temperature still allowed outdoor exertion, before the heat pressed in for the day.

He didn't need to go to his mom's. He'd seen enough of her, and she'd seen enough of him on Monday night. So he jogged in the direction of the town square. From there, he would circle the park.

He stretched at the bottom of the stairs and headed out at his warm-up pace. Reaching the square, he circled the courthouse, appreciating the hawthorns, crape myrtles, and strong columns on the front of the hundred-year-old building. It all reminded him of Lou. Good old Auntie Lou.

Heading down the one boulevard in town, a street that led into the city park, Charley was running at a steady clip. He heard an engine idling behind him. One reason he never ran with earbuds in both ears was so he could hear all the subtle sounds. For the next block, he assumed the idling truck—he could tell by the engine sound it was a large pickup—was waiting for him to pass a driveway so it could turn in to one of the rambling ranch-styles that lined the street. But the truck was still with him when he reached the park entrance.

He hated to stop since he'd just gotten his second wind for the turnaround and the jog back home. Damn it. But he looked over his shoulder to see what was on his heels.

Bo Buchanan and his cow-catcher grille. Double damn.

It would feel silly and pretentious to jog in place while Bo stopped the truck and got out. So Charley stood with his hands on his hips and wiped the sweat that was dripping from his hairline since he'd stopped moving. At least Bo didn't want to run over him. He would have already done it if that was his intention.

"Hey, Charley." Bo walked toward him. "I was back in town today to see Darla before she left for A&M." Bo studied Charley's face to see if this news was a bomb being dropped.

"Howdy, Bo. Yep, gonna miss Darla while she's gone, but she's got some important things to tend to."

Bo nodded. "Mind if we take a walk?"

"Well, I've dropped my pace, so we might as well."

Bo fell into step, and they turned into the park.

"Darla says she's known you—or who you were—most of her life."

"Yep. It kind of scared me at first—like, why would she keep up with me? But girls are different, aren't they?"

"Sure are. I spend most of my time trying to figure them out."

"Me, too. Darla's a good one, though. You and her mom and stepdad—all those people that've raised her—have done a good job, as far as I can tell from a couple of dates and a haircut."

Bo cut his eyes over at Charley. The look told Charley he'd corroborated Darla's version—which was true, if you used the term "date" loosely.

"I just want you to know I look out for Darla. She's made some mistakes. I don't want her to get hurt."

"I know. So've I. Made mistakes."

"I know that, too."

Charley shrugged. "Can't change the past, can we?"

"I'd like to call you sometime for a cup of coffee."

Aw, shit. "Sure, Bo." Charley gave him his number, which he entered slowly with thick fingers into his phone. Darla hadn't gotten his hands, thank God. The strength maybe, but not the link-sausage fingers. "So were you looking for me, or was I just a deer in your headlights today?"

"I went by the salon, but they said you'd already gone home and were probably out running—either over to your mother's or around the courthouse and down to the park."

How helpful his coworkers were. What if Bo had been a bill collector or an IRS agent? But nothing about Bo would clue them in to either of those worries.

"Those women are a fount of information. . . .I'll tell you what!" The impulse to kid Bo took over. "Ask Dorothy Pinkfield for a date, and she'll tell you my life's story. She owns the salon and she's divorced. Her ex is in prison."

"I'm happily married, Charley."

"Oh. Well, Darla and I haven't gotten around to learning that

much about each other's folks. Like I said, just a couple of dates."
Charley patted himself on the back for his restraint. He wanted to
shout in Bo's face, "What kinda nut are you to follow me like this
and act like you're some kind of investigator?" But he didn't. And,
he realized Bo was the one with the problem. Charley was Darla's
boyfriend. For now.

"Call me for coffee, or if you want me to cut your hair without scalping you."

Charley waved goodbye and jogged off. What a control-freak
dad.

13
Black-Sheep Nephew

IT HAD BEEN A LONG MONTH.

Charley was still trying to figure out who, and what, he should tell about his newfound family. He hadn't even told Wayne yet. Lou was keeping quiet, and April . . . she wouldn't be telling stories at any cocktail parties.

At their weekly breakfast meet at the Navaho, Wayne looked serious.

Charley put down his coffee cup. "What?"

Wayne shifted in his chair, folded his paper napkin into a small square, and stuck it under the edge of his plate. He cleared his throat. "I've been meaning to ask. . . . Are you going to start seeing that little Darla Buchanan regularly? You can say it's none of my business."

"That's okay. Yeah, I think Darla and I want to make a go of it. . . . Why? You're not thinking of asking her out, are you?"

"No, no! Here's the deal . . . . Dick Raney is Lou Trainer's landlord. You know, she's living at the old Middleton place. Dick bought it twenty or so years ago—it's a nice old rock house with fifteen acres around it. Dick's only used it for a guest house. Anyway, he's leased it out to her."

Charley wondered what this had to do with him and Darla.

"Anyway." Wayne was finally getting to the point. Not like him to hem and haw, so for once Charley was entertained by Wayne's discomfort instead of the other way around. "Anyway, uh, Dick bugged me to meet up with Lou for coffee. He thinks she's first-class. Said he'd ask her out if he was single."

"So?" Charley relished being the cool one.

"So. . . I wanted to make sure you weren't making a play for Lou. I did meet her for coffee, and she's lined me up to come out to her place for dinner. She mentioned that y'all went to Lubbock not long ago to pick up beauty shop supplies and break in your Skylark."

"So?"

"Okay, Charley. I guess I'm clearing it with you. So it doesn't get complicated between us."

Charley decided not to keep Wayne dangling any longer. "Yeah, Wayne. Go ahead. Date Lou with my blessing. Not only is she too old for me, she's not my type."

"Since when did you have a 'type?'"

"Since when did you?"

They stared at each other a moment, each of them offended. When the truth hit them, they both guffawed, causing people at nearby tables to inspect them to see if they could see what was so damn funny. When he got tickled, Wayne liked to rap his fork in the middle of his plate, so his clattering added to the noise-making. They caught their breath.

Wayne said, "Lou's not too old for you; she's too mature."

"I agree. So is Darla. So I better get busy growing up, don't ya think?"

"Yeah, Chippie. 'Bout time."

Charley ignored Wayne's use of the nickname Lou had given him. He had a better bomb to drop. "All that said, I'm just not into dating relatives."

Wayne froze in mid-chew. "What?"

"Yep, it turns out Lou is my mother's long-lost half-sister. I thought she was coming on to me. Remember that first night when I got you to give me a ride to Ladies' Night? I thought Lou was chatting us up for a reason, but I was wrong. It's because she was getting to know her little ol' nephew before she got around to introducin' the subject of a father that my mom hadn't known about."

Wayne stared blankly for a moment while he put together that Charley's mother and Lou shared a father. As it sank in, he looked puzzled. Finally, a smile spread over his face. He was genuinely pleased. Charley considered that Wayne was proud for him to have such a worthy family member as Lou—she was good people. Talented . . . and available. "How did you keep this from spreading all over town?"

"Only me, Lou, and my mother know, and you know Mom— she doesn't talk to people much."

"Well, I'll be damned."

"Anyway, I'll tell you more about it all—or Lou will, when you go to her place for dinner. She's a great lady, and if y'all get married, then you'll be my Uncle Wayne."

"That's premature. . . . But the idea of having you for my black-sheep nephew does warm the cockles of my heart. Chippie."

They were trading insults and laughing when the door swung open. Before Charley could catch his breath, Bo walked toward their table.

"Howdy, Charley." Bo pulled out a chair and sat down, un-invited. "Sorry I haven't gotten back to you for that cup of coffee."

"That's okay." Charley sure didn't mind letting go of that obligation. He introduced Wayne, glad that Wayne would be able to see what he was up against.

Wayne never minded anyone waltzing up to his table, ex-cept for Larry Bob. He could shift his social gears quickly and in-clude the new arrival in the conversation. Recognizing Bo's name, Wayne said, "You're the owner of the tire dealership, right?"

"Yeah, we do retail and distribution on some brands."

"I've been wondering—can I get my tires straight from you off the Internet?"

"You wouldn't save any money over getting them from Jarod, once you paid the shipping. You're talking pickup tires, right?"

"Couple of pickups, my mom's car, couple of trailers, tractor, backhoe."

Wayne's list of vehicles and equipment impressed Bo. So sad, Charley thought, that he had to get secondary Brownie points with Darla's dad just because Wayne used a lot of tires, running the ranch.

"Bo is Darla's dad," Charley interjected.

"Is that right?" Wayne immediately picked up the role of rooting for his would-be nephew to the father of the girlfriend. "You ever go over to Hopper's?"

"Not much. Been a couple times in the last five years maybe."

"Charley comes from a talented family. There's a great lady drummer playing in the band that's bringing them in at Hopper's. She's his aunt."

"I just might check that out," said Bo. Then he said, with manners surprising to Charley, "Well, I hope you'll forgive the interruption. Just wanted to say 'Hey.'" He went to his own booth and sat with his back to them.

Wayne looked at Charley. "That guy stalking you?"

"Maybe," Charley said, uneasy at Bo's ability to material-ize just at the moment he had his guard down. Pretty creepy, he thought.

14

Goodbye to The No

JAROD WAS GOOD on his word about the Renault. People stopped on the street to stare as the flatbed trailer and truck hauling the handsome, broken-down car passed by, carrying The No on to fame in someone's classic car collection. The cashier's check was made out to Charley. He headed straight to the bank and deposited it. Then he headed straight back to Jarod's with another cashier's check as a commission and repayment for his efforts to fix the unfixable. Only a bare spot at the side of Jarod's shop remained as evidence of the Renault disaster.

As Charley entered the shop, he speculated that he might have a calling, going to used car lots and finding vintage models that he could resell to collectors and quadruple his money. But he admitted to himself that the No miracle was a one-time deal— pure good fortune. Easier to go gambling in Shreveport.

Jarod protested when he saw the check. "Now, Charley, you know I don't want this money."

"Too late. It's made out to you. Take it, or I'll tell Sue you turned down five hundred dollars."

Marriage helped out a would-be blackmailer. Jarod gave up arguing about the check and folded it into his shirt pocket with a simple thank-you. "So, are you coming out for the centennial railroad celebration?"

"Absolutely not." Charley's answer was as quick as a cap pistol. "See you later. And you better cash that check. I'll be following up with Sue." He shut the door to further argument.

Sulfur Gap was celebrating the hundredth anniversary of the first freight train arriving at its depot. The railroad had put the Gap on the map and spawned a business boom that died during the Great Depression and stayed dead because of periodic droughts. But the townspeople celebrated what they once were. They gathered to remember that they managed to survive as a community with its own character, even if half the businesses on Main Street were boarded up and many of the finer homes were crumbling away on once-posh residential streets.

Charley hadn't thought about the centennial. Dorothy would insist on opening the salon late so that everyone could see the small parade—a few horse-drawn hay trailers, side rails removed, and occupied by the local Boy Scouts, the high school drill team and cheerleaders, the Friends of the Library, and the Lions Club. The high school band would pound a rhythm down the street behind some curvy twirlers, and all the bystanders would cheer them on.

Charley avoided parades and celebrations. They mystified him. He always wondered how in the hell folks could think it was fun to stand out in the heat and wave like maniacs at people they saw every week. Waving an arm off because they were on a parade float made from a flatbed trailer trimmed with hand-painted signs. He didn't get it.

The antiques stores on Main would be open, with special discounts on sidewalk sales. Rusty wagon wheels leaning against lace tablecloths topped with kerosene lanterns and Candlewick crystal would be on display. There would be a dunking booth, too. The mayor was usually the prime victim. If only they could get Sheriff Larry Bob Sparks. Larry Bob would bring in a fortune if people could pay for a chance to dunk him. Wayne would be at the head of the line. Charley smiled at the thought. Wayne and

Larry Bob had always clenched their fists and faked a smile at each other, nourishing an old grudge. They grated on one another's nerves, especially in the case of Larry Bob getting to Wayne.

A small traveling carnival would be offering rides, shooting galleries, and ring tosses. People would come from surrounding towns, even some antique hunters from Austin. One lady was reputed to have bought cheap a bunch of old pearl snap-button cowboy shirts at the festival and then sold them on eBay for a hundred dollars each to a costuming contractor for Hollywood movies.

Thinking about it made Charley bilious. He smiled and nodded and kept cutting hair whenever the salon buzzed with the excitement of the coming festival.

As he was driving away from Jarod's, heading for the salon and his afternoon appointments, Darla called. He'd been counting down the days till her return to Sulfur Gap. Three more to go, as of today. And he'd set aside a bit of the proceeds from the sale of the No to take her out on a really nice date to celebrate.

"Hey, Charley, I have an idea," she said. He had grown fond of the sound of her voice on the phone these past weeks.

"Yeah?" Now Charley perked up. He liked Darla's ideas.

"Let's go hang out at the railroad centennial this Saturday when I get back."

He deflated like a speared blowfish. "Really?"

"Yes, really. I think it would be fun."

Darla had been busy getting her veterinary internship started. They hadn't seen each other since their dinner at the Navaho. Since he'd had time to process what he was learning about his sweetheart, Charley figured that her escapade with the professor must have been a bigger blow to her than she admitted. She seemed so capable in everything she did. This huge life mistake must have put her in a tailspin. He guessed it was harder for an achiever like her, with high self-expectations. Heck, he'd landed on his feet almost instantly after his divorces, but then his self-expectations weren't high. He'd continued with his usual vague sense of disappointment and emptiness, lightened by his work and his friends.

Charley held back the groan surging from deep in his stomach. It felt like trying not to throw up. He wanted to take Darla somewhere, but certainly not to a lame small-town festival. "Yeah, okay," he heard himself say. Good old Charley. Always agreeable. "How about we start the weekend at Hopper's on Friday?"

"No, you go ahead and have a good time. I'll be driving in Friday morning and will need to rest up."

"We could trade Hopper's for the festival," he bargained, still holding onto hope.

"No. I'll be wiped out Friday, but glad to be home. And I'm too susceptible to hanging on a good one when I'm that tired. One more night, and it'll be worth the wait."

Damn Darla and her damn self-discipline.

So the date was on for the centennial festivities. Jarod would give Charley a hard time. Sue would smile, but at least Wayne wouldn't know Charley was ending his festival boycott to be with Darla because Wayne wouldn't be anywhere near the celebration. Of course Dorothy would know. Her radar would pick up all kinds of signals. Wayne, on the other hand, missed a lot of the gossip mill in the Gap because he made himself unavailable. He wasn't the kind of guy people went up to and started a conversation with "Did you hear about so-and-so?"

On Friday night, Charley found a pool game at Hopper's. A few out-of-towners timing family visits to coincide with the centennial celebration thickened the crowd with people coming by to kill time and check out the new band.

The Crew was in top form. Their expanding repertoire included newer songs with the old standards. The blended vocals, the sounds of the steel guitar, rhythm, bass, and fiddle, driven along by Lou's drums, all seemed effortless. A right decent band. They could make it in a larger city if they cared to, but fortunately for Sulfur Gap, they didn't care to. Wylie and Lou could harmonize like an old married couple, and Charley smiled to realize that he didn't feel territorial about Lou any more. He hoped she and Wayne could get together. He smiled again at the thought of having an Uncle Wayne.

Charley and Lou had made plans to go together for the next regular Wednesday visit to his mother. Lou would diffuse the painful atmosphere that hung between Charley and April. Another person in the picture would be like diluting a toxic mix with a gush of fresh, cold well water. Then Wayne might join them someday. Charley would have a whole team on his side.

He was playing some eight-ball tonight. A self-satisfied Austin yuppie type was convinced that no Sulfur Gap rube would be able to beat him, especially not one wearing Wranglers instead of designer jeans. Not being a hustler—he knew that sort of shenanigans could hamper future friendships and endanger his well-being—Charley always kept the stake money to a minimum, when he played for money at all. The Austin man pulled a fat money clip from his pocket beneath the tail of his carefully and casually wrinkled shirt and put out a hundred-dollar bill, but Charley said, "Let's play for fifty."

Austin man snickered and pulled out a fifty. "Okay, if that's all you can afford to lose," he said through his nose.

Charley rolled the cue ball the length of the table and stood aside with little concern until it banked off the far end and returned to stop less than an inch from the near bank. Austin man's lopsided smartass grin faded a little. His cue ball hit the bank hard on the return, so Charley won the break, sank the four and the fifteen balls, and called solids. Ordinarily, he didn't clean up so fast because he savored a game and threw many away so that he would have a few friends left at the pool tables in Sulfur Gap. But he wanted to be rid of this guy like a skunk on his heel. So he proceeded to sink all the solids and called for the eight to go into the corner.

Game over.

The small crowd that gathered to watch the bloodbath between Charley and the unwitting stranger erupted into applause and shouts of congratulations. Planning to call off the bet, Charley waved to everyone to cut it out and offered his hand to Austin man. But the city boy turned on his heel with a parting comment, "I'll be sure to warn everyone coming through here that there's a crooked bunch of pool hustlers in this shithole."

Jarod and Sue were part of the audience, and Jarod couldn't resist the retort, "Oh, and don't forget who wouldn't let you lay down your Ben Franklin." Sue grabbed his arm and pulled him onto the dance floor for a round of "Cotton-Eyed Joe."

Charley decided it was time for a beer break, so he sat at a table close to the band. It was the first time that evening he'd looked closely at the bandstand. A keyboard with its cover still on it stood beside Lou and her trap set, and he wondered if her next trick would be to whip out a number on the ivories. Come to think of it, it wouldn't be all that surprising. *Not* being surprised by Lou would be a switch.

Jarod and Sue finished their dance and joined Charley as the band followed up with "I Love This Bar." The floor filled up with dancers singing along, celebrating the diversity of the different ages, stages, and cultural backgrounds of Hopper's clientele. Everybody in town who wasn't a Church of Christ (Southern Branch) or in AA—and even some of them came to dance to the Crew and sip club soda—came to Hopper's on the weekends.

Unless the management at the VFW started booking some competitive bands, it would dry up and blow away except for the small group of smokers who were allowed to fog up a back room and play gin rummy all afternoon and evening.

As the song ended, Wayne appeared at the club's entrance. He leaned out to hold the door open for a small woman in a western hat and a god-awful sequin jacket. As they walked toward the table, Charley realized it was Darla. He stood up as she rushed to him and threw her arms around his neck. "Surprise!" she shrieked in his ear. His heart jumped for joy at the sight of her, but he was confused. He gave her a welcome-home kiss and returned her hug, but after the greeting, he stood back, trying to understand what was going on.

He frowned at Wayne. What was he doing escorting Darla to Hopper's if he was dating Lou? Or had that gone south? Wayne picked up on Charley's displeasure right away, while Darla looked at Charley, perplexed by his mixed reaction.

"Evenin', Charles," Wayne said pointedly. "Look who I found in the *parking lot*."

Well, that clears up the part about Darla and Wayne, he thought. But what was with the getup? Knowing better than to mention the jacket except in the most flattering of terms, he reached for her hand and squeezed it. He pulled out a chair for her. "I'm glad you made it after all. But why did you want to surprise me?"

Darla didn't squeeze back, perturbed by Charley's greeting. "The surprise is that I'm gonna sing with the band," she said.

"Don't kid me now," he said.

This time Jarod jumped to Charley's rescue. "She kids you not. I bet this little lady has some pipes."

"I can do a good Miranda Lambert imitation," she said, with a tinge of bashfulness.

"I love Miranda Lambert!" Sue chimed in. "Hi, Darla, I'm Sue. We haven't officially met. And this is my unmannerly husband Jarod, who forgets about introductions."

"Sorry, sorry," both Charley and Jarod muttered at the same time.

The band started its break, and Lou headed toward the table. Wayne and Darla scooted apart to pull up a chair for her. Wayne put his arm on the back of Lou's chair.

Wayne saw the curiosity in Charley's eyes and wiggled his eyebrows villainously. Well, good for Wayne. Good for Lou.

"So you're a singer, too?" Charley asked Darla.

"Just for fun. Do you sing?"

"Oh, not me. I'm about as much fun to listen to as a buzz saw. I meant, you're a singer like Lou."

"I'm not nearly as good as Lou. She can fill out the low notes lots better than I can."

"Wait a few years, honey, and your voice will drop, too, along with a few other things," Lou said.

Darla explained to Charley, "Wylie and my stepdad, Ed, are pretty good friends. So Ed was telling Wylie how I used to always sing in church and with the chorale in college. After I got back into town earlier today, I practiced a few numbers with them."

"And she's remarkable," Lou said. "I think she could be a regular with any dance band, including ours—if she didn't have to keep studying for that vet degree."

"Thanks," Darla beamed.

Charley felt proud. He was still a bit miffed that the first thing she did wasn't to run to see him. But he had to remember, he was in new territory with a different kind of woman, the kind who set her own priorities—healthy ones, mostly.

The other couples leaned their heads together to talk to each other, and Charley turned to Darla. "I'm sorry I was a jerk just now. Frankly, I've missed you so much, I *was* a little jealous when you walked in with Wayne, and I stepped in it."

"Don't pull that one again," she said, poking him on the arm with a forefinger that felt like a cattle prod. "You need to learn how to accept nice surprises."

"That's a promise. I don't relish being an asshole. You nervous?"

"Well, sure I am, but so what?"

"You don't mind being nervous?"

"No. If I screw up, I screw up. Not the end of the world. It's not like I'm auditioning for my big break with the Grand Ole Opry." She elbowed Charley. "Anyway, if I faint on the bandstand, Charley, you can carry me off."

They clicked their beer bottles in agreement, and Charley basked in the contentment that Darla was back in town. They would have the rest of spring and the whole summer to be together.

When the break was over, Darla prissed to the bandstand and swept the cover off the keyboard. Standing behind it, she adjusted a mic and checked the settings. Her god-awful sequin jacket glittered from the recessed lights that cast a dim glow over the band.

This was certainly a night for surprises. They hadn't even gotten around to the part about Darla accompanying herself on keyboard. But she did, as she sang "Famous in a Small Town." Charley listened to every word, and he relished the idea that everyone is famous in a small town. It was a celebration of small-town life, where it was all right to have your picture on the front page of the newspaper for getting the first buck of the deer season, and it was a given that someone would have something to say regarding anything you did, whether it was being late to church or locked up in jail. No secrets, no shame. Like being a celebrity.

The song stopped the dancers. They wanted to watch this new singer. Darla's amateur status wasn't apparent until the end of the song, when Wylie gave the signal to wrap up, but Darla started into an extra chorus on the keyboard. She stopped abruptly, flashed a sheepish smile, and said "Oops." Everyone laughed and applauded as she curtsied and left the stage. Shrugging out of her jacket, she walked straight to Charley, who was beaming with pride.

No doubt now in this small town, the two of them were an item by now. Charley felt that twinge of self-consciousness he hid so well. He waved to Dorothy and Loretta from work. Some of their friends joined them, waving to Charley and Darla. It was a parade-float moment. Two observant coworkers would be sufficient to fan an unrelenting interest at the salon in this new chapter of his love life, he thought. This time, though, he didn't feel the shame as though he were living under an interrogation lamp with critical observers judging his every move while he screwed up. Instead of thinking of their eyes watching him, he thought of his inner eye watching himself.

He and Darla danced every dance the rest of the evening, getting more in sync. Darla lengthened her stride to match his, and Charley shortened his to match hers. Lou sang "Stand by Your Man," with the new fiddler ripping into the chorus with her. Wylie sang "All My Rowdy Friends Have Settled Down," while the older members of the crowd held up their one and only beer of the night in salute. Lou sang "You Ain't Woman Enough to Take My Man," and Charley looked up in time to see her wink at Wayne, who was sticking around for a change.

After the band finished playing and the bartender rang his cow bell for last call, Charley walked Darla to her car.

He bit his tongue. She drove a Prius. At least it didn't have a sticker saying "Namaste" on the bumper.

"Want to come to my place?" he asked her. How could she not?

"I would love to, but then we won't want to get up and make the centennial tomorrow."

Damn the damn centennial. "Sure we would."

"Let's save it for a more special time," she said.

"What could be more special than your Sulfur Gap singing debut?"

"It's not that big of a deal. Besides, I do need some rest now."

"Okay. But there's no time like the present." He eased two fingers down behind the waistband of her jeans and pulled her into him. "Just so you know, I hope that special time is tomorrow and not next month some time."

He stayed quippy so he didn't pout. Pouting was unattractive. He knew this from listening to his clients and coworkers at the salon. There should be a diploma in "What Women Don't Like." His coursework for the bachelor's degree completed, he now tackled the internship.

They leaned against her Prius and kissed.

Shoot. She was sure worth waiting at least twenty-four hours for. Even another month or longer.

As Charley unlocked the Skylark after Darla drove off, he spotted the now-familiar truck with the cow-catcher grille parked back under the overhanging branches of a live oak. Well, fine and dandy. Bo could skulk around all he wanted. Tonight, all he'd seen was a friendly kiss good-bye. He gave a cheery wave, unable to tell if Bo really was inside the cab with a pair of night-vision binoculars. Maybe he'd come by to watch Darla sing, keeping out of the way after too many interruptions in the flow of Charley's social life. He decided not to find out. Bo could stick it as far as he was concerned.

15
Helluva Celebration

CHARLEY ARRIVED AT DARLA'S promptly at 9:30 a.m. as instructed. He couldn't remember for sure if he had crossed paths with Mrs. Barta since the second grade. A faint mental image made him think he'd seen her in the Shop Tight Grocery, which had closed after the United opened. But he was never on the alert for teachers in the store.

He smiled, remembering the old store. The owner had wanted to convey by the store's name that the prices were reasonable, so that if you were tight with money, you'd like the store. But everyone instead joked that the name meant you were supposed to have several belts of bourbon before you could steer the wobbly shopping baskets over the sloping old floors. Anyway, the faint memory of his second grade teacher picking out bananas at the Shop Tight could be a real one, he thought.

Mrs. Barta could be a salon customer, a client of Charlene or Bethany. He was racking his brain. He remembered that she looked sort of like Darla, with a rounder face, bigger teeth, and short brown hair. He simulated a mental image of her aged by eighteen years. She should be a bit older than April. That gave him a frame of reference.

The person who answered the door could not be Mrs. Barta. She had shoulder-length bleached blonde hair and wore shorts and a tank top that showed off an even tan. No sign of aging. Damn. Older women were getting better looking all the time.

"Charley Bristow!" She opened the glass storm door to the porch and grabbed his arm, pulling him into the entryway of her neat, stucco bungalow. Once he was inside, she grabbed his other arm and leaned back to take in his height. "Hot dog! Have you ever grown up! So how are you doing?"

"Great! And how are you, Mrs. Barta?"

"It's Janet. You can call me Janet now that we're both grown-ups. Anyway, I'm glad Darla dug you up. I've thought of you on and off all these years and I'm happy to hear that you're doing so well!"

She sounded a bit too surprised at how well he was doing. Faked enthusiasm might be a way to get over how low Darla was stooping for someone to go out with.

"Thanks," he said. By now she had pulled him into the living room. "You know, you gave me my first book, *High Plains Indians*, written for early readers. I still have it."

"Oh, I'm so touched! You still have it?"

"Yeah. I've added a few books to the collection."

"What's your favorite book?"

"I don't have a favorite. I like Hemingway, and Faulkner, when I can figure him out, and *To Kill a Mockingbird*, for sure." He stopped himself. He didn't want to sound like he was trying to impress his former teacher. But he was.

"Have a seat and I'll grab you a mug of coffee." She gestured to a wingback chair in the corner. Walking toward the kitchen, she yelled—and this is how he remembered her as his second grade teacher—"Darla! Ed! Charley's here! Get in here and visit with our company!"

Yep. That was Mrs. Barta. Bubbly and bossy.

A handsome gray-haired man appeared from the hallway. He looked like a Ken doll dressed for yard work. Boat shoes. Khaki cargo pants. Cotton T-shirt. Old Yardman Ken. He beamed a white smile at Charley and shook hands.

"Charley! Good to see you!" he said, as if they were old friends. Charley couldn't remember ever meeting him. "Ed Barta!"

"Sure, sure!" Charley tried to act as though he recognized the name. Where was Darla? She needed to get her butt out here so they could get on over to the parade. Even the parade was better than making chit-chat with parents of a woman with whom you'd enjoyed raunchy sex and with whom you were doing your best to have another go at it—and soon.

"So what are you doing with yourself these days? Cutting hair? What?"

Uh. Gambling. Trading cars. Having disasters with dogs. Creating chaos with cheating chicks. None of these sounded like the cleverest thing to say under the circumstances. "Oh, trying to grow up," he said, not believing he said it.

"Ha! That's a great goal! Aren't we all?" Ed shook Charley's hand as if to congratulate him.

Charley settled into the wingback and Ed squatted on a nearby ottoman.

"You'll have to excuse my attire, Charley. Janet and I are getting ready to do some yard work. Spring trimming and mowing."

"It's that time of year." Charley wondered how long he would have to keep this up. He felt like a high school kid being vetted by the parents. He was trying to think of what he could say about yard work that didn't involve the challenges of the trailer park or scooping dog poo, when Darla bounced in.

Charley stood to greet her. She pushed him back down and perched on the arm of his chair. Janet came in with a tray of coffee in steaming mugs. Everyone settled in for a visit. He felt like a treed raccoon. Should he cover his eyes the way raccoons do?

"So," Janet said, "Darla says we might be seeing quite a bit of you this summer."

"I sure hope so." Charley looked up at Darla.

"Does your mother still live here?" Janet asked.

Boy, she got right to it. "Yes, she does. Same neighborhood, same trailer." Charley didn't feel like mincing any words. "She doesn't get out much anymore. Health problems."

"Oh, that's too bad," Janet commiserated, as if she hadn't heard any rumors. "No other family?"

Charley hesitated. Now would be a good time. Yes, it would. The moment unfolded.

"Well, yes. Not long ago, I discovered I have a whole family out in Oklahoma." If he was going to hang out with the Bartas, he would rather not indulge in idle chatter. He did it all week at the salon.

"What?" Darla turned to stare at Charley.

"Yeah. I was gonna tell you as soon as you got back, probably today. Well, here we are. It's today."

"I hope it's a good discovery," Janet said.

"Oh, it is. I'm still trying to get my head around it."

"Tell us about it," Ed said, rubbing his chin like a psychologist. Oh, right, that's what he was—a psychologist. Psychologist Ken. His practice was in Big Spring.

"I'm not sure where to start," Charley said. "Let's see. Long story short. My mother grew up not knowing who her real father was. He died recently and told his other kids about her in his will."

"That must have been hard on everyone," Ed said.

"Yeah," Charley said. "He was a professional drummer with a daughter and two sons."

"Wow, I bet that put you on tilt," Ed said.

Darla and Janet nodded. They waited for Charley to go on. "So how did ya'll make the connection?" Darla asked, breaking the silence.

"He left information about where he thought she lived and her maiden name of Bristow. April Bristow. It didn't take Lou long to find her."

"Lou? Of Lou's Crew?" Darla yelped. Janet giggled. They looked at each other and gawked in astonishment. Like a couple of sorority sisters.

"Yeah. Lou's the drummer's daughter."

"Sure! That makes sense. Natural talent! So she's your aunt?" Darla clapped her hand over her mouth. "And I thought she *liked* you. Like, wanted to *date* you." Darla and Janet gave each other the wide eyeball. Ed refolded his fingers around his chin and tilted a curious head at Charley.

Charley laughed. "Well, she does like me. But not as a boyfriend."

"When did you learn all this?" Darla asked.

"Lou told me a few weeks ago, right before you came into the shop to get your hair done."

"Oh, I remember you were distracted when we went to dinner. I guess you were pretty blown away."

And, Charley thought, you still don't know about me driving my grandmother's Buick.

They all sat a moment.

Ed reached over and patted Charley's knee. "Wow, Charley. I suppose we shouldn't say anything about it until you and Lou decide how you want to introduce yourselves to other people."

"Yeah, that'd be nice. Thanks."

About that time, they heard the clash of cymbals and the pounding of a bass drum. The band was on the march. A cloud moved from blocking the skylight, and the sun shot a yellow glow into the room.

Darla jumped up. "We should go. We'll miss the whole parade!" She grabbed Charley's hand. Janet stepped in and gave him a quick hug. Ed waved a casual salute as they whisked out the door. "It's only a few blocks. Let's walk it." On the sidewalk, Darla started off in a quickstep, boot heels clicking, so that Charley used every bit of his long stride to keep up.

"Wait! Hold up!" He put a hand on her shoulder. She stopped.

"What's wrong, Charley?"

"I was wondering how Ed got to be your stepdad. What happened with your mom and your real dad?"

"Oh! He and my mother got an amicable divorce when I was three. We'll go see him at his house, sometime when we get a chance."

"So you got to go see him a lot growing up?"

"Sure. Every other weekend. And he was close enough to come to all my school functions. Then I decided I wanted to live with him during middle school. That's when I moved away. Sure was nice that everyone was pleasant about it. Helped me out."

Darla waited for more questions, but Charley had enough to chew on. He thought how much of an advantage it was when divorced parents got over themselves and made peace. Good to know that Bo had an agreeable side.

As they drew closer to Main Street, the music grew louder and the sound of mingled voices—kids screaming with excitement, friends hailing one another—drifted toward them. Eventually the smell of popcorn taunted him with the revived memory of nights at the old drive-in movie on the highway between Sulfur Gap and Briargrove. He'd sat on two pillows in the middle of the scratchy seat of the pickup, between Eldon and his mother. They passed a box of popcorn back and forth between them as the images flashed across the screen.

On the final block of their trek to the parade, Charley's legs went stiff at the sight of a familiar van parked near the intersection. April's old Dodge Caravan. Before he caught his breath, he saw her familiar bulk sitting on the driver's side, alone in the van. The nostalgia of the popcorn smell vanished, replaced by a cold clod in his stomach. He was faced with the choice of walking Darla past the van and not acknowledging his mother's presence, or stopping to say hello and introducing the two of them. The thought of the first choice made his heart flutter with the shame of heaping more pain on his mother, adding to the burden that he had sensed in her for as long as he could remember. The second choice made his guts roll with embarrassment for both himself and April. He thought of her sadness wafting toward them on the fumes of cigarettes and booze as she would roll down the window to say a reluctant hello, embarrassed as much as Charley to be caught out in public.

He wondered why April was parked on this particular corner. He couldn't imagine that she was parked in a prime spot to watch the parade from her car. The parade must have cut off a booze run to the drive-through Party Warehouse, leaving her no choice but to pull over.

He decided on the spot that if meeting his mother would cause Darla to sense a basic wrongness in him and to conclude that the relationship was a no-go, it would be better to find out now than later. Neither Joyce nor Vicki had expressed any curiosity about his mother, and they were content not to meet her during their brief marriages. Darla would probably want to be introduced if for no other reason than the provocative story he had told at her parents' house. Scooting past his mother without stopping would prove him to be a jerk, acting like a junior high kid who tried to pretend he didn't have a mother when in fact one was lurking nearby.

Charley took the plunge. He grabbed Darla's elbow.

"Hold up. I see my mom," he said. This felt right to him, like he was manning up.

Darla slowed and began looking at the crowd for someone that could be Charley's mother, someone that resembled her own mother. Well, she would strike out using that filter to process the possibilities.

"She's in her van, parked up here," he said.

Darla spotted the van as they drew nearer. Her eager smile dropped to a questioning gaze as she took in April's profile.

Charley stepped to the curb, tapped on the window, and waved to April. Darla followed as he walked stiffly around to the driver's side window. It felt as though they were approaching roadkill to see what kind of critter it was—possum or armadillo?

April rolled down the window. To Charley's surprise, no fumes reached out to greet them. In fact, he thought he detected a faint talcum smell. His mother was mashed behind the steering wheel, the gathers of her muumuu held straight. Her hair was clean and combed, and he thought she'd even applied some make-up that hid the dark circles under her eyes.

"Hey, Charley."

"Hey, Mom."

After a pause in which they looked at each other, not believing they would meet on the street of their own hometown, Charley said, "Are you enjoying the parade?"

April was looking at Darla with more curiosity in her eyes than Charley expected. She pulled her attention back to him. "Oh, sure," she said.

Darla reached a hand through the window. "I'm Darla Buchanan, a friend of Charley's."

April held Darla's tiny hand in her sausage-shaped fingers. "I'm April, Charley's mother."

Their eyes met for a longer time than Charley could stand. He jumped in.

"Why on earth are you watching the parade?"

"I could ask you the same thing," said April. "This is the last place I thought I'd see you."

"You, too."

April let the question go and gazed again at Darla. "Are you Miz Barta's daughter? I remember she had a little girl, name of Buchanan."

"Why yes, Janet Barta's my mom."

"You know, she was my Charley's second-grade teacher."

Charley was stunned that April was putting this all together. The chance meeting was going well, but Charley didn't want to push the luck.

"Gotta go, Mom. Nice to see ya. Enjoy the parade." He waved and whisked Darla away by the elbow.

"Why don't we get her to come walk around with us?" Darla looked back over her shoulder.

"She has trouble with her knees."

"Oh."

Charley's insides exuded a sigh of relief that Darla didn't want to pursue the subject of his mother. But he was wondering, still. Why was she interested in the parade? Not like her at all.

The parade was short, and after the pep squad brought up the rear to conclude the march, Charley and Darla crossed the street to the large parking lot dedicated to the various booths. A tight knot of people gathered around the dunking booth. Cheers and heckling drifted over the heads of the onlookers. "Come on, you're throwing with the wrong hand!" someone yelled.

A gap in the shifting crowd revealed the hapless target of the heckling. It was Wayne Cheadham. He was standing sideways with a baseball in his hands, looking at the target on the dunking booth's lever as if it were the strike zone of a top-rated batter and he was about to make the deciding pitch in the World Series.

Sheriff Larry Bob Sparks, the true target, sat on the plank above the water. Wayne and Larry Bob had carried a grudge from high school, started over a girl. Wayne had told Charley he was weary of Larry Bob's little sideswipes, when his bruised ego brushed into Wayne's sphere with ploys for attention and attempts to deliver put-downs. Mostly ignoring him, Wayne did sometimes take the opportunity to play with Larry Bob's insecurities, like a bored cat swatting at a passing caterpillar.

"You can't hit the broad side of a barn. You can't hit a bull in the butt with a bass fiddle!" goaded Larry Bob. So far, he was still dry, and some of Sulfur Gap's finest had already paid to take a pitch and failed to dunk the sheriff.

Charley was correct that a dunking booth with Larry Bob would be as tempting to the ball-throwers as would a dart game with the Sheriff of Nottingham as the target in Robin Hood's day.

Larry Bob's last heckling inspired Wayne's last throw. His form took shape as he hurled his final ball straight at the target with the right speed to send Larry Bob plopping into the water tank.

The crowd whistled, hooted, and cawed as the sheriff pulled himself up the ladder, soaked to the bone in his track suit worn for the occasion. Wayne tipped his hat at Larry Bob, who nodded grudgingly before Lou and Wayne took off arm in arm to look at the craft booths. Charley and Darla watched Wayne and Lou walking together toward an antiques display, the same height, almost the same gait. Charley was surprised to see Wayne, to tell the truth. He and his friend occupied the same boots—those of a kidnap victim, dragged to the railroad celebration.

The gathering dispersed while Larry Bob toweled off and waited for the next person he had ticketed or irritated in some way to seize the opportunity to knock him off his perch into a symbolic watery grave.

* * *

Charley vaguely remembered Wayne's first wife, but he got an idea why the marriage failed when Wayne said, after Charley divorced Vicki, "Don't marry for sex. Sometimes the sexiest ones are the craziest." Charley had ignored him.

Wayne had described his second wife to Charley. "Cynthia was a church-singer-Bible-quoting Southern lady who was so tangled up in applying her religion, she confused herself and everyone around her. But she meant well." Wayne's failings, although not as crowded as closely in time as his own, made Charley feel better about his downfalls.

Lou let go of Wayne's hand to pick up a glass bowl. She set it down and moved on to a carved mesquite totem almost as tall as she was. She ran her hand over the polished surface. Charley could see that while Lou admired the wood carving, Wayne was admiring her. Charley imagined the love birds chirping around Wayne's head.

Wayne had clung with the grip of pride to the second marriage, but then Cynthia, driving home one dark night from a visit to San Angelo, had run head-on into a speeding drug dealer driving with his lights off. For Wayne, that marriage was like giving CPR for hours, only to have the patient die. His efforts were taken from him, snuffed like a candle, along with Cynthia's life. Wayne resigned himself to bachelorhood, and he had lain low for several years. Lou brought him out of hiding because she lacked the scent of a predator.

Nearby, Darla spotted Andrea Harper, the veterinarian. Darla gave Andrea a cheery wave just as Jarod tapped Charley on the shoulder. They exchanged pleasantries with him and Sue and moseyed on. Wayne and Lou saw them and looped back to form a friendly knot on the sidewalk.

As they walked the street, they waved to the people they knew. Parents gathered to let their kids see the old railroad engine, music lovers tapped their feet to the bluegrass band, and shoppers browsed the quilts, carvings, and homemade pies and cakes. Charley eased along with the crowd, feeling a surprising fluidity as he meandered through the stream of life. Again, he felt the voice that told him he belonged—on the street of his hometown with ordinary, everyday people he had known all his life.

Charley breathed a sigh of relief that Bo hadn't decided to join the fun, and they were heading back to Darla's house, having survived the hoo-haw. But he stopped in his tracks. Darla walked ahead a ways before she missed him and twirled to find him staring as if he had spotted a coiled rattlesnake.

"What's the matter?"

"Who's that guy?"

Darla followed his gaze. "Beats me."

A thin, stooped man with gray, wispy hair and wearing a baggy, threadbare suit was standing and leaning in the window of April's van, which was still parked at the curb. As they approached, they could hear his honeyed voice. The words were mostly unintelligible, but his tone was mocking and wheedling, like a bully extorting a weak kid's lunch money, enjoying his victim's fear. Charley heard "you *must* listen" and something about "urgent lessons."

He covered the remaining distance in a few long-legged bounds. He grabbed the old man by the shoulder and pulled him back. Tears were running down his mother's cheeks, and terror pinched her eyes into little buttons.

"Leave my mom alone!" Charley roared.

People walking nearby stopped to stare. Charley felt like he was in a theater-in-the-round, with the audience pressed near him. He remembered the desperate feeling when he was a little boy and could do nothing to stop the boyfriend of the moment from saying or doing as he wished with his mother. This time, though, he was bigger than the bastard that was messing with her. The thought flashed across his senses and inspired him to rise to his full height while the shrunken man cowered. Who was he? Some bum who thought he could browbeat a lone woman into giving him her purse money? Some salesman thinking April was a captive audience?

The old man backed away but didn't make a move to leave. He stuck his scrawny neck toward Charley and attempted an ingratiating smile.

"So here's your boy!"

He held out a hand to Charley, who refused to take it.

"Mom, are you all right?"

April clutched the steering wheel. She looked up at Charley through teary eyes. "Make him leave me alone," she begged.

Charley took a few steps toward the man, who began backing up. Charley wondered what he would do to make the guy leave if he didn't want to. He was good at staying out of fights and sometimes at finishing them, but he wasn't sure how to expel the guy from the presence of his mother. He was relieved to hear Larry Bob's voice behind him.

"Is there some kind of problem here?"

Charley never thought he would be so happy to hear from Larry Bob.

The sheriff had dried off and put his uniform back on, along with his badge, gun, handcuffs, and taser—lots of tools that seemed unnecessary for the streets of Sulfur Gap but part of Larry Bob's regular attire. For once they might come in handy.

"I'm this lady's father," the man said, nodding toward April. "Frank Bristow."

What a month. His family tree had blossomed—sort of. Now here stood a rotten apple—the man who had posed as April's father and thought he could still get by with it.

"Well, she doesn't have to talk to you if she doesn't want to," Charley said. He felt Darla's fingers in his belt loop. This time it reassured him to have her holding on. He saw Wayne off to the side, poised and ready to back Charley up. He sensed Jarod was nearby as well.

"What kind of person rejects a father?" The old man's voice rang with the judgment that should fall on a child who violated the commandment to honor one's father and mother.

"You're *not* her father," Charley said calmly. "If you're Frank Bristow, you're not her father, and you're not my grandfather. You're a mean, pathetic old man who once posed as a preacher and made life a living hell for my grandmother and mother. I'm glad I was able to grow up without you around, and I wish my mother had, too."

"You are a blasphemous fool!" Frank bellowed, his eyes shining with anger. All he lacked was a pulpit to pound on. If Charley rolled his eyes like he wanted to, he would sprain all the muscles in his eye sockets.

Frank took several steps toward Charley, fists at his sides, but Charley stood his ground. "Keep coming, Mister, and I'll flatten you."

Larry Bob stepped between the men. "All right, we don't need to have an altercation here. It's a festival, not fight night. You guys tone it down. Miz Erwin? Do you want to file a complaint against this man? We can start the process to get a restraining order."

April was gazing at Charley as if seeing him again after a long absence.

"Miz Erwin? I can give Mr. Bristow official warning to stay

away from you."

Finally, April moved her eyes to the sheriff. "I'm sorry, Sheriff. I was shocked to see that jackass after so many years."

Frank turned his head sharply to glare at her. "Now, Missy, I wouldn't use that kind of language if I was you."

April pounded her fist on the steering wheel. *"Shut up, Frank."* Her eruption brought a stillness to the crowd.

After the moment soaked in, she said, "Just a minute, everybody. I need to get out of this van." She ran her seat back far enough to release her seat belt. Opening the door, she swiveled her legs out and plopped her swollen, sandaled feet onto the pavement. She smoothed her muumuu and faced Frank, who, though still silenced, was beginning to smirk with judgment as his eyes took in the expanse of her.

April didn't give him a chance to remark. "Now I have someone to stick up for me. I have Charley. I have the law on my side. And I have some new dope on you, asshole."

Frank gaped at her, but he stood straighter to dominate her.

"You can't intimidate me," April said evenly. "I owe you nothing. Nothing! You are a cockroach of the worst kind. First you pose as a man of God. Then you pose as my father. And now you pose as someone I owe something to. I can't believe the gall of you, coming back after all these years to see if I have anything of any worth that you can take from me. I do have something. I have my son, my Charley, and you can't get a thing from him. Not a nod, not a howdy-do, and certainly not a single penny. We owe you nothing. I know you're not my father. My father was a decent man, and you kept him from me."

April pointed to Lou, standing beside Wayne. "See her? She's my sister! She found me, and she's back in my life. And I have two brothers, too."

"People can claim to be anyone," Frank argued, seeming far

less sure of himself.

"Sure they can. Just like you claimed to be my father. And where is my mother? I know you killed her. Where is she? Where is my mother, Frank?" April kept her voice steady and firm. The small crowd around them clung to the scene.

Frank shot a haunted look at the faces that pressed in. But he was not completely daunted. "You're making a public spectacle of yourself," he hissed, making a show of pity and compassion for this miserably ungrateful daughter. "You should be ashamed. It's you who should be answering questions about how you could stoop so low as to accuse me. . . ."

"Miz Erwin, do you want to report a missing person?" Larry Bob asked, breaking into Frank's speech with an all-business tone, dismissing him.

"Yes, I do. Her name was Ann Bristow, and she has been missing from my life for twenty-six years. And this man found a way to make her a captive for many years before she went missing. He has an assault and battery record in Briargrove. Or attempted murder."

"That's ancient history. Statute of limitations applies," Frank shot back.

"So you admit to assault and battery?" Larry Bob cupped his hand over his night stick.

"No, I admit nothing, you idiot!" Frank couldn't control his rage. His face was splotching red, and a low, involuntary growling came from his throat, like that of a caged badger.

Charley figured that Frank had planned to renew his relationship with April, possibly find a place to land for a while. The con man probably didn't believe his luck when he drove into town and spotted her sitting right on the street in her van. It would have been simple to spy on April over the years. She had lived in the same trailer park ever since her high school graduation. He must have expected her to be as easy to push around as when she was a helpless child. Obviously, Charley had diverted Frank from his plans. He hadn't counted on Charley, or the sheriff.

Larry Bob proceeded calmly, as if Frank hadn't called him an idiot. "Now, Miz Erwin has pointed out that her mother has been missing for twenty-six years and that you are the last person seen with her in these parts. Unless you can account for the whereabouts of Miz Erwin's mother, you've got a problem."

Frank said, "I want a lawyer. I'll be happy to discuss whatever you have to ask, as long as I have a lawyer. I will not be railroaded."

"You're not under arrest, sir, but I think at this point we should take you in to answer a few questions for the record. I might overlook the public disturbance you've created. Will you come willingly, or do we need cuffs?"

Frank Bristow put on a bold face. "Lead on, sheriff."

"Okay, folks, let's get back to the party. Nothing more to see here!" Larry Bob waved away the crowd and walked Frank down the sidewalk to the sheriff's office in the next block.

April put her arms around Charley's waist and leaned her head on his chest. He returned the hug for the first time in . . . twenty years?

Darla dabbed a tear from her eye as April reached a hand toward her.

Letting go of Charley, April said, "I'm so sorry we had to meet like this."

Darla took her hand and patted it. "Well, I don't think you need to apologize. That Bristow fellow started it all."

"Yes, he did, a long time ago, the bastard. I can't believe that the first time I try to take part in anything, even remotely, along comes Frank to put a stain on it."

Charley looked up the street as Frank and Larry Bob disappeared into the sheriff's office. "Me, too, Mom. I've avoided these railroad anniversary celebrations and parades all my life. We both show up, and then so does Frank. Go figure."

Darla alerted to this last remark of Charley's. "What? You mean you don't like these festivals? Why didn't you tell me?"

"I wanted to be with you, darlin'. Even if it meant puttin' up with a festival. And I was having a pretty good time until Frank crashed the party. I was glad, though, that Lou made Wayne come, too. And Wayne probably feels like it was worth it since he got to dunk Larry Bob."

"And I got to meet your mother." April smiled shyly and put her fingers to her lips.

Even with all the drama, this day's unexpected upward turns landed it in the plus column. And now there was a chance that April could find out what happened to her mother. It was as if a great, dark, secret monster was chased into the sun to die of light exposure.

Charley and Darla promised April a visit soon.

"I'll be cleaning up and fumigating as fast as I can," April said. Charley winced at her frankness. Too much info. "What I mean is, I decided to quit smoking. I'm wearing a nicotine patch for now, and I'm going to gradually withdraw from that. Now that I've got a half-sister back in town, I want to make myself more presentable. And if Charley's going to introduce me to his girl-friend for a change, then I need to turn over a new leaf."

They waved goodbye as April pulled away from the curb and pointed her van toward the trailer park.

Darla held Charley's hand as they walked slowly back to her parents' house.

Charley said, "I'm glad Mom wants to get cleaned up in case you visit. She never wanted to clean herself up for me."

"I'm sorry, Charley. The timing sucks, but she probably felt pretty bad about herself all these years. It wasn't your fault."

Charley gave her a wistful smile. He put his arm around her shoulders and pulled her into a closer walk. "Yeah, if I was her, I'd feel bad, thinking that nutball weasel was my dad. Better to have no dad."

"I can't imagine, really I can't," Darla said. "I'm happy for both you and your mother that you've found your real family. It must help to know they're out there."

"Yeah. But I'm not getting my hopes up about Mom turning over a new leaf, as she calls it. I've seen her try to quit smoking before, and she replaced the cigarettes with extra beer and gin. Then she's told me she needs to start smoking again to protect her liver." Charley's bitter laugh died on the quiet street. He kicked a pebble off the sidewalk.

Darla reached around his waist.

Charley felt his equilibrium returning. "I'm beyond arguing or trying to make sense of what she does. Every week, I spend a little time visiting with her and running her errands to keep my conscience from grabbing me."

Now, the noon sun was tilting off to the west, and cocktail hour neared. Charley knew that April would face a far bigger challenge if she decided to give up the booze, too. He hoped that if she did, she didn't find a worse crutch. He caught himself imagining the worst and hoping for the best simultaneously. He thought it was time to concentrate on his own life.

Back at Darla's parents' house, they fell on the couch. Janet brought them iced tea and sat down to listen to what happened.

After all the details were told and processed with sympathetic sounds from her mother, Darla checked her watch. "It's lunchtime. I have an idea. Let's pack a picnic and go out to the windmill."

Charley composed his face, not wanting Janet to see how the

idea of Darla and a trip to the windmill charged him up. "Yeah, okay," he said, managing to sound interested, but not overly enthusiastic. Only two late Saturday appointments were in his book, and they could be canceled if necessary.

Darla made sandwiches and packed them up with a thermos of iced tea, a jar of pickled okra, and a bag of tortilla chips. Charley and Janet sipped their tea. The adrenaline charge from the confrontation with Frank was subsiding. Ed came in from the back yard, finished with planting his rosemary along the fence.

Innocently enough, he asked, "How was the festival?"

Janet let Charley decide how to answer.

"It was interesting," he said, and Ed let it go at that.

16
An Interrupted Picnic

THEY FOUND A GOOD SPOT near a large, old, leafed-out mesquite. The lacy leaves announced that no late freezes were expected, at least not by the mesquites, the last Texas tree to bud after a winter sleep. They lazed in their camp chairs borrowed from Ed's storage building. "Keep them in your trunk as long as you like, Charley," Ed had said. "We'll be traveling a lot this spring and summer and won't need them for our destinations." Travel Agent Ken.

The windmill creaked and clanged with the breeze. An occasional fly invaded their space, but they enjoyed this brief time of mild weather—not too hot, not too windy, and not too many insects.

Charley mentally categorized the day's disasters. He considered it a disaster to have to go to a festival and schmooze around on a Saturday morning, but that turned out fine. He thought running across April was a calamity, but that went surprisingly well. The thought of the scene with Frank brought a flush to his face, and he felt the dangerous mix of shame and anger that surged into his fists. Frank was fortunate that Larry Bob had walked him to the sheriff's office, or Charley would have punched the old windbag and been charged with assault on a senior citizen. He could be spending the rest of the day in the Sandstone County jail. He sighed with the relief and reached for Darla's hand.

"So who is this Frank Bristow?" she asked.

It was time for Chapter Two of his long-lost family story and why it was long lost.

"My mother grew up thinking he was her father. I've read about religious abuse and how it's mixed in with other kinds. And he was an expert abuser. Super-crazy. Spoke in tongues and started churches in backwater towns all around the Southwest and into East Texas, from what I understand. Kind of hypnotic to some people. When he ran out of credibility in one spot, he moved on."

"I wonder why April's mother stayed with him." Darla looked puzzled.

"Her mother had to be in a mess of some kind to let him get a foot in the door in the first place. I think, though, that he's gotten worse over the years. Surely he hasn't always been that creepy. Once he started acting crazier, she probably figured he'd kill her and April if she tried to leave." Charley stopped a moment and considered his own messes. They paled in comparison to the trap Ann and April had fallen into in Frank's clutches. For a moment, he was almost grateful for Vicki and Joyce.

Charley told Darla more of his mother's story and how Frank's arrest in Briargrove landed April in the girls' home.

"Looks like a good chance to escape Frank's abuse," Darla observed.

"Frank got out on bail and he and Ann split. Mom says she knows he killed Ann or she would have heard from her."

Darla shook her head in sympathy, or maybe disbelief.

"I guess you could say he's ruined a few lives," Charley concluded.

Darla sighed. She came to Charley's chair and sat on his lap and put her arms around him. The day was beginning to take an interesting turn.

It was an unfamiliar comfort, Charley realized, to have her

hold him. Time to cancel some afternoon appointments.

Charley's cell chirped. It was April. Now what?

"Hello, Mom." He heard ragged breathing. "Mom?"

Finally April's voice came through. "Charley, I need help." She was gasping.

He jumped from his chair, almost dumping Darla on the ground.

"What's the matter?" Darla asked, but before Charley could say more, April's voice came across the phone again, her words clear and unmistakable.

"I shot Frank," she said. "He's dead."

Bloody hell.

* * *

Charley stood on the sidewalk beside the emergency room entrance. After he had verified that a 911 call had been made—he didn't know whether by April or a neighbor—he and Darla threw the remains of their picnic and the camp chairs into the trunk and sprayed dust and gravel as they drove away. He called Wayne to give him a heads-up that he was dropping Darla at his house. Wayne was good at listening and not talking, and Charley was grateful for that, telling him that Darla would explain. Lou was there, and the three of them would wait to hear from Charley.

Once on the main highway, Charley had called Larry Bob, who said, "Go to the ER. Your mom will need to be checked for injuries, and we can keep her in custody there. Don't come here to her house and block the ambulances. There'll be enough gawkers." Charley had obeyed the common sense of this request. He called Dorothy next and asked her to cancel his afternoon appointments. "It's a huge emergency—you'll hear all about it. I'm fine, my mother's fine, but there's a big deal going on." That was all he wanted to say. He ended the call.

Waiting outside the ER was a challenge. He hated not knowing what had happened, whether his mother was hurt, or if she had indeed killed the slithery little man who had accosted her earlier in the day.

Finally, two ambulances made the turn off Main Street. They weren't using their lights or sirens. Larry Bob followed in his cruiser. No doubt a funeral procession. A lump thickened in Charley's throat, and he swallowed hard at the idea that April could be dead—she could have suffered a heart attack in all the excitement. Hope, though, fluttered within—please, God, let Frank's be the only dead body!

Charley went to the first ambulance as its rear doors opened. Two EMTs hopped out and began working the gurney out with a special lift. Thank God for hydraulics, he thought, after he saw his mother blinking in the sunlight.

"Hey, Mom, you okay?"

"She'll be all right," an EMT said. "She's pretty dazed and shaken, a little shocky, but she doesn't seem to have any injuries."

"Oh, Charley, I killed Frank," April groaned.

"Don't say anything yet." This instruction came from Wallace Derby, local criminal lawyer and ambulance chaser. Wallace had driven up behind Larry Bob and was now leaning past Charley to speak.

"Hello, Mr. Derby," Charley nodded. "Is she in big trouble?"

"Don't know yet, but I'll be with her when she talks to the sheriff."

"I will, too."

Derby shot Charley a look.. "You sure?"

"Never surer."

They followed April's entourage into the ER. Charley looked behind him as the glass doors slid shut. The other ambulance sat closed up. He heard the EMTs reporting at the intake desk—a DOA, they said. Something about the coroner's office. Frank was dead, no doubt about it. Charley would be comforted, knowing that this monster was no longer out there at large in the world. If he felt that way, he could only imagine what a burden would be lifted for April. If only she had not been required to take him out herself. He hoped his mother would not pay dearly for it.

Charley and Wallace waited outside the exam room while nurses checked vitals and changed April's blood-spattered clothes for an extra-large hospital gown. Charley stuck his head in the door when he knew she was safely covered and waiting for the doctor.

"You okay, Mom?"

"Yes. You can go home or wherever, Charley. I don't want to take up any more of your time."

Typical of Mom. Kill someone, arrive at the hospital in an ambulance in shock, and dismiss your son. Charley stepped in and grabbed her hand. "I'm not going off and leaving you here. You've got law enforcement and lawyers circling, and you need some family support. So that's me."

Doctor Fletcher tapped on the door before April could answer Charley. He swept in, all business. "You've had a big shock, my dear, from what I'm hearing. We need to do some X-rays and blood work. Did you sustain any injuries that you know of?"

"No, he never touched me," she said.

"We'll need to give you a look-over, see how the ticker sounds. Then we'll do some X-rays and a head CT." He turned to Charley. "Out you go, Mister."

Charley was only too happy to join Wallace Derby in the lobby, where Charley found a *Smithsonian* to go through the eye motions of reading, even though nothing sank in with his mind full of the day's events. Derby sat across from him and jiggled first one knee, then the other. He looked at the clock, then his watch, scratched his head and stretched and then started the jiggling routine again.

Finally, to get away from Derby's constant motion, Charley stepped into the hall to see if his mother was back from X-ray. Just then, her gurney squeaked around the corner, with two orderlies steering and puffing. Sheesh, these guys needed to work out, Charley thought. You'd've thought the stretcher had no wheels.

April was looking more relaxed. They must have given her a tranquilizer. Or she could be relishing the moment, the beginning of all moments of her life with Frank definitely never coming back. Hard to know. Charley rejoined her in her exam room, ready to hear from her exactly what had happened, but Derby followed him.

"April, can you talk to me now?" Derby stepped half into the room, waiting like a vampire to be invited.

"Come on in, Wallace," April waved him in.

A speck of blood on her temple began to trouble Charley. He moistened a paper towel at the small sink and dabbed the blood away—Frank's, it looked like. He suppressed a shudder.

"Do you want me to defend you if you're charged with murder?" Derby didn't beat around the bush.

April's eyes widened. "*Murder*? You think I need a *lawyer*?"

"Oh, yes ma'am. You shot someone and he's dead. That can be construed as murder or manslaughter."

"But I had to or he would have killed me—eventually."

"That's good. You can tell the county attorney that, and you might not get charged at all. Or they might have to convene a grand jury to decide. But if you want to retain me and have attorney-client privilege, I'll need $1,000."

"Whoa! Hold on, Mr. Derby," Charley jumped in. "We don't know if we'll need you yet. The truth is on our side. We'll take our chances telling the whole story to Larry Bob, don't you think, Mom?"

April nodded. "If you want to be a stand-up guy and witness or be a kind of advocate, we could use your help, but I don't think we need to shell out at this point."

Derby withdrew to a stool in the corner as Larry Bob tapped on the door.

"I need to take a statement. You up to it, Miz Erwin?" The sheriff looked for a seat, but Derby was claiming squatters' rights. "You servin' as Miz Erwin's attorney?"

"No, but I could be. I'm here for now as an advocate." Derby sounded noble.

"All right, then." Larry Bob explained that he wanted to record a statement and pulled a small device from his front shirt pocket. He told April that she was not being arrested, only questioned, but that she should hear her rights since she might be charged.

"Okay, L.B." April was ready to talk. Charley noticed that her hands were shaking. Could it be that she needed her afternoon snort, or was it all the adrenaline still hanging around after a shooting? Or was it fear? All of the above? He should say something, so they could be prepared in case she started having d.t.'s or convulsions. His usual numbness was settling in, and he was glad. It kept him calm but observant.

"Okay, Miz Erwin," Larry Bob was saying, "can you tell me what you did after leaving the downtown area today?"

"Call me April, please."

The sheriff nodded.

"I was real upset and shaky, and I drove home from the festival with my eye on the rear-view mirrors. I expected Frank to come right after me, as soon as he finished talking to you."

"Why is that?"

"Frank never let other people change his plans. He was like a pit bull. He would come after me to say or do whatever he came to Sulfur Gap for. He would want to even the score, too. We pretty much humiliated him when he tried to talk to me in town."

"Then what happened when you got home?"

"I rushed into my house. I made sure to lock both deadbolts. I checked the window locks, too. I was out of breath and had to rest. I could hear my own heartbeat, I was so scared."

"You feared for your life?"

"Yes!" April shot a sharp look at the sheriff, as if he hadn't been listening to a word she said. She was getting impatient.

A knock at the door broke everyone's concentration. A nurse traipsed in with a blood pressure cuff. "Sorry," she said, seeing Charley's irritated look. "We're supposed to monitor her blood pressure."

As soon as the nurse made some notes on a clipboard and left, April said, "Where were we? Oh, yes. I sat down to catch my breath. I had a 9mm pistol in the end table drawer. I took it out and put in the clip. Before I clicked the clip in place, I held my finger over the trigger and pulled, to remember how it felt when I practiced."

Charley started to worry about the gun being registered. "I've been wondering when you got that gun, Mom."

April frowned slightly, remembering. "As long as you lived at home, I didn't feel like I needed a gun. When you were small, I always managed to keep a man close enough so I didn't feel so afraid. I lived in terror after Frank and my mother disappeared. I figured Frank had killed her. The idea—not knowing—has haunted me all these years."

Charley scooted his stool closer to April's gurney and took her hand. "I'm sorry, Mom. I never knew."

"I didn't know how to tell you," she said.

"April, why didn't you get the law involved sooner?" Wallace asked from his corner.

"After Charley was born, I tried. I'd married Eldon, and I felt more secure. I visited Sheriff Sparks—your dad, L.B. I was too ashamed to tell him how bad it was—the way I grew up. I was afraid to say too much. If Frank got picked up for evading the assault charges, he would come for revenge."

"You were stuck on the horns of a dilemma," Derby said.

"Yeah," she said.

"So you've been afraid of Frank Bristow all your life?" Larry Bob asked.

"Yes!" April's impatience surfaced again. The sheriff stopped the recorder.

"I'm sorry to ask such obvious questions, April," Larry Bob explained. "I want to be crystal clear on the threat you were feeling today." He clicked the recorder back on.

"Okay," April said. "I'll try to explain how evil Frank was. He was capable of catching a sack of rattlesnakes and dumping them through a window at night. His comment over the dead bodies would be something crazy like, 'He who is righteous need not fear the serpent.' And in Frank's twisted mind, he would feel that he was fulfilling the role of a prophet when he spoke those words. He was capable of finagling his way into the good graces of the school secretary so she would let him take Charley out of class. No telling what could happen from that point. He might stalk me at work and create scenes like the one at the railroad celebration today. He could get Eldon fired with a convincing lie to someone he worked for."

Quite a speech. Charley realized that protecting him from Frank had always been April's priority. She had told the sheriff only that she thought her mother could have run into some foul play. She asked him to investigate. The sheriff made some calls, but nothing turned up.

April was saying, "I was tormented by the idea that if I'd been braver and told the sheriff what kind of man Frank was, I could have saved my mother." A sharp breath of regret shuddered through her. "It felt like a miracle when Lou told me Frank wasn't my father. I started feeling this tiny little seed of hope that life could get better, a little at a time.

"Deep down, I knew my mother was dead. I dreamed about her—I could see her face when I was asleep, but it wasn't a face that existed in this world." April shook her head. "It's hard to explain. But I didn't see the face if I drank. I didn't have to think about my mother."

"And so this afternoon, you had your gun ready?" Larry Bob prompted.

"Yes. It was pure luck that I had time to get ready. I was determined that Frank Bristow would not set a foot in my home."

She explained how she sat with the loaded pistol in her lap, watching the door. A passing car on the lane that led to the back of the trailer park lot bounced spots of light from reflected chrome onto her ceiling. She tensed, but when the car moved by, she relaxed. Only a neighbor. Her mouth began to water at the thought of a strong gin and tonic, but she prayed aloud, "Not now, not now. Please, not now."

After hours in which the light penetrating the thin curtains dimmed as the sun angled behind the trailer, she finally heard the slow approach of a car. The gravel pinged against the undercarriage.

He was coming.

Here, April stopped for a drink of water. She cleared her throat and continued. "I figured he would want to explain why he and Ann had stayed away. He would have a story cooked up about how Ann had died, probably in his arms and in his tender loving care, according to him, leaving out that he gave her one too many concussions."

"You knew it was his car?" Larry Bob asked.

"Yes. He pulled into the driveway behind my van. I heard the door slam and the clomp of his boot heels, first on the sidewalk and then on the steps leading to my door. He stopped on the porch. I could see his silhouette through the curtains on the small window in the door."

April continued on her own, telling her story, while the men listened.

Frank had knocked.

"Go away, Frank," she said.

"Now April, honey, you know you should call me Daddy," he answered.

"Go away," she said, louder.

"April, open this door." He was turning the knob now, pushing against the deadbolts. She knew this old man at least couldn't break the door down. But still she wasn't safe.

"Go away," she said again, her voice steadier.

"April, I insist that you hear me out. You are being unfair. I raised you. I cared for you when you and your mama needed a man around."

"Go away."

"April, I can't let you get away with this. You can't decide this on your own."

Glass shattered. A monkey wrench pulled a bit of the curtain through as it was withdrawn. An arm reached through. A gnarled hand began searching the door panel for the locks.

"Frank, I have a gun, and I *will* shoot you if you break into my house."

The searching hand stopped a moment.

"You're bluffing, April. You're not going to shoot me, and

you know it."

The hand found both dead bolts, turning first one, then the other, with a finesse that surprised April even in her shock. The arm drew back through the window.

Frank turned the doorknob and pushed the door open. He stood framed by the warm afternoon light, the monkey wrench hanging at his side. He put first one boot and then the other over her doorstep, stopping to let his eyes adjust to the relative darkness of the trailer. His bold, self-assured look meant he thought he would be able to have complete control of the situation. He began moving toward her.

Hesitation vanished, and full resolve took its place.

She held the pistol in both hands, arms straight, and took aim, as practiced. She squeezed the trigger and jumped at the slight recoil and pop. Frank stopped. The wrench clunked to the floor. She still aimed at him, unable to tell if she had hit the target. Now that she had stepped into the job of killing Frank, she wanted to see it finished. His face was a mask of rage. He gripped his chest and took another step as if to lunge at her, but he was falling. She fired again. Her second bullet had entered his forehead as he went down.

April closed her eyes as she finished the story. The sheriff turned off his recorder and said, "Thanks, Miz Erwin. I'm assuming the doc will want to keep you tonight. The investigation will be finished by tomorrow, and then you can get back in your home. Two deputies are working it. I'll include in the report that Bristow fled from assault and battery charges in 1982 and that he's under suspicion in the disappearance of his wife, Ann. I'm also opening an investigation on that."

The sheriff paused. He looked down at the floor. "I'm real sorry that fella came straight after you, but I didn't have anything to hold him on. Kept him as long as I could. I was going to drive by and check on you, but the call came in before I got to my car. He knew exactly where you lived, didn't have to take time to look at addresses."

Charley shuddered outright this time.

Derby spoke up. "If he killed her mother, there's no way a jury would convict April of anything. Besides, she was acting in self-defense against a home invasion."

Sparks nodded agreement. "As a matter of fact, I've already put out a query to law enforcement in five states to see if there's a cold case Jane Doe, a woman in her mid-thirties, dating back to 1982 to 1985."

April thought a moment. "It'd be closer to 1982. Frank probably didn't let her live long after they left Briargrove," she said with conviction. "The only thing I'm sorry about is that I killed him before we found out anything helpful."

"Between all of us?" Larry Bob looked around. Derby and Charley nodded.

"What, Sheriff?" April asked.

"If it was up to me, I'd give you a medal and dedicate the next railroad celebration and parade to you. You're my hero, Miz Erwin." He took off his hat and held it to his heart.

April waved him away with a hand but began to cry.

Charley dove for more paper towels, and Derby and the sheriff backed out with promises to be in touch.

* * *

The doctor read April the riot act. She must stop smoking and stop drinking if she wanted to live another year. Her liver counts were so bad, he was amazed she hadn't developed a full-blown case of cirrhosis. She would need a special diet to heal her liver. Her oxygen level was low, but there miraculously was no sign of emphysema. "You must come from strong stock," he said. "It's a blessing and a curse. Genetics like yours keep you alive longer while you're trying to kill yourself."

"I do come from strong stock," April said. Otherwise, she gave him an indifferent look, like a cat marveling at the idiocy of human beings.

Charley was allowed to carefully enter her home to get what she needed for a night in the hospital. He tiptoed past the puddle of blood on the living room floor, grabbed a plastic grocery bag from the stack on the kitchen countertop, and jerked open her underwear drawer to find what he needed. "Bloomers and a double parachute," he thought to himself, using only his thumb and forefinger to lift the unmentionables. He found a voluminous nightgown in the drawer below the bra and panty stash. A fresh muumuu hung in her small closet. He ducked into the bathroom and quickly spotted her toothbrush and hairbrush and toothpaste. He rounded up a pair of house slippers and beat a hasty retreat, grabbing her purse from the counter that separated the living room and kitchen. Taking the gin bottle to her went against his grain, but the heft of her purse assured him that a full emergency flask lay in its depths.

Charley helped April get settled in her hospital room. He told the charge nurse to put up a "No Visitors" sign and to hold all calls. Lou would be coming to check on her sister, and she was allowed, but if Don Runion wanted to get the scoop for the local news, he'd have to wait.

Comfortably ensconced in her hospital bed, TV remote in hand and her supper tray in front of her, April waved Charley out the door. "You go see Darla and Wayne and Lou. Tell them I'm fine. Too bad you can't tell 'em the sheriff wants to pin a medal on me."

"Lou's on her way to see you, so I'll check with you tomorrow." He let the door to April's room ease shut behind him, and he stood a while in the hallway, taking deep breaths and staring at the polished floor. With a new perspective, he thought about the day's catastrophes and sighed with relief that he and April were alive.

* * *

Charley's people had moved on to Hopper's for the evening. They all wanted each other's company as they shared their mutual concern for Charley. Dorothy, Charlene, Loretta, Jarod, and Sue had joined Wayne and Darla. He hugged the women and shook hands with Wayne and Jarod. As he settled into a chair, he heard Wylie's voice on the sound system. "Folks," he was saying, "we're gonna be about fifteen minutes late getting started. Lou's had a family matter to tend to, but relax and have a good time. We'll be playin' for you in a few."

When Lou came through the door, she hurried to hug Charley. "How ya doing, kiddo? Hasn't this been a helluva day?"

She handed Wayne her purse to hold under the table for her. Charley thought how much they already behaved like a married couple. She squeezed Wayne's hand, waved around the table at the gathering of friends, and headed for the bandstand. A smattering of applause erupted when people saw that Lou was back behind the drums.

Darla flagged a waitress and got him a beer.

Taking a sip, Charley said, "Thank you, and thank you for being such a good sport with all this. It sure wasn't my idea for how to spend our first day back together."

"You sound like you're apologizing. Don't. I feel like we're in the middle of some pretty big changes, and I'm along for the ride. We'll have plenty of time to celebrate."

People walked by the table to say, "Charley, you okay? Your mom all right?" and Charley nodded with responses of "We'll be fine. Things are gonna work out okay. Thank you. I appreciate it." And he meant it. He kept his phone set to maximum vibrate in his hip pocket, in case his mother called, but she didn't seem to need him tonight.

He danced with Darla five straight songs in a row, and then invited Dorothy, Charlene, Loretta, and Sue to dance in turn. During her break, he danced with Lou when "True Love Ways" echoed over the sound system. They laughed and belted out the lyrics together as they swayed around the floor. Wylie should put this in the Crew's repertoire, they said.

When they returned to their table, Wayne mock-grumbled, "Lou, you need to get a day job."

"I *have* a day job, ya numbie," she said, and ruffled his thinning hair.

"Well, my day has done me in. I'm gonna have to get some . . . sleep?" Charley grinned at Darla.

"If you want a notice on the bulletin board, you won't get far," Darla warned, smiling sweetly.

"Let me take you home, then," Charley demurred.

As they walked to his car in the yellow light of the parking lot, he said, still hoping, "Where to?" It seemed like a long time since the windmill, and only her busyness and his family business kept him from focusing on getting her in bed.

"Oh, you can take me on to my house," she said, offhandedly.

Charley stuffed his disappointment. For tonight, he ached to have Darla to hold on to. But he knew he could survive. The more frequently he hung on by himself despite the urge to envelop Darla, the more convinced he was that he possessed a substance of his own that countered his neediness.

When they pulled up at the Bartas' house, the garage was closed—unusual for them. All the lights were out but the front porch light. Were they gone? Hope fluttered.

"Where's Mrs. Barta and Ed? I mean Janet and Ed?" Charley asked, as he turned off the ignition.

Darla assumed her best casual expression. "They decided to drive down to Fredericksburg and shop and spend the night. They won't be back until around noon tomorrow. That means total privacy," she said, sliding her hands down his chest and around his waist.

Dear God, please let her not be teasing me, he thought.

"So?"

"So come in, Mister Bristow."

"You'll have to start calling me Mr. Trainer soon," he countered. "I've decided to change my name."

"I approve totally," she said. "Something wonderful will come of all this, I know, and I never claim to be able to tell the future, but I feel good about how it's lining up."

"Well, it's about time, don't you think? I mean, the law of averages and all."

He kissed her, and she reached across him and opened his door.

"Get out," she said. "Get out of this car and up on that porch and into my room, Mr. Trainer."

And so he did.

17
All in a Name

THE SUN ROSE OVER Sulfur Gap a bit earlier than the day before, and early risers noticed the increments in daylight brought by the advancing spring. Gentle rays filtered through the mini-blinds in Darla's room as Charley woke up. She was still sleeping, her back snuggled into his side. He turned to spoon with her, hoping not to wake her up.

If only this moment could stay a while, he thought, and then tried to remember the country-western song with that same idea. He'd have to ask Lou. He hoped Lou and Wayne were enjoying a similar embrace, and he even let his mind tiptoe around thoughts about how his mother had passed the night. He worried about her trembling hands, pushing the possible scenarios into his brain's denial vault. This was no time to rob the moment with worry.

He looked around the room. It was all Darla. He was relieved that vestiges of her girlhood were scarce. It would feel weird to wake up in a room with a hot pink bedspread and a bulletin board tacked over with mementos like pom-poms and CD covers and concert tickets. She did still have her white wicker headboard that must have been around since she was in junior high, and her antique-white dresser, but the matching bureau was moved off-center on the wall to make room for a computer desk and shelves containing massive books with intimidating titles. The room was orderly, much like Darla. Uncomplicated, straightforward. A comfortable place to be. He wondered if the smarter a person is, the more simple their approach to life. If that was true, he would rank in the moron category.

Darla stretched and wiggled her hips against him.

She yawned and turned to face him. "You still here?" She laughed and snuggled into his chest. "So what do you want to do today?"

Glory hallelujah. But wait. What do I want to do today?

"Be with you," he managed. He was so happy, he thought he would burst.

"Let's go to the Navaho for breakfast, and if there's time, run over to church in Briargrove."

"Church?" He accidentally sang soprano on the word. "Which church?"

"The Methodist. I need to go scope out a service before next Sunday."

"Why?"

"I'm supposed to sing in their choir—help out with the special music—and then do a solo."

"Why?"

"My mother is friends with the choir director there. She's a music teacher that worked with her for a while. You wouldn't know her. She knows about my singing experience, and she wants to beef up the choir."

"Oh."

Darla rose up on her elbow. "What's the matter? Are you against going to church?"

"No. I don't have a lot of experience with it. Of course my mother won't go to church. Her past with preacher-types isn't too good, you know."

"If you don't want to go, that's okay. I can see you later."

"I don't have any church clothes with me."

"It's real informal."

"I'd have to wear the same clothes I wore yesterday."

"That's okay. You can borrow a shirt from Ed."

Charley drew the line at borrowing Ed's shirt. It wouldn't be cut long enough anyway. "No, I can shower here and run by my place after breakfast to change."

"Still, you sure are reluctant. I hope it's not another deal like the festival, which you hated the idea of but went anyway. You know, you can be blunt."

"No. It's not that."

"What, then?"

"I guess this is as good a time as any to tell you what I found out about *my* father."

Charley told Darla about his mother's marriage to Eldon Erwin, about knowing that Eldon wasn't his real dad, although not a bad one as stepdads go. Charley knew he didn't have much to compare Eldon to, but he was a far better man than the boyfriends who came along for a while after Eldon died.

"The good thing about Lou coming and finding Mom is that Mom started talking . . . well, it did take her three years. But the other night, I asked her who my dad was, and she finally answered me. I always hoped *she* knew. It was kind of scary. I was afraid she was going to tell me it was Frank Bristow. He was such a creep. Luckily, at least, Frank was a lot of things but not a pedophile."

"Thank God." Darla's earnest face on the pillow next to his reassured him, so he went on.

"So she told me she dated a boy in high school in Briargrove, while she was in the girls' home there. He broke up with her, but she was pregnant. The guy who dumped her went off to college and only came back a couple years ago to preach at the Methodist Church."

"No shit?!!!!" Darla yelled. She grabbed his shoulders. "Really?!!!!" Now her face levitated over him, eyes wide. Then she collapsed back on the bed and, with sudden modesty, pulled the sheet over her body.

"What's the big deal?"

"You need to be sitting up for this." So they sat cross-legged on the bed, naked except for the shared sheet.

"Okay, shoot," he said, and cringed at his choice of words.

"Well, you know my stepdad's a psychologist?"

"Yeah."

"That Methodist preacher refers clients to him sometimes. They have a professional relationship, go out for coffee. I've heard Ed talk about him. . . . What's his name? Woodford? Wood something."

Now here was something Charley didn't know yet. His actual name.

Darla's eyes focused. "His first name sounds sort of Swedish. . . . Gunnar! That's his name. Gunnar Woodruff!" Darla pronounced the name, satisfied with her ability at recall. Then, she frowned a little. "Does your mother know for certain?"

"She didn't at first," Charley admitted. "After I got older, she could see I looked like the guy that broke her heart."

"Oh, this is so interesting!" Darla was wound up at the idea of a new research project. She looked like she was thinking about DNA comparisons, genetic data. Her eyes glazed over for a moment. Then she refocused on Charley. "Aren't you anxious to see him?"

"As a matter of fact, I've been thinking I should pay Briargrove First Methodist a visit. Sit in a back pew and look at my father."

"But are you ready for that?"

Charley considered. This was definitely the day the Lord had made, and he was rejoicing, like that Bible verse said, but no, he didn't think today was the day to take a look at Gunnar Woodruff. While arriving at this conclusion, Darla had let her share of the sheet slide down.

"Let me think about it during breakfast. But first . . . ." He scooped her up and kissed her good morning properly — with all the trimmings.

He still hadn't told her about driving his grandmother's Buick, but that could wait.

* * *

Knowing he didn't want to sit anonymously in a back pew and spy on Gunnar Woodruff, Charley also acknowledged he couldn't stuff another "big reveal" into his psyche at the moment. Enough drama surged around his life without stalking the reverend. Forced introductions were coming along all by themselves, leaving him feeling dazed, as if the paparazzi were following him, flashing cameras in his eyes. Darla could do her reconnaissance mission to the Briargrove Methodist Church while he took care of weekend errands and checked on his mother.

April was ready to go home when Charley stopped at the hospital, but she said the sheriff had already sent a deputy to take her home.

He made his weekly trip to the grocery store and Laundromat. At home, he put away his underwear and socks in the drawer, towels and sheets in the linen cabinet. He hung his clean shirts, T-shirts, and jeans in their places on the closet rod, and he put his milk, eggs, cold cuts, and tomatoes in the fridge, coffee in the canister next to the coffee maker. His fresh jar of peanut butter and box of crackers went into the cabinet in the usual spot. It was all a pattern, but he felt like he was doing everything for the first time.

He felt the pulse of life in his hand as it held a dust cloth. The sharp, clean smell of the freshly rinsed mop drifted up as he hung it over the balcony rail to dry. The satisfaction of an orderly life visited him like a long-lost friend.

It was time to check on Mom.

April looked rested when she answered the door. Her hands were still trembling; otherwise, she looked better than usual. A flush crept across her cheeks, but it gave her some color.

A neat plywood insert covered the window Frank had broken. There was no crime scene tape, no sign of blood, no hint of a killing. Frank's car had been towed away. Only a faint smell of bleach remained.

"The sheriff's deputies started my housecleaning for me," April said. "I've got a few years of tar buildup to wipe off the walls."

"Do you think Larry Bob will find out what happened to your mother?" Charley asked, feeling like a spy as he appraised April's housekeeping.

"I hope he turns something up," she said. "He said I shouldn't expect to hear anything for at least a week."

Charley looked around the trailer house. It did smell better. Several empty liquor bottles gleamed on the counter beside the sink.

Following his line of vision, April said, "I'm *really* cleaning up."

Charley nodded, no idea what to say. Way to go Mom? How can I help? Best wishes? Such spoken sentiments felt insincere, so he didn't even launch them, knowing how short of the mark they would come. Instead, he hugged her. The second time in two days, and the third time in almost twenty years.

18
Truth in Gossip and DNA

THE TOWN OF SULFUR GAP was behind April Bristow. There was some hesitation at first. The idea of shooting your own father gave a few people pause. But the word was getting around that Lou was April's sister, related through their father. Frank was a poseur, as April had announced in front of God, the sheriff, and everybody within earshot at the railroad celebration. Charley was known to be the best source for more information, so even more clients than usual called for appointments.

Sondra Chilton, who usually got her hair done at an upscale salon in Dallas, called to wheedle an appointment, her voice full of the privilege she held in Sulfur Gap society and the assurance that Charley would be eager to please her.

"I can't get you in until Saturday, ma'am," Charley said.

"Surely someone won't show up, Charley," she said, sticky sweet.

"I don't have many no-shows, Mrs. Chilton, but I can pencil you in and call you if someone cancels. Would you be able to come with, say, thirty minutes' notice?"

He could hear her balking at the idea.

After a hesitation, she said, "Write me in for that Saturday afternoon appointment, and then call me the first minute you get a whiff of an open space in your schedule, even Saturday morning. I've got company coming for the weekend, but I'll have to leave them on their own while I run to get my hair trimmed."

Charley didn't bother to tell her that there were two other people of lesser social standing on his waiting list before her and that he would be calling them first.

He called to Janet Barta, who was waiting on the bench at the front of the salon.

As she settled into his chair, he said, "I haven't cut your hair before, have I?" He thought he would remember cutting his second-grade teacher's hair because he would have really focused on someone like that.

"No, Charley, I've been meaning to get myself worked into your schedule, but I usually go over to Briargrove." Janet had made her appointment three weeks ago and had graciously waited her turn. He appreciated that she wasn't here to see what she could pick up about the man April shot and all the juicy details to go with the story.

After a brief hair consultation, Charley decided he would give her a dry cut this first time to get a feel for her head and hair.

"How are you doing, Charley?" she asked, genuinely concerned.

"I'm pretty good." He was leaning behind her to get a look at her reflection in the mirror, his face reflected over her shoulder. Their eyes met, and he winked at her. She smiled. It was a moment. He knew that Darla had told her, with his permission, more about April's history with Frank Bristow. Charley gave her his blessing to tell her mother anything she wanted to, but Darla said, "No, Charley, there are some things that're your business to tell. I'll let you be the one to say that Gunnar Woodruff is your dad, if and when you want to announce that. I know Mom and Ed wouldn't ever gossip about it, but it's a matter of principle—it's your story."

Charley loved Darla more and more. He was accustomed to the veiled urgency some people showed when it came to telling what they knew, no matter who they knew the dirt on, as if letting others know a detail about someone's life—especially an episode that was lurid or provocative—raised their stock, made them seem knowledgeable, or at least interesting. He was used to gossip of all varieties. Something about sitting in the chair and talking at a reflection in the mirror loosened tongues, while some didn't need the encouragement but were probably born with a long-lived battery implanted in their jaw that kept it working and working on telling and embellishing stories about people they hardly knew.

Darla, on the other hand, didn't have the compulsion to talk or to discuss other people's business. He loved her, admired her, and lusted for her. He hoped she took him as seriously as he did her, but he didn't want to push. Of course she would go back to college to finish her degree, and of course she would have many dazzling opportunities that would accentuate the bleakness of settling in Sulfur Gap.

If she still loved him by then, he would be staggered with gratitude. If not, he didn't want to miss being with her now.

He still puzzled as to why she would care about him—a barber in a faded little West Texas town. One with a genealogy lost because of the intrusion of a budding sociopath. One with a father he didn't know because of the backwash from April's early life with the same sociopath. And a mother who had killed said sociopath and heaved a huge sigh of relief. Darla should be running away, and fast . . . and yet, she stuck around. The Bartas accepted him. He couldn't understand that. Surely they wanted something better for their daughter.

"How's your mom?" Janet asked, as Charley began sectioning off her hair and clipping the layers so that he could work each one into a nice blend.

"She's better than I've ever seen her. I don't get it. Most people would have to go to bed for a few days after having to shoot someone. You'd think that seeing Frank again after he disappeared so many years ago would put her in a coma or total shock, but it didn't."

"She's had—what?—two or three years to process that he wasn't her father."

"Yeah, that must have been a relief. And she was pretty enraged, too. That got her going. Sometimes being pissed off can motivate a person. I hope she finds out what happened to her mother. The news probably won't be good, but she'll know something."

Janet fell silent as Charley snipped, letting him concentrate on her emerging hairdo. They kept their voices low, and Charley knew how voices carried as the blow dryers' hum came and went. Charlene, in the booth closest to his, was much less talkative with her own clients these days, hoping to pick up some more information with her radar dish ears.

Dorothy watched as subtly as she could from her manicure table but didn't try to eavesdrop or ask a lot of questions. During a couple of lulls, the women of the salon gathered around him like mother doves over one chick. He told them, as if they hadn't heard it, about Frank's confrontation with April at the festival. About her accusation that Frank had probably killed her mother. They knew all this, but they wanted to hear Charley's version of it. He also added, to their great satisfaction and to alleviate their sincere concern, that Larry Bob had contacted law enforcement agencies in a wide swath to find out if any unidentified murder victims fitting Ann's description had been found. And that April's case would have to go before a grand jury, that it would be a reluctant presentation by the county attorney, to go on record that April did not need to be prosecuted.

"Well, I never!" Charlene was indignant. "I can't believe she has to be put through that."

"Oh, she won't have to be there."

"Still," Bethany said, "why must the grand jury even hear the case? Everyone knows there's no crime committed."

"The county attorney told Mom that when there's a dead body, it's best to have the grand jury decide not to prosecute, rather than for him to make the call on his own. It's a formality."

The weekly Sulfur Gap *Echo* finally hit mailboxes, and its readers eagerly unfolded the thin paper to see Don Runion's writeup. Runion did not disappoint. Across the front page, the banner headline declared, "Man Killed by Gunfire at Sunset Estates; Investigation Ongoing."

The story added no details that hadn't already made it around town. A shorter version appeared in the Abilene, San Angelo, Big Spring, and Lubbock papers. News about the railroad festival was relegated to a position below the fold of the *Echo*.

* * *

On Wednesday evening, Lou picked Charley up at his apartment. They were keeping to their plan to visit April together. Darla decided not to go. She didn't want to overwhelm April with too much company, and she pointed out to Charley that this was family.

The glass panel in April's door had already been replaced by a handy neighbor whose curiosity made him more helpful than usual. Inside, the fumigation project still persisted, despite Charley's doubts that she would stick with the plan. She had cleaned the windows and cleared off the countertops in the kitchen. On the bar that separated the living area and kitchen, a large scented candle wafted a piney odor. Everything was dusted and neat. April's hands still shook, and her breathing was more labored than usual, so Charley registered his concern and stored it beside the little bit of hope that he hadn't dared to have before. Concern and hope canceled each other out, and he was comfortable with that. His mind hovered in the familiar position of no expectations.

Her couch was usually piled with unfolded laundry in various stages of filth removal, but now it was cleared, so he and Lou sat down. April had news from the sheriff.

"Sheriff Sparks called today and told me there was a Jane Doe case in 1982 out in East Texas. It could be my mother."

"How are you feeling about all this?" Lou asked.

April looked at the spot where Frank's blood had formed a puddle such a short time ago. "I've been waiting twenty-six years to know what happened to my mother. Not knowing for sure has been awful, even though I could feel deep down that she was dead. I was keeping back the sorrow all this time. Now I can have the sorrow." She folded her hands across her stomach, pulling at her fingers occasionally. Charley knew that one curse of quitting smoking was figuring out what to do with your hands.

"Why didn't you ask someone to look for her sooner?" Charley asked.

"I was afraid of Frank. I started getting some courage after meeting Lou and my brothers. That gave me the courage to start trying to change. I knew I needed to talk to someone that could help me, so I've been seeing a psychologist over in Big Spring."

"You . . . what?" Charley nearly choked on his Adam's apple.

"I started going twice a week over two years ago and talking to Ed."

"Ed . . . Barta?"

"Yes, you know his practice is in Big Spring. It's not that far. He said I might need residential treatment when I decided to quit drinking. We'll see. He told me I'd make a lot more personal progress without the booze. Boy, was he right."

Charley thought of how Ed had sat with his hand on his chin when he told the Bartas about his family discoveries. And Charley was proud of *his* poker face. That guy was like a statue when he needed to be. A Ken doll.

"And Candy has been giving me rides to AA."

"Candy? My friend Candelario Vasquez? How long?"

"For the past few weeks. Counting here and Briargrove, there's a meeting nearly every night. So far it's helping me not take the first drink."

April seemed to enjoy Charley's jaw being on the floor. The more flabbergasted Charley was, the more she smiled.

Lou was laughing and clapping. "Oh, April, you're giving Chippie a shock!"

All this heavy revelation—and these women were ganging up on him and laughing.

"When Lou moved back to town, I started feeling more like getting out. Ed was encouraging me. He said I had PTSD and needed to learn not to isolate."

Remembering Joyce's PTSD diagnosis, Charley wondered if he had been attracted to women like his mother.

"So," April was saying, "I thought I'd be okay sitting in the van, just to watch the parade go by. When I saw Frank, I was scared to death, but then you came running up the sidewalk, and Darla was there behind you, and then Wayne and Lou and the sheriff. I realized I could say it out loud to everybody. Frank killed my mother, and I didn't care if he came after me. . . . So it was odd. I expected to be afraid of seeing people, but I was glad to see people, under the circumstances."

"What's the next step?" Lou asked.

"Sheriff Sparks says I need to come in and give them a DNA sample. If the samples from 1982 haven't degraded, they can see if the Jane Doe is my mother. They'll have to exhume the body if that doesn't work. If there's a match, they'll give us the details in the case file."

"You want me to take you down to the sheriff's office tomorrow?" Charley asked.

"No, Charley. You've got work, and I can drive, you know. I'll be in and out. I'm going to run some other errands, too."

Charley smiled at the idea of April "running" anything—errands, the two-foot dash, or the table in a pool game. It would be good exercise if she could push her own shopping cart around the United. Or, for starters, she could learn to drive one of those basket buggies. If that worked, he wouldn't be saddled with getting her groceries and picking up her prescriptions.

19
Face-to-Face Encounters

CHARLEY'S SATURDAY was finally over. He had cut more hair than any other week of his barbering career, except when he was getting his license and gave five-dollar haircuts for practice at school. He had even worked in Sondra Chilton early, and she registered her irritation at the inconvenience of having no more than thirty minutes' notice to rush to the salon by ten a.m. But she seemed happy enough with the results and gave Charley an extra tip. When she asked how his mother was doing, he told her the truth, as he had with other curious ones. He said April was better than ever. She was glad to find out about her family and had been hovering on making some serious life changes, and killing Frank was the exact boost she needed to get the ball rolling. This shortened version of events satisfied even Mrs. Chilton.

As she pressed his fee, fattened by the tidy tip, into his hand, she said, "I'm starting to realize I've wasted my time working in my haircuts around shopping trips to Dallas." Her glance swept ever so subtly from the top of Charley's head down to his crotch as she added, "And please. Call me Sondra."

Charley thought how much fun it would be to respond with "Please. Call me Mr. Bristow." But then, he wasn't sure how much longer he would be Mr. Bristow. He might go with Trainer, and he could even choose Woodruff for a last name. Hell, what if he married Darla and took her name? Convention be damned!

At the end of the day, when Charley finished sweeping his

station and folding his load of towels from the dryer, he waved goodbye to Dorothy.

Darla was expecting his call.

"How about we take in a movie over in Big Spring or Angelo?"

"Why don't you come over for dinner? Mom and Ed decided to make a run to Big Bend while the cactus is still in bloom. They lucked out and got a room at the Gage Hotel—a last-minute cancellation."

Charley needed no further persuasion. To hell with the movies.

* * *

It was the Sunday of Darla's singing engagement at the Briargrove Methodist Church. Charley would have enjoyed seeing her in a choir robe, belting out songs, but he didn't want to see the Reverend Woodruff. When he had a chance to give it a thought—with everything else that was going on—he was mostly mad. Why hadn't Gunnar Woodruff come looking for him? Hadn't he ever run into April? There weren't that many people in Sandstone County. The highway kept up the constant exchange between the two towns—people came and went to see doctors and lawyers, do their banking, take care of county business in the courthouse at Sulfur Gap, buy cars in Briargrove, and shop at Wal-Mart in between.

He wanted to check out his grandmother's house. He'd been pondering the logistics for a month. His smart phone would guide him straight to her. He could drop Darla off at the church and go do some surveillance on his grandmother's neighborhood, even get a picture of her if she was outside. He still hadn't told Darla he was driving his grandmother's Buick—it hadn't come up—so he told her he would pick her up after the church service, after he scouted a couple of places that would make a good site for a salon, in case he got around to starting his own, in case he ever in a million years had the money to start one or buy one.

He drove down Broadway, Briargrove's main street, with its storefronts. There were a couple of boutiques, a few offices—a lawyer, an optometrist, and a dentist—a bank, a bakery, and a sandwich shop. Further on were an Edward Jones financial advisor and a couple of insurance agencies. A small hardware store sat on one corner, and most of the next block was taken up by a lumberyard that had closed down. As the businesses scattered out and the speed limit increased to introduce the highway leaving the town, oil-field supply yards and a welding shop and yard took up the open space, with an old, converted Dairy Queen lodging a well-known steak house. There was a county library, a clinic, and Irma's used-car lot where he had bought the Skylark. Down a side street that held a few small antique and gift stores, he spotted a modest building set off the road. It was adobe and stone, with a copper-colored metal roof. There was a paved parking lot around it. All it needed were a few pink yuccas at strategic places to soften the corners. And the best part about it—there was a sign in front: "For Sale or Lease."

Charley pulled over and jotted down the number of the real estate agent, knowing that he was going through the motions to prove to Darla that he had in fact been scouting for a possible business location. And he had no idea what kind of remodeling would be needed to make the location suitable for a salon. And what about Dorothy? He always felt a surge of guilt when he thought of abandoning her. Even pretending he was thinking of abandoning her. He wasn't sure, though, how much was pretense. He could start his own salon. He could support it with his own reputation. His finances were in better shape than they'd ever been, and here was the irony—he'd been in a relationship longer than ever before—and without getting married. Relationships usually meant that he started blowing money. But he hadn't.

He told Darla, "When we have a sleepover, I feel bad that it's always your place. You could come to my place, but then before that happened, I would need to refurnish."

Darla leveled her gaze at him and said, "That's why I'm not going to your place. Not because I'll see shabby furniture, but because you would think I shouldn't see it and go out and buy a bunch of crap you don't need right now so that I wouldn't know that you have not invested wisely in home furnishings. So give it a rest, Charley. I'll come to your place only when you're comfortable with me seeing the way it is right this minute."

Since she put it that way, it was a challenge to him. But he wanted to prove to her that he had good taste. He didn't always put it to use, though. Darla would like this little shop. He'd have to drive her by after church.

He made a U-turn to head back to the heart of Briargrove and followed the voice of his phone navigator as it took him past an elementary school, a park, and two large Victorian homes that were still preserved and had belonged to some of the early ranching families in the area. He had never ventured around the residential part of Briargrove, but several of his clients made the drive from here to Sulfur Gap for him to cut their hair.

He turned onto a smaller street with smaller houses, a tidy little neighborhood. Some of these houses looked as though they dated to the 1920s, with narrow brick archways over the porches, awnings over the windows, steep shingled roofs with attic gables, and real shutters. He admired a house that was so quaint, he expected the Seven Dwarves to march up to it, singing a ditty as they returned home from a day's work. His phone said, "Your destination is on the right." It was the dwarves' house.

Here was a house that he could have visited as a child,

a house with a real chimney and a fireplace that he could have imagined Santa Claus coming down to deliver toys at Christmas. A house with a yard that probably had a good dog in it. He drove further up the street, and as his eyes filled with tears, he pulled over to the curb to clear his vision.

He adjusted the rearview mirror so that he could look back on the house, when a tall, thin woman with short white hair stepped out the front door. She wore capris and a tank top, and she carried a hoe. Leaning the hoe against the porch, she picked up hedge clippers that were lying on the lawn and began lopping the boxwoods with the energy of a Tasmanian devil. Her quick movements were invigorating to watch. "Must be my grandmother," he thought. "Will I ever get to meet you?" He was being careful of his time so that he could pick Darla up from the church, so he checked his watch and leaned down to the floor to pick up his notepad with the real estate agent's number.

It wouldn't hurt to call and find out about the asking price. He didn't know how much money he would need to start his own salon. Should he buy or lease a property? How much would remodeling cost? Should he leave Sulfur Gap at all? He didn't want to leave Dorothy, didn't want to go into competition with her, and knew that leaving the Wild Hare would create a vacuum there that would be hard to fill. He pondered for a moment and looked up to see how his grandmother's yard work was progressing.

Startled by an aggressive knock on his window, he turned to see the white-haired woman aiming a blue-eyed glare through the glass. He rolled down his window.

Before he could say anything, she demanded, "Who are you and why are you spying on me in my old car?"

Charley lifted placating hands toward her, as if she had said, "Stick 'em up!"

"I'm the guy who bought your car. Irma Bridges sold it to me."

"Yeah, I recognize my old car. So? Why are you casing my house?"

Charley remembered that she worked at the prison in Matilda. She was tough enough to be a guard, but he figured she was probably a teacher or social worker. Still tough. "I wanted to see where you lived."

"And why is that?"

At this point, Charley realized she had been holding a cocked pistol in her hand, and that she was releasing the hammer, having decided that she wouldn't need to shoot him. Jesus God, he could have wound up like Frank Bristow. Still too many women with guns.

"It's a long story," he offered lamely.

"Let's hear it, or I'm calling the police." With long, strong fingers, she pulled a cell phone out of the waistband of her capris.

"Do you remember April Bristow?"

Now she was flummoxed. She tilted her head to one side and then leaned toward the window of the car to get a view of Charley without shadows.

Her eyes widened and her chin quivered when she took in his face.

"Oh, my," she said quietly, letting the gun drop with a clatter to the pavement. "You're the baby."

Charley opened his door slowly, and his grandmother backed up to let him get out and rise to his full height, never taking her eyes from his face.

"You look like your father," she said, and placed a calloused hand on his chest.

"That's what my mother says."

They stared at one another for a full minute. She broke the trance when she remembered the gun lying on the street. Bending to pick it up, she checked the safety and stuffed it in the waistband of her capris as if she did this every day. For all Charley knew, she did, considering that she worked with convicted felons. That could jade a person.

Charley said, "I'm sorry I scared you. I found out only a few weeks ago about you, and it's a coincidence that I bought your car. I know you have a lot of questions."

"And so do you," she said. "But for starters, what do I call you?"

"Charley," he said, "and I should call you . . . ?"

"Doris."

They shook hands.

"I'm sorry," Charley said, "but I have to go pick up my girl-friend from church. She's over at the Methodist—"

"You do know who the preacher there is?"

"Yes, ma'am."

"At least tell me how you found us. You can't run off this minute with no more said."

"Well, I came over here to find a good used car, and Miss Bridges sold me the Skylark. Part of her sales pitch was that the car belonged to the Methodist preacher's mother. I guess she thought that sounded like the car had been in responsible hands. It didn't mean anything to me at the time, but it wasn't long until my mother told me about my dad being the Methodist preacher in Briargove."

"And you realized whose car you were driving!" Doris was a quick study, he could tell right away. They laughed, and the tension melted.

"Anyway," Charley continued, "I always knew my mom's husband wasn't my real dad. My stepdad died when I was five, almost six."

"Oh, I'm sorry!" Doris put her hand to her cheek.

"Yeah, my mom sort of shut down for the next twenty years,

you could say. Here lately, she's been more open, and I took the opportunity to press her about who my dad was. She said a boy that dated her when she was in the girls' home here. That he dropped her."

"Oh, I know about that! I overheard him telling her that his father and I didn't want him to date her any more. I was so mad at him. He took the coward's way out. I've had a hard time watching him develop into this preacher that everyone loves, knowing he fathered a child and didn't take responsibility."

"So he knew?"

"Damn straight he did. I told him."

"How did you know?"

"I saw her at the clinic, and I knew one of the counselors at the girls' home. She swore me to secrecy when I asked her. I thought April looked like she was just starting to show. She was so cute and willowy, a baby bump was hard to hide from a prying eye like mine," she said proudly. Charley thought for a moment they must have a mix-up. April? Willowy?

"I couldn't say anything to April—I wanted to—but I had promised the counselor, and she assured me that the girls' home would see that she got prenatal care and help her graduate. She convinced me that it was up to April to contact me. I kept hoping she'd do that."

Charley took this all in. "To tell the truth, she wasn't totally sure your son was my father until I got old enough for her to see the resemblance. When he broke up with her, it seems she found some consolation in someone else's arms, and so my parentage became confused." He didn't hesitate to tell Doris. They had to get past the secrets and miscommunications and missed opportunities. A feeling of urgency prompted his words, but they came easily with the sense that he and Doris were surrounded here on the street by a bubble of safety. The familiar grip of shame seized him, but not as tightly as usual. And he coped as usual by shifting mental gears and pretending that he was describing someone else's life.

"I heard she got married and moved to Sulfur Gap," Doris said. "I always wanted to find her and get to know you, but she'd moved on, and I didn't want to interfere. And my son was off at college." She looked at the ground. "I . . . I guess we both dropped the ball. Can you forgive us?"

Charley was shocked at the question. He hadn't thought about needing to forgive anyone besides April. He had blamed only April. Compassion edged its way into his heart, into a small cleft that was opening more and more for his mother. "I don't know what I'd be forgiving. I didn't miss what I didn't know I had."

Charley thought over his last statement and decided it made sense, at least to him. "I had a decent stepdad for a while, but Mom didn't have a support system after he died, so it was rough. People took me under their wing." He thought of Wayne—his older brother in spirit—and Wayne's parents—surrogate grandparents. They always made sure Christmas didn't disappoint him. And the guys who taught him to play pool. And Dorothy. And Jarod and Sue.

"Have you been to see Gunnar?"

"No, I wasn't ready for that. I wanted to see where you lived. I thought I'd find you first and introduce myself. I thought it would be awkward, but not nearly this awkward." They blushed and laughed. "I've listened to your tape of the Skylark song, so I at least knew something about you. And I've been driving your car for a while."

Doris laughed. "If I can help, let me know when you're ready. You could come to my house. I know he'll be happy to see you, but you'll both need to choose the right time. I'm glad you didn't

show up at his church. He would have fainted behind the pulpit
if he looked out and saw you." She chuckled at the idea, and then
frowned. "He and I have been mad at each other off and on. He
and his wife, Celia, haven't been able to have any kids. They can't
help it, but then that makes me mad I didn't get to have grandkids. I start telling myself that he ruined it. Oh, it's so much crap.
We're a mess. I'm a stubborn old woman a lot of the time." Doris
was as comfortable talking to Charley as he was to her. They were
strangers to one another, but they shared like the old friends they
should have been.

"I'll think about how we need to meet. I do want to meet.
You'll tell him, I guess. I don't want to surprise him the way I did
you," he laughed.

This reminded Doris of the story in the *Echo*. "Oh, my God! I
was almost forgetting—how could I?—the story about your mother shooting that nut case that tried to break into her house. What
a life she's had! Poor April!"

Charley looked at his watch. He didn't want Darla to have to
wait and wonder on the church sidewalk. "Yeah," he said, "all this
is sort of tied together. Mom and I are both sorting out the family
tree."

Doris picked up on his itch to get away. "Well, that's a whole
other can of worms, however they may be related. I'll let you go
get your girlfriend, who, by the way, is welcome any time you
come. One more question. What do you do for a living, Charley?"

"I'm a hair stylist."

She grabbed his face with both hands. She was delighted.
"No!" She danced a little jig. "You're *that* Charley? The magical
hair stylist? I'm always hearing people talk about going over to
the Gap to get a Charley-cut."

Charley appraised her short, white hair, and thought it could
be beautiful if he ever got a chance to shape it.

She ran her fingers through her thatch. "I never cared enough one way or another to try to get over there for a cut." She dropped her hands. "If only I had. But you can't make a silk purse out of a sow's ear. If I had cared more about hair and gone over to the Gap, I would've met you sooner."

"I guess the timing is better this way. And speaking of timing, I'd better be off to pick up Darla." He turned to his car. It would be better, he thought, to leave it up to the Reverend Woodruff to get in touch with him. He could wait a while, leave the ball in his court, see if he would punt, slice, or scratch. His frequent lessons in waiting would hold him in good stead. He knew that just appreciating the moment he was living in was the best way to wait . . . or not wait.

"Hold on," Doris said. "Let me get your number, and I'll give you mine. You need to come over and have supper some evening. And you don't get out of here without giving me a hug."

He didn't have to bend far, as she threw her long arms around his neck and hung on for several seconds.

He belonged here and always had.

* * *

At the church, most of the cars had vacated the side lot, so Charley had no trouble finding a place to park out of the way. He knew Darla could spot the Skylark in a heartbeat. His timing was impeccable, because as soon as he cut the engine and began wondering how the stained glass windows looked from inside the church, she walked around the corner.

"How'd it go?"

"It went great. There are some pretty good voices in that choir. It was hard not to stare at Reverend Woodruff, though. I wouldn't have goggled, but knowing he's your father, I could see how much you look alike, and I wanted to analyze his looks to decide if that's how you'll look in twenty years."

Twenty years? Oh, be still my heart, Charley thought. Does she want to be with me twenty years from now?

He said, "If he's good-looking, then of course that's how I'll look in twenty years."

"Oh, you!" she said, and scooted across the seat to hug him. Charley wasn't about to waste the moment, so he hugged back and tried to start one of his long, indulgent kisses that he loved so well with Darla.

"Not here!" she protested, wriggling free and pushing away. "We're in the church parking lot."

"Let's make a run for the windmill, then."

Hot damn. Forget everything. To the windmill!

* * *

A mix of excitement followed by disappointment swept over Charley as he neared the windmill on the narrow dirt lane.

Lou's red pickup was parked in the best shade.

Charley had hoped for some peaceful, quiet time with Darla. Time to play with her hair and talk, their fingers interlaced. Time to walk across the pastures with a view of the horizon as they shared their life stories with one another.

When he spotted Wayne, standing with Lou twenty yards beyond the windmill, the two of them looking like a married couple surveying a landscaping project, disappointment vanished.

They waved as Charley and Darla walked toward them.

"Y'all look like you're planning something," Charley said as they joined their friends.

"Yep," said Wayne. "Lou's got an idea. Tell 'em."

Lou swept her arm toward the windmill. "This windmill

shouldn't sit idle. It can pump water. I'm thinking Wayne could get a concrete tank built over there." She pointed. "We can put a good fence around an acre or two to discourage the feral hogs. We could make an entertainment spot—plant some vines to grow over trellises for shade and set out some tables and chairs."

Charley deflated at the idea that his wild, special place would be demolished. Darla had an opinion, though. He could always count on Darla to come up with an opinion.

"That's a great idea, Lou! Wayne could have parties and family gatherings here."

"I'll have to get more social if I expect to come up with a guest list for any kind of party," Wayne said. He looked at Lou. "Should we tell them now?"

"You just did," Lou said, punching Wayne on the arm.

Charley got it right away and saw Darla did, too, by the way she clapped her hand over her mouth. She grabbed Lou. "Congratulations!" she yelled into Lou's ear as the taller woman bent down for a hug. Charley pumped Wayne's hand.

"Yep," Wayne said, "We figure there's no point in putting off tying the knot."

"We could live together, but that's so *conventional*," Lou said.

"I need to marry her so it won't be too easy for her to pick up and leave when she meets the extended family," Wayne smiled.

"So you're having the ceremony here? At the windmill?" Darla looked around.

"Yes, so far that's the plan. Don't know if Wayne and I can get all this work done by July."

"Sure can," Wayne said. "Concrete tanks and windmills are my specialty."

Charley thought Wayne was being optimistic and showing off a bit, but hey, who could blame him?

20
Summer Heat

THE DAYS OF SPRING melted toward shimmering, hot summer. Pink yucca on the corners around the old courthouse square sent up shoots topped with buds that proclaimed the hot and hotter weather. People parking their cars outside offices and stores left their windows cracked so they could breathe air that wasn't stifling and touch their steering wheels without burning their hands when they returned to move on to the next errand in the waffle-iron heat. Winds up to thirty miles an hour were much appreciated because they stirred the air. Gales above thirty brought too much dust and blew trash across streets to collect between buildings and pile against fences.

But everyone was accustomed to it. Ceiling fans churned while the ACs ran nonstop, and the tropical ice vending stands offering thirty flavors opened in both of their usual locations— empty lots on different sides of town, where the weeds would be trampled and scraped away by the restless feet of children and their parents.

April waited. She called and left a message for Sheriff Sparks. He called back to say that it would take a while to hear about the DNA results. The county had reopened the investigation. There would be lots of paperwork and review. She knew all this, because she had signed off as possible next-of-kin on some of the forms.

She waited some more. Then Larry Bob called her to say that

no exhumation was necessary, and investigators were waiting on the DNA comparisons to establish that the Jane Doe found near Marshall was Ann Bristow.

While April waited, Charley kept up his busy schedule. As his workday ended, he looked forward to plans with Darla. He had arranged a debut dinner for her at his apartment. The chili in the slow cooker and the DVDs from the Redbox rental awaited them. He would point out to her that he had resisted the urge to run up to Abilene to buy an updated HD television and Blu-Ray DVD player, augmented by the best in Bose speakers. Anyway, he hoped they wouldn't make it past the movie's opening theme song before they headed for his fresh sheets.

He swept up his last haircut. As he hung the dustpan and broom back in their places on the wall and waved goodbye to Dorothy, his phone vibrated in his pocket.

Crap.

It was April. *Please don't torpedo my plans, please don't*, he prayed. "Hey, Mom," he tried to sound chipper rather than put-upon.

"Charley! You've got to come over!" She was insistent, excited, downright urgent.

"I've got a date with Darla—can it wait?"

"It won't take long. Bring Darla. Come on, and then y'all can go about your business."

Charley picked up Darla at Dr. Harper's office. The vet clinic looked like a good place to take a pet. Darla had repainted the trim on the adobe building. She'd chosen a mud color that wouldn't work anywhere except with that particular adobe, and stenciled "Sulfur Gap Animal Care" across the front wall. Big pots of foxtail fern at the corners set off the building. Charley wondered how she found time. She certainly wasn't one to sit filing her nails during a break.

"So what's up with April?" As she got in the car, Darla wafted the smell of the antiseptic that permeated the clinic. That would dissipate, and if not, he could coax her into the shower. He wouldn't even think about Joyce's patched bullet hole presiding over the scene . . . he hoped.

"No telling," he said. As far as he knew, April was still abstaining from her bad habits—or addictions—he wanted to think of them as addictions, to be honest and not put a shine on her problems. She was also still keeping house and getting out to take care of her own business. She walked up the road and back every day to get her mail, rather than wait for someone—namely Charley—to bring it.

"We'll see what she called about and then get the evening going," he added, fingers crossed.

April was standing beside the door.

"Welcome, Darla!" She greeted them and swept a hand for them to come in. Every time he went to her home, he saw improvements. This time the furniture was rearranged, with added throws and pillows. The wobbly captain's chair was gone, replaced by a club chair that could be the anchor piece for further redecorating. Everything still smelled pleasant. Her candle wafted jasmine.

What surprised Charley was that April was wearing jeans. Her weight was down by a good twenty-five pounds in the last month or so, and Charley guessed she weighed in at under 250. Still big, but the weight loss had inspired her to buy some jeans. She wore a long, loose tunic that covered her rolls.

"Sit, sit," she said. They perched on the couch and she lowered herself into the new chair. Her hands weren't as trembly. How long—two months?—with no cigarettes? A month, at least, without booze? Charley marveled at her courage, surprised at his new admiration for his mother.

"I need to tell you this in person," she began. "They've found my mother."

"What? Alive?" Charley sat up straight.

"No, nothing like that, I'm afraid. But remember the DNA sample I gave?"

"Yeah, that was fast, if they got the results already," Charley said.

"Well, they did. It was a match to a sample from a Jane Doe found murdered and left in one of the back bayous of Caddo Lake in late 1982. She's not a Jane Doe anymore."

April looked into their faces to see if they comprehended. Satisfied, she continued. "They sent samples from the original investigation to a lab at Texas State University. Since the match with my DNA came back, we can find out what they know from that investigation. I'm the family."

"What have they told you?" Charley asked.

"Just that a man fishing the back bayous on Caddo Lake in East Texas found her. There wasn't any evidence to go on. The sheriff's office and police department put a sketch of her face in the papers, but no one responded. It probably didn't look like her. They couldn't find any prints or any clues at all."

"When will you know more?"

"That depends on whether I wait for a written report or go there myself."

"Why would you want to go there?"

"I can ask more questions face to face. The man that found her body is still alive—really old now, I understand. I want to know as much as I can. I also have to decide if I want to bring my mother's remains here or leave her grave in Marshall."

"You're so brave, Mrs. Erwin," Darla said.

"You better call me April, honey. I haven't been Mrs. Erwin ever, except when Eldon was teasing me. Anyway, I feel like I've been hiding in a little pup tent and somebody came along and lifted the flap so I could crawl out and stand up and enjoy the view. I know I'll cry, but it won't kill me."

"A lot of people would crawl back in the tent," Darla added.

"It's not easy, but it's easier than what I've been doing." April leaned back, closed her eyes, and took a deep breath. She looked at them and smiled.

"So, do you want me to take you to Lake Caddo?" Charley asked.

"Yes, if you don't mind. I'll get on the phone and see if I can meet with the man who found her. He lives in Marshall, which is a good thing since the Harrison County sheriff's department did the investigation, and their headquarters is in Marshall. They'll have someone walk me through the investigation. I want to go to the lake, too—it's right up the highway from there."

"All right, then," Charley said. "Thanks for keeping me in the loop."

He hugged April and stood aside while she and Darla hugged. April drew back to look at Darla. "You're so precious," she said, cupping Darla's cheek with her hand. Charley thought that wonders never ceased. They stepped off the porch hand in hand, trying to appear unhurried.

"I can't believe your mom will find the answers she's been waiting for," Darla said, clicking her seat belt on.

"I know. I'm actually looking forward to the trip with her."

"You get to discover another grandmother. But it'll be bitter."

"Filling in the blanks," he said, and squeezed her hand. Time to change the subject. That pot of chili was waiting.

Charley could feel Darla's excitement. He was charged up, too.

At the apartment, he ushered Darla up the stairs.

Inside, she looked around while he held his breath. She put her hands over her eyes and screeched in mock horror, "Get me out of here! I can't stand the décor!"

They both laughed, and he scooped her up and into the bed-room. He tossed her onto the bed and then pounced.

The chili could wait.

21

Eastbound

THEY SET OUT FOR MARSHALL in the Skylark early the next Sunday morning.

"When's the last time you made a trip this far?" Charley asked April.

"Probably when we went to Vegas that time and I met my real father." April gazed ahead at the road. She looked excited, almost girlish. Charley's heart broke for her as he thought of their mission—to learn about her mother's murder.

She had let Charley trim her hair so that it could begin growing into something that could actually flatter her. She'd been using a shampoo he had recommended, and her premature grayness was turning to a silver shine. The pouches under her eyes had shrunk, along with the other parts that had been inflated by the booze. The biggest change, though, was her hope. It was the first time that he remembered his mother having hope.

They settled in for the seven hours down the Interstate to East Texas and the Marshall exit.

"You want to hear the theme song for my car?" Charley asked.

"Sure." April's new curiosity still surprised him.

He popped the tape into the player and turned up the volume. They listened through all the repetitions of "Skylark," and when it stopped, she said, "That's a sad song, but it's a good song. I think there's a little bit of joy stirring around in there."

Good summation, he thought. Maybe like her life will turn out. A sad song, but a good one, with a little bit of joy finally stirred in. The song now made him happy, rather than hurting the way it did when he first heard it on the trip up the caprock with Lou.

They stopped for lunch in Eastland, where April ordered a grilled chicken salad and Charley wolfed down a bacon cheese-burger. He had skipped breakfast in his haste to get on the road. While they were alone and face to face in a booth, he decided to satisfy some of his curiosity.

"Mom, you can tell me this is none of my business, but I was wondering what happened to the twenty thousand from Darrell Trainer."

"It's your business, too, Charley. It's all about your business."

"What's that mean?"

"I knew you wanted to have your own salon, so I invested that money in hopes it would grow into a nice fund to start a business."

"You invested? How?" Charley assumed she'd paid off credit cards with the inheritance. But come to think of it, there was never much in the trailer to show for high credit-card indebtedness. He had assumed, based on his own spending habits.

"I went and talked to the Edward Jones guy over in Briargrove, Leland Hicks. He gave me some stock tips and let me decide."

"You played the stock market?" Charley couldn't believe it. He hadn't thought of April as a gambler.

"No, I didn't *play* the stock market. I made an informed decision and bought stock in Apple."

"But the market's crashing. That's all over the news. Everything's going to hell. Did you lose it all?"

"No. I bought a little over 4,300 shares at about $4.60 back in early 2005, right after Lou brought me that check. In January of this year, the share price was $28.46, so with dividends reinvested, that twenty thousand has turned into $140,000. All in three years."

"But what about the market crashing?"

"Apple fell a little, but Leland called me at the right time and talked me into taking out half and holding the cash for a while. He said there would be buying opportunities."

"Buying opportunities."

"Yes, then he called me again the other day and told me we should jump on Priceline.com. He expects it to multiply many times over in the next few years. With that and Apple, my account should be worth a half million if all goes the way we expect."

"And I guess he takes a big fee every time you buy and sell."

"Well, he gets a commission, but I couldn't have done any of this by myself. He's a nice guy who realized I never had any money in my life, and when he found out I was willing to take the risks and invest aggressively, he gave me his best advice.

"I've seen the ads on TV for the websites where you can do your own investing," she said, "but I don't have a computer and don't know enough not to blow it all. I don't mind paying the commission."

"What if we lose it?" Charley warmed to the idea of "we."

"Well, we're no worse off. I'm sure you can start your own business without the money, but with it, you won't have to go into debt. Anyway, the account's in both our names, so if something happens to me, it's automatically yours. But I'm going to indulge myself a little bit, too.

"I've decided I'm going to use some cash I set aside and buy myself a laptop and whatever I need to have Wi-Fi so I can get on the Internet and do research. Not just the price of stocks, but other news. You can find any recipe you want on the web, attend an online AA meeting. And you can even find family records so I can trace my family. There are some computer classes coming up at the community center, and I'm going to sign up."

Charley was so floored, he stopped chewing. Wonders never ceased. He couldn't comprehend having $140,000 ever in his life, and here was his mother casually sitting on that much. Of course, she could sit on a set of encyclopedias and they would go undetected. He shook his head to clear the image.

"So when do you want to buy into a business?"

"Oh, when you're ready. I figure Dorothy will want to retire in a couple of years, and you'll be able to make her a solid offer. But we shouldn't count our chickens. Still, these iPhones are taking the world by storm, and no telling what else Apple will come up with."

"So you've thought this all out?"

"I've thought about a lot that would surprise you, Charley." She smiled mysteriously, and for a moment, he thought she looked like the Mona Lisa with pink lipstick.

Buying the salon from Dorothy, if she would sell it, would get him over the guilt hurdle. Dorothy would have her retirement nest egg, and she could stay on and keep doing nails if she wanted. If he and Darla were still an item—and he hoped so—he could open a shop wherever her career took her.

Lots of "if's." Seemed like the only thing that was certain was uncertainty. Might as well get used to it. But maybe he should think of the uncertainty as possibility.

Back on the road, he kept glancing at her. She was a genius. With no experience, she had quickly begun to understand the workings of the stock market. Now she was interested in learning about computers. Lou could call him "Chippie" all she wanted. His mother was the block. And she rocked.

* * *

They stopped a couple of times at convenience stores. April stuck to black coffee and overpriced, unsalted pistachio nuts. Charley indulged his weakness for Cheetos on the road to the point that his cuticles were orange, but he was satisfied.

Charley had anticipated miles of silence, and there was that. April never felt obliged to make conversation. She brought along a book with a heavy, tooled leather cover, and from time to time, she would open it and read, then close it and look off out the window.

Finally, he asked, "Whatcha readin', Mom?"

"The AA Big Book. My sponsor gave me this cover so I can read it wherever I go and people can't see what it is."

"Oh." Charley wondered who her sponsor was. Surely not Candy.

Finally, she slipped the book into her shoulder bag on the floor between her feet.

"I shoulda brought something more entertaining to read."

"I've got the latest Grisham in my overnight bag. You can start on it if you want. But I'll wrestle you for it if you get hooked and don't give it back when we get to the hotel."

"Don't bother. I'll borrow it from you when you're finished."

"So . . . any interesting activity in the trailer-hood?"

April thought a moment and laughed. "Well, you know that little old man and woman that live two lots up from me?"

"Yeah. The Klukowskis?"

"Yeah. I call 'em the Kluks. She's pulls crazy moves like driving up to the wrong place and trying to get in their door. The other day, she walked in on the Tylers' daughter and her boyfriend making out on the couch and demanded they leave her house at once. They said it wasn't her house. And she said, 'Don't change the subject! I'm telling your parents.' And stomped out."

April unreeled a peal of laughter that surprised Charley. He laughed, too, trying to remember her ever having a sense of humor. When she had, it was long ago.

Fifty miles from the exit to Marshall, April turned to Charley. "You want to hear the story I've made up about my mother?"

"Story? What for?"

"Just for me. I know it's a story, but I also know something sort of like it probably happened."

"Yeah, okay."

April turned a little to face Charley and laid her hand across the back of the seat. "Here's what I think happened. My mother waited for Darrell Trainer to come back from his tour. Sometime after he left, she realized she was pregnant but didn't tell him when he called. This was back in the day before *Roe v. Wade*. Getting an abortion could be dangerous. She wasn't sure she was going to keep the baby, but the first trimester passed. She was afraid to tell her own parents, afraid to lose their approval. But she needed to start making plans of her own. She decided she couldn't go through with an abortion. She would get help from her parents. She knew Darrell would want to be involved, but she didn't want him to leave his music tour and get a bad reputation and lose some opportunities to get back into doing what he loved."

Charley figured April was as qualified as anyone to make this story up. After all, she was the only person around who had known Ann. April narrated her story as if she had written it down. "She told her neighbors and friends she was going to Alaska to work on landscape painting, while she planned to go home to Amarillo and stay with her parents and put the baby up for adoption, or even keep it and marry Darrell when he got back. She might still go to Alaska someday. It was a longtime dream anyway."

Charley couldn't believe it. She sounded like him when he talked about his life. Like it happened to someone else. And she could even refer to herself in third person—"the baby." She had built a detailed fantasy. Well, it was how she coped, he guessed. Didn't make her crazy—she knew the difference between being clueless and making something up to fill in the blanks.

"She left her forwarding address and her parents' phone number with her neighbor, a young man who had moved into the duplex next to hers. He seemed nice and responsible. She told him some letters would come from Darrell, and asked him to hold those until he showed up. And she waited for two days right by the phone for Darrell to call. She would tell him the plan. It just happened that those two days she waited before she left were the only two consecutive days of Darrell's whole tour that he didn't have a chance to call. The band was on the road between gigs, and pay phones were few and far between. By the time he did call, there was no answer, even though he tried over and over."

An eighteen-wheeler blew by so fast, his back draft shook the Skylark. April concentrated on her story. "She told the guy next door that her parents would know where she was—to please give their contact information to Darrell when he came by, along with a letter she had written. She would also leave Darrell a note on the door. Going to her parents—pregnant, a college dropout—was horrifying to think about. She wanted to get it over with.

"The neighbor had her letters from Darrell and forwarding address and phone number in a file on his desk, but he had a party one night. There was a keg and lots of hard liquor, and the next day, his place was trashed. He cleaned everything up, but he could never find the file folder. He looked through all the trash bins up and down the street. He was so embarrassed, he took down the note Ann left for Darrell on the door of her empty duplex. He figured Darrell would find her on his own, and he didn't want to have to explain himself. So a lame coincidence and a lame college kid with no sense of responsibility kept Darrell from knowing where Ann had gone."

This was as good an explanation as any, Charley thought. Everything got FUBAR'ed.

"Darrell knew she had family in Amarillo, so when he got back and couldn't find Ann, he drove up there and called all the Smiths in the phone book. What he didn't know was that Ann's mother answered one of his calls and denied knowing anyone named Ann. She was still having her own temper tantrum about her daughter. When Ann came home pregnant, her mother simmered with resentment. Her dad stayed out of it, wimp that he was, but her mother blurted mean observations and acted as if it was all about her that her beautiful, talented daughter would have her life derailed by an unwanted pregnancy. She was also concerned about what her friends in Amarillo would think. The drama was too much. Ann decided she would be better off on her own rather than under the shadow of judgment cast by her mother. She would take her savings and head out for . . . oh, Kansas City. She would find a home for unwed mothers. That's what they called those places back then."

Good idea to bring in a mean mother and weak-willed father blocking Darrell and Ann's reunion, Charley thought.

"And she did go to a home. She let her parents know where she was, but by then, Darrell had decided that the trail was cold in Amarillo. She spent the last five months of her pregnancy with a bunch of high school girls at the home. She felt abandoned by Darrell. Her parents had abandoned her emotionally, and if she stayed with them, there would be a blowup to make it official that they didn't want her or her baby. She cried and grieved and wondered what would become of her and the baby.

"It turned out there was a handsome, charismatic chaplain that worked part-time at the home, name of Frank Bristow. Through the final months of her pregnancy, he made himself available. He was steady, said all the right things. She confided to him that the father of her child apparently didn't want to take any responsibility. She hadn't heard from him, in spite of her attempts to let him know where she was.

"Frank was only beginning to blossom as a sociopath. He was ready to start a family, and he saw a wonderful opportunity here to acquire an instant one. First, he talked her into keeping the baby and not putting it up for adoption. He sincerely believed that a baby is better off with its birth mother.

"Ann developed preeclampsia and almost lost the baby, but Frank stayed at her side, holding her hand, reassuring her with a tenderness that she longed for. She felt safe and cared for. She was so grateful, she agreed to let him drive her back to Amarillo after she regained her strength. But he made several stops along the way, and he was such a reassurance to her and seemed to be so talented, she was lulled into trusting her future and the baby's future—at least for the time being—to this man. Her hormones were raging, her maternal instincts were telling her to seek protection, and the thought of going to her mother for any kind of help or support was galling.

"She let Frank find one excuse and then another to keep from taking her home. He always came up with the money to stay in nice places—cabins at lakesides and charming B&Bs in places she had never seen. By the time the baby was six months old, she realized Frank had no intention of taking her home. She argued that they at least go for a visit to her parents. He would throw it back at her that they had abandoned her. Why would she want to pay

them a visit? He began to insist they get married for appearances'
sake and to do the right thing in God's eyes, too, by the way.

"She didn't know what else to do. She was beginning to be
afraid of Frank. She had seen him sneak tips off the tables as they
left Cracker Barrel. And he had a wallet full of credit cards that
he kept hidden from her. She tried not to think of that. She would
figure out a way to get away from him, but she was feeling vulner-
able with the baby. Remember, women were only starting to burn
their bras then.

"Eventually, she gave in and married him, thinking if he felt
she had made a commitment, he would relax and she would find
a way to give him the slip when she needed to. Rather than making Frank nicer, marriage made him more possessive. His control
escalated and kindness faded. He had grabbed her hard a few
times, but the slapping and twisting and hair-pulling were introduced after the wedding vows, and they became a weekly event.
She even feared that if she did not comply with whatever Frank
wanted, he would hurt the baby somehow, and even make it look
like it was her fault. And he made sure to instill that fear as deep
as he could. Everything was her fault—according to him, anyway.
Brainwashed, she believed it more and more. All this developed
over time.

"The years went on. When he was released on bond in
Briargrove, they headed for East Texas. She felt bolder since her
daughter was no longer with them. Frank couldn't hurt the girl
when he raged. The years with Frank taught her a few tricks, and
she could confuse store clerks when making change, turning a
five-dollar bill into a twenty. She lifted purses from the backs of
chairs in restaurants and cleaned out the cash in the bathroom
stalls. She had a stash of money and intended to buy a bus ticket
back to West Texas.

"Frank caught up with her at the bus depot and sweet-talked

her into taking one last ride with him. Said he understood that she wanted to get back to her daughter and that it was time for them to part ways. He made her believe it somehow. She thought it would be nice if they could reach a resolution of sorts and say good-bye so she wouldn't be looking over her shoulder from then on. Then he took her to the lake and killed her, and he left her body to be eaten by alligators."

Charley had pulled over at a rest stop so he could listen. April's story caught the essence of what had happened between Ann and Frank. Maybe Ann told her some of the early story, and she could have overheard things that lingered in her subconscious mind and came together in the last three years since she learned that Frank wasn't her father. He could certainly see how that could happen. Children have a way of sensing the grief and fear in their parents, and without knowing it, they can absorb their unspoken pain as if it belonged in their own tiny hearts.

A ring of truth echoed in the substance of the story, even if the details were made up.

"So. Let's get back on the road," April said with finality.

22

Hezekiah

THEY PULLED INTO MARSHALL with the afternoon sun still slanting high in the sky, in time to check in to the Fairfield Inn, drop off their bags in adjoining rooms, and proceed with the next leg of the journey.

Charley checked the directions on his phone, and they drove through town and out the highway toward Caddo Lake. At the edge of the city, they spotted the building they were looking for because of its unmistakable shape—one long wing across the front with a fake plantation look, and three other wings shooting off behind. Seeing the familiar layout filled Charley's nostrils with the imagined smell of disinfectant, urine, and feces, all rolled in one odor unique to what today were called "rehabilitation" centers. This would be the most dreaded part of the trip for him. He could purge the lice from a filthy scalp and work around dirty ears, but he became squeamish at the thought of going to an old folks' home, a nursing home, the last stop before the funeral home.

Fittingly, the name of this one was Caddo Sunrise Rehabilitation Center. Charley remembered a few stops at the nursing home in Sulfur Gap, when his mother went to visit one of the old geezers she'd gotten attached to at the VFW. The old man was younger than he looked, but a hard life and a bad hand dealt from the gene pool left him helpless and wizened, dribbling tobacco juice from a toothless grin when April came to his little room with its potty chair beside the bed. She always held

Charley's hand tightly to keep him from bolting.

Today, it felt like she still had him by the hand. Did he ever want to bolt. *Man up*, he told himself.

They stepped into a cool lobby that smelled surprisingly normal. At the nurses' station, April asked for Mr. Hezekiah Mayfield.

Charley braced himself for a walk down one of the wings, where he would keep his head down, eyes averted from doorways where unwelcome sights lurked. But instead, the woman behind the counter said, "Mr. Mayfield? Right over there," and pointed to a tall, white-haired, very black man sitting at a game table across from a bald Humpty Dumpty man who was so white, all his color seemed to have been absorbed by Mr. Mayfield. The two were playing chess. Both men wore track suits. They must have just come from physical therapy, Charley thought.

April approached and tapped Mr. Mayfield on the shoulder.

"Excuse me, Mr. Mayfield," she said. "I'm April Erwin. I hope you remember that I called you a few days ago. . . ."

Mayfield started a bit and turned to her. He looked at his watch. "Oh! I beg your pardon, Mrs. Erwin. I lost track of the time. I was watching for your arrival and became totally absorbed in my chess match with Mr. Halfmann here."

After introductions, Mr. Halfmann said, "Okay, Hez. We'll finish this game later." Nodding to Charley and April, he backed his motorized chair away from the table and sped off down the hall.

"Thank you for seeing us, Mr. Mayfield."

"Call me Hez—that's what my friends call me. And we are friends, I think you'll agree."

"All right, then, Hez." April was uneasy with the name.

"I was named after the Old Testament prophet," he explained. He looked at Charley and said, "You can call me Hez, too."

"Okay," he said, "but my mother is probably going to do all the talking."

"Oh! So is that how it works?" Hez winked at April.

"Not usually," Charley said, feeling the need to defend her.

April dismissed Charley with a hand wave. "He's right. I've probably talked more in the last month than in the previous ten years put together. Finding out what happened to my mother has been a big part of it. It's been a relief to start putting this puzzle together."

Hez smiled. "I've wondered why in the hell God hasn't sent me to my reward before now, and this could be the reason. You know, I'm ninety-seven." He paused to give them time to show surprise at his age, as if accustomed to giving people time to respond to the news.

Charley appraised the man. His hair was snow white, and he wore thick glasses, but his skin was relatively smooth and unblemished. His hands were gnarled with arthritis, but the dark skin on them was smooth as well. It seemed his main concession to age was his motorized wheel chair. He didn't even seem to be wearing a hearing aid and was keeping up with the conversation.

"You don't look ninety-seven," Charley said. "At least how I would think someone that old would look. I've never known anyone that old." Then he backtracked, "What I mean is . . . well . . . ."

Hez laughed. "It's all right, son. You don't have to pretend I'm not old. Hell, I have socks older than you!" Then he gazed at April. "Are you ready, honey?"

"As ready as I'll ever be," she said.

"Well, okay. Here goes. After I retired from Wylie College, I was free to revive some of my favorite activities. My old granddaddy used to take me canoe fishing up in the bayous and through the cypress swamps on the edges of Caddo Lake. He knew the lake well, because he helped build lots of the levees. He was born a slave, but by the time I was born in 1911, he'd been sharecropping for years. I felt at peace on the water in the flat-bottom boat with Pampa—that's what I called him.

"Back in the late summer of 1982, I was making my slow way up a bayou, around where not many people went. It was getting close to school starting, and the families of campers had pretty much cleared out. Most people couldn't take the heat and humidity. I was always resistant to that, and the mosquitoes never liked me much, so I could enjoy myself any time of day. I stocked up the boat that day so that I could pitch a tent and spend the night at the lake edge if I decided to.

"So I was moseying up that bayou with the big roots of the cypress trees all around and their tall trunks reflecting in the water. Couldn't hear a thing except birds calling, frogs croaking, and my paddle pushing the water. I was going past some logs lying side by side—about three of them where old trees had fallen over to look like someone had abandoned a raft-building project.

"A white heron I hadn't seen took off and flapped away right in front of me. She had been sitting on a low branch, above those logs. I looked at where she came from and saw in the shadows a woman lying on the logs. Wouldn't have noticed her at all if that heron hadn't started out from that tree.

"Right away, I knew it wasn't good. There was no reason for a woman to be lying like that, right by the water, way up in that bayou. But I called to her—'Ma'am? Ma'am? You okay?' Of course she didn't move or say anything. I knew she was gone. She was so still. Her hands were folded on her stomach, I could see that, and she didn't have any shoes on, but other than that, she was dressed in her Sunday best, all laid out there. When I got close enough, I could see why she was so still, why she was gone."

At this point, Hez stopped and searched April's eyes. Again

taking her hand, he said, "You sure you want to know the rest?"

"Yes," April said. "You know I killed the man that did this to my mother."

"Yes, you said that."

"Well, if I ever start to feel bad about doing that, and I could, I'm so used to kicking myself—you know, old habits die hard— I'll remember what you're telling me today and I'll forgive myself for taking a life."

Hez said, "From what I know, you had to defend yourself from a home invasion."

"That's true. But I want to know what he did to her so that I don't imagine a bunch that's not true." April's voice quavered on her last sentence. She reached for her purse and drew out a tissue to dab her eyes.

"All right. . . . I wish I'd never seen it myself. The cruelty. . . . But if this is helping you, then it's helping me. I drew my boat a ways up the bank to find a place to make land. Once I was on the bank, I found a hiking trail that led down to the logs. I saw that the way the logs had settled made it easy for a person to walk across them. And midways, there she was. Only this time, I was seeing her from the other side. The side where her head was bashed in. That side of her face was disfigured—mashed in. Didn't look like a face any more. It looked like someone took a swing at her with a mallet or a baseball bat. And gave her more than one blow."

At this, April flinched. "I could have guessed. He loved to use that bat. Do you know if they ever found a bat?"

"No, honey. From what I remember, they decided whoever did it threw the murder weapon in the water or out in a stand of kudzu. Anyway, she was wearing a sleeveless lavender dress. The investigators said it looked like she must have been wearing a jacket over the dress that kept most of the blood off when she was hit, and then her killer took that off to leave her looking better. She didn't have any jewelry on, so they thought robbery could have been a motive."

"Oh, Frank would have wanted to hock whatever little bit of jewelry she had. I'm surprised he left her clothes on her." April rummaged nervously in her bag and then abandoned the instinct. "God, I forgot for a minute I've quit."

"Investigators said the killer was probably someone she knew who laid her out as best as possible out of remorse."

April spluttered. "Bullshit! No way did Frank have one iota of remorse for anything he ever did!" Then she composed herself. "I'm sorry, Hez. I don't mean you're bullshitting. I mean the investigators don't always know as much as they pretend to. Frank was probably taking one last look at her to have his own pleasant memory. It wasn't out of any respect for her. Everyone was a mark to him, someone to be conned, and he looked at my mother the same way, as a possession that he would keep as long as she was useful."

Charley wondered if April's perspective might mellow eventually and allow her to concede that Frank just might have had a tad bit of sorrow after he killed Ann.

Hez said, "Well, that's the way I found her. She hadn't been there long, maybe since right before sunrise. I was glad the scavengers or a gator hadn't gotten there. I lit out up the hiking trail and luckily found some campers. They took me to a phone so I could call the police. It worked in my favor that I had sense enough not to touch the body, because they sure looked at me, all suspicious."

"Why on earth?" April asked. Charley thought how naive she was.

Hez pointed a crooked finger at his cheek. "What color is this skin, honey?"

"Black," she said.

"Well, in these parts, especially more so back in '82, being black made me the first suspect. Discrimination was less prevalent in '82 than it was in '42, but there was still plenty of racism, and there still is today, don't let anyone fool you. Anyway, they ruled me out pretty fast when my brothers from Wylie College came to the police station and brought me a lawyer."

"Brothers?" Charley asked.

"I mean my fellow professors. I was retired, but I still had friends who knew how to make a constructive ruckus."

"Oh, so you were a professor?" Charley thought this fit with how articulate Hez was, along with his regal bearing.

"Yes. Economics. Howard University—Washington, D.C."

"So you came from a sharecropper family, went to Howard, and came back here to teach at the college?" Charley was impressed.

"Well, my granddaddy was a sharecropper, but my daddy eventually owned his own farm, and we saved and saved so I could get out of the county and get an education. And I did. Got some scholarships. Got my doctorate. One of the first black men in the country to get one."

"Why don't you have everyone call you Dr. Mayfield?" April asked. "I would, if I had a Ph.D."

"Because by the time you get to be my age, that doesn't matter. Oh, I'm glad I did it. And I'm proud. But I don't need everyone calling me 'doctor' to help me remember I'm worth something." He leaned toward April, fixing her with his bright stare. "Did you learn what you came for?" he asked, redirecting the conversation from himself and back to April.

"Yes. But can I call you again or come see you?"

"Why, sure you can, honey, but you know, I could be outa here any day now." Hez grinned and pointed upward.

The lobby door jingled and a tall, handsome woman walked in with a girl who looked to be about ten. They both had long, black hair hanging in shining waves around their shoulders, and both were dressed as if for church.

"My dears!" Hez called to them. Turning to April and Charley, who were getting up to leave, he said, "Hold on. I want you to meet my granddaughter and great-granddaughter. There are three generations of my descendants on the ground in these parts. Makes me feel grateful."

Charley and April shook hands with the woman and the girl, and then April had an idea. "Hez, would you take us to the spot?"

The granddaughter jumped in protectively. "Granddaddy doesn't drive anything but that chair. Where you wanting him to take y'all?"

April smiled, trying to reassure the granddaughter. Hez was smiling at the idea.

"I thought Charley could drive us out to the lake some time tomorrow, and Hez could show us where to walk down to find the spot where he found my mother."

Hez's granddaughter was eventually assured that Charley and April were decent people and that it would be okay to take her grandfather out for an hour. He loved to go for the occasional drive, especially over to the lake.

"We'll come by in the morning after we finish at the sheriff's office," April said. They left Hez with his family around him.

23

Finding Ann

THE NEXT MORNING, Charley and April arrived at the Harrison County sheriff's office for their nine a.m. appointment. A woman at the front desk told them to have a seat, and she buzzed the detective in charge of cold cases.

A portly man in khakis, run-down boots, and a belly straining against the buttons of his shirt came down a hall crowded with a copy machine, water cooler, extra chairs, and an abandoned file cabinet. He introduced himself as Ross Flynn and ushered them back through the gauntlet of bureaucratic debris into his small office. Charley thought Flynn looked to be one rib eye short of a heart attack.

After they were seated, the detective rummaged through some files on his desk and found the one he was looking for. Pulling his reading glasses from his shirt pocket, he looked at April.

"This case was investigated pretty thoroughly, probably because it was so unusual. It's never happened around here that a body was discovered so soon after death in such a remote area and in such good condition. It was like finding a needle in a haystack. The discovery of the body was so circumstantial that at first it looked like Hezekiah Mayfield had to have been the killer. But that theory didn't hold up, especially when his colleagues from the college and all his friends vouched for him so strongly."

He turned through several pages. "These are the documents

from the justice of the peace releasing the body to the medical examiner." He stopped on a report.

"I'll give you copies of these pages if you want them."

"I only want the death certificate," April said quietly. "I appreciate you going over all this."

"Sure, it's like notification of next of kin—in this case, twenty-six years later."

He went on as if he were giving a book report. Charley thought about how this man had cultivated his objectivity over the years, a necessary posture for a detective, just as his own image was easygoing, eager-to-please. What good fortune for him to escape a career that required telling a family member how their loved one was victimized. But then, he would be the first to admit that he would never even consider a career in law enforcement.

"There were no immediate signs of trauma to the body other than the obvious severe head wound," Ross Flynn was saying. "Once the body got to the medical examiner, several healed fractures were discovered—ribs, a cracked tailbone, an old hairline fracture of the jaw. Injuries that would have healed on their own but would have been painful while they were healing. Evidence indicated that she was probably a longtime sufferer of domestic violence."

"I can corroborate that," April said.

"There was no evidence of drugs or alcohol in the toxicology report. Tissue and blood samples were taken and preserved." Flynn turned more pages. "Fibers didn't provide any clues. No finger or handprints in the blood on or around her. An abandoned canoe was found not too far from where she was lying. It had been stolen from the rec camp, sometime during the night. No one saw or heard anything. No dogs barked that anyone remembered. There were too many vehicles around the rec camp during the day to find any definitive tire tracks. Footprint evidence didn't give any leads. She was probably brought to the lake in the trunk of a car and put in a canoe and dropped back in the narrow bayou where she was found. Then her killer abandoned the canoe and hiked back to the car. It would have been a five to ten-mile hike. If he stayed on the trail, he slipped past the campers that helped Mayfield later. They hadn't heard a thing.

"A sketch of her went out in the newspapers. It was all the talk about who this Jane Doe was. Made the statewide news and some national news outlets."

Detective Flynn gave them directions to the cemetery that had donated a place to bury Ann, and he told them where to find the plot. The conversation had taken twenty minutes. Now April knew the official version. She signed an affidavit saying that her mother's name was Ann Martin Smith Bristow and that her step-father, Frank Bristow, the probable killer, was dead.

Leaving the office, April wiped the palms of her hands to-gether, dusting away the last of the mystery.

"I can't think of another question," she said, as Charley held the door for her.

* * *

They stood beside a tall pine tree on the fringes of the cemetery. It was quiet, with the occasional vehicle swishing by on the narrow highway. The only marker on Ann's grave was a small concrete block with the plot number engraved. Someone mowed—April would find out if it was a constant care cemetery or if the county kept it up. She would buy a nice headstone, too.

The place was peaceful and almost groomed. It got rain. It was better than the windswept cemetery in Sulfur Gap, where the groundskeepers had to watch for pincushion cactus that could disable a person who didn't watch where he stepped. A watering system in the Gap would be a waste of a precious resource, so everyone graveled and installed curbing around their family plots. The unvisited graves were left to the whims of nature, with weeds that sprouted in creative combinations that were sometimes beautiful but mostly sad.

Here, the whims of nature were kinder. But Charley had brought insect repellent on the trip to be prepared for chiggers. He anticipated that April would want to visit a grassy cemetery like this or walk through a variety of ground cover near the lake. He knew that chiggers loved him—had learned the hard way during one rainy summer when he went skinny-dipping in one of Wayne's water tanks and had an enjoyable roll in the grass with a sweet girl named . . . oh, how could he forget? He never again went to the great outdoors without insect repellent. An ounce of prevention was worth a pound of cure, he said.

Here in the cemetery, April, protected with a layer of Charley's insect repellent, stood over her mother's grave. A breeze swayed the pines and ruffled the kudzu, as though a spirit sighed over them. She began wiping her eyes with the backs of her hands as she cried silently with her head bowed. Charley stood close and put his arm around her. She turned to him and began to cry into his chest in great, gulping sobs. Charley leaned his cheek on the top of her head and cried too, more silently. They shared their grief for what had been stolen from their lives, while they formed a new bond, both determined to heal from the past.

* * *

Hez was waiting in his wheelchair on the broad front porch of his rehab center. April had re-powdered her nose and touched up her mascara after the cry at the cemetery. Wonders never cease, Charley thought.

She wanted to sit in the back seat with Hez, so Charley drove on, feeling like a chauffeur. Hez was a competent guide. At one point, he missed a turn, not recognizing a road, now paved, but rutted dirt the last time he drove down it. They came to a wide spot where jeeps and SUVs were parked. Signs pointed to campsites and a marked hiking trail.

"My, my, they've sure cleaned this up since I was last here. But that was a long time ago. To tell the truth, I didn't ever come back this way after finding your mother, but I'd learned the way long before that. I'm sure that if you follow that trail about a mile, you'll come to the water's edge on that bayou. And if those downed trees are still there, you'll know it's the spot. They should be there unless they decided to clear it for hikers. Takes a long time for cypress to rot away."

"But can we leave you here in this hot car long enough for us to walk down and back?" April was concerned.

"I'll be fine, honey. You can leave the windows rolled down and I'll lean back and have me a nap."

Charley thought about the activity that had gone on in the back seat of that Buick. Never in his wildest imagination did he think that a ninety-seven-year-old black man would be napping there.

The trail was easy—level and wide. The rocks were cleared away, and the greatest hazards were the occasional tree roots that forked across the path.

April said, "I've been trying to walk a mile a day lately, thinking I would wind up doing something like this."

She was out of breath, but she was keeping up with their slow pace. They reached the water's edge sooner than expected.

"They must have straightened some of the switchbacks out of the trail. That was no mile," Charley commented.

They looked for the path to continue along the bank. Here,

the trail was narrow, but the trees were further apart, the brush much more sparse. They stepped more carefully, moving as far as they could until the trail ended abruptly. The sun, high in the sky, pierced the shadows of the cypress swamp and glinted on the still water. The three old trunks lay before them, now covered with green moss. They were larger than Charley had pictured them, but they were undoubtedly the bier that had borne Ann's body. He reached for April's hand, and she squeezed his. They stood a moment, listening to a child's voice carrying from a campground across the water, the caw of a crow echoing through the air, and the slap of a bass striking a bug on the surface and diving back into the reeds.

A white heron dove from a perch high in a distant tree and skimmed above the water. At first, Charley felt that the bird was aiming for them as she sailed in their direction, tilted under some branches, and lit on a low branch above the midpoint of the three fallen trees. She became so still as she looked out at the water, Charley would have thought she was some kind of decoy or ornament set in the tree had he not seen her coming. But as soon as he entertained the idea, she tilted her head and spread her wings to resettle them along her body.

"Life everywhere," April said. And, wiping away her tears with the back of her hand, she turned and headed back up the path.

24
In-Laws and Outlaws

ON THE WAY TO BRIARGROVE, Charley and Darla were feeling silly. So they sang. And since they were making a trip to Charley's grandmother's house, they sang, "Over the river and through the woods, to Grandmother's house we go." When they forgot the rest of the words, they started over. Darla's segue into Bo Diddley's "Look at Grandma" didn't go far. She broke down in giggles trying to sing about grandma doing the funky chicken. Charley gave her a slow-head-turn stare.

"You know," he said, in his most serious tone, "this is a somber occasion. My first Sunday dinner at my grandmother's house."

"I'm nervous."

"Me, too."

When Doris had called Charley to set up the Sunday lunch, she invited April. Charley groaned inwardly, thinking, "Too much, too much!" To his relief, when he relayed the invitation, April said, "I'm not meeting any of them until I lose more weight. Anyway, you need to meet them first. I can come into the picture later. Or not. We'll see." That was a relief.

As they pulled up to the Seven Dwarves' house, they parked along the curb. An old Ford Taurus sat behind Doris's Regal.

"That's probably the preacher's car," Darla said. "They always drive cars like that, unless they're Episcopalians or ministers at giant Baptist churches. The Episcopalians drive used Mercedes they buy from their parishioners, and the Baptists drive new Caddies. Methodist preachers in small towns don't make that much."

"How come you're so knowledgeable about preachers' cars?"

"I've done a lot of church singing where I have applied my sharp powers of scientific observation. The conclusions are irrefutable."

They were still sitting at the curb. Charley hadn't reached for the door handle.

"Are we going to do this?" Darla asked.

"At the moment, I'm tempted to drive away. I wish I could be a fly on the wall and spy on them for a while. . . . I feel like I'm walking into a maze or something."

"I bet you do. It's easier for me. I'm here to support you."

"I can't even begin to think about what to expect. It's a big vacuum. I'm stepping off a cliff into it."

"You can run back the other way any time. We have a getaway car." Darla scooted to his side and patted his cheek.

Charley opened his door and got out, taking Darla's hand. He didn't let it go as they walked up the front walk, picturing the family rowed up behind the front window, watching their every move. They took the steps up onto the porch, and Charley punched the doorbell. Silence. No footsteps growing louder as the expectant hostess hurried to answer. The stillness from inside the house pressed against the front door. Charley rang again. They waited.

Darla looked up at him. "She's in good health, right?"

"Totally. Scary good."

Charley peered into the living room window. He could see the comfortable setting—a Sunday paper, probably the *Abilene Reporter-News*, was spread out on the couch where someone was separating the ads from the news. A light glowed from a hallway that must lead to the kitchen.

"I can't tell if anyone's home," he said.

The sound of older kids playing a game, their voices pitched for teenage trash talk—"You spazzed!...Shut *up*!...See how you like this! . . . Oh yeah?" followed by hoarse laughter from boys and squeals from girls—drifted from a nearby backyard.

Then Darla spied something. "Look," she said. "A note fell off the door."

She opened the glass storm door to reach for the paper. She read, "Dear Charley and Darla—Come around back. Gate's open. Forgot when we made plans that I'd told Gunnar he could use my backyard for a cookout for the high school Sunday School class, so we will all have to be chaperones for a while. Apologies. —Doris"

Note in hand, Charley felt like he was carrying a hall pass. They ventured down the drive, and, sure enough, a gate in a tall fence opened into a large backyard. Lawn chairs were scattered on a covered patio. Doris sat in one, keeping in the shade, with a dark, slender younger woman beside her. Further out in the grass, two portable charcoal cookers smoked with grilling hamburger patties. A card table nearby was covered with a checkered table-cloth. Underneath the protective cloth had to be the buns, mayo, mustard, lettuce, tomatoes, onions, pickles, chips, and dips that would make a patty into a solid meal.

Gunnar Woodruff was flipping burgers with a practiced flair.

On the lawn, three boys and five girls played volleyball. The sagging net was held by long ropes tied to two well-spaced pecan trees.

Doris saw them first. "Look! It's Charley and Darla!"

The dark little woman looked up, a hand automatically reaching to smooth her hair.

Gunnar was balancing a plate as he hefted hamburger patties

off the fire.

"Hang on, ya'll. Be right there. Gotta get these burgers off before they burn!" He called over his shoulder.

The little woman scurried to take the plate from him. "Gunnar, you go on. I'll finish this up."

Doris hugged Charley and turned to Darla. "Welcome, Darla," she said.

The kids playing volleyball stopped their game, as if some unseen hand shushed them. All eyes were focused on Charley and Darla.

Gunnar faced Charley. He was Charley's height, with a thatch of thick blond hair. Charley's hair still caught the glint of the sunlight, while Gunnar's was duller. Charley was lean, while Gunnar's small paunch straining against his barbeque apron bore testimony to too many covered-dish suppers. Gunnar reached out toward Charley and clapped his hands together. For a moment, Charley thought he was about to lead a prayer or a round of applause, but the preacher brought his pressed hands to his face and looked over them at Charley as if he were marveling at a fireworks display or standing at the edge of the Grand Canyon.

Charley stood still, presenting his best poker face. Both men had been told they looked alike, but they were startled. The little woman deftly slid the platter of burgers onto a place on the table.

Gunnar tore off his apron and broke the silence. "Charley, I'm Gunnar Woodruff." He extended his hand and walked to his son.

The two men shook hands.

"Gunnar, this is Darla, my girlfriend." Saying the name felt strange to Charley—*Gunnar*. He had rehearsed his lines at home, looking in the bathroom mirror.

Gunnar shook her hand. "Pleased to meet you, Darla."

He turned to reach for the little woman who was now standing beside him. "This is my wife, Celia."

"Hello, Charley. Hello, Darla." Celia's smile was warm.

The preacher turned to the audience of watching teenagers. "Hey, everybody. These are some friends from Sulfur Gap, Charley and Darla. Please be civilized for them!"

The kids waved, the boys trying not to show Darla their enthusiasm.

And so the meeting took place in a way Charley hadn't expected. No spontaneous embraces. An audience who for the most part were in the dark about what was going on. Feeling that it was the most important introduction of his life, Charley thought the meeting certainly was understated.

So many events beyond Charley's wildest imaginings had happened lately, and this was the most unlikely—that he would meet his living, breathing father, at a Sunday School gathering, no less. The butterflies were coming to rest in his stomach. He was here, and Darla was with him. The feeling grew in him that he wasn't on one side and his father on the other, nor his father's wife. And Doris certainly was no adversary. They were all on the same side. They longed for family and the ties that involved family. They all hoped that they could at least become friends, while they hoped for more but knew many years of history had been lost and would never be captured. They were starting fresh, as if they had entered a dark and unfamiliar room and a light had been suddenly turned on, temporarily blinding them. They would stumble along, trying to familiarize themselves without barking shins and stubbing toes and falling over footstools.

Charley didn't know what to say, so he hadn't rehearsed many lines. Everything he'd tried sounded lame. He had finally decided that everyone else could do the talking, and he would join in to prop up the conversation, as he did every day at work. He was a bit put off that there were eight teenagers watching the meeting, but they were soon distracted by the sight and smell of food. The kids descended on the table like a flock of hungry buzzards. They had taken quick note of Charley and Darla and had moved on to their own agenda. The boys occasionally eyed Darla, making sure the view remained.

Doris motioned Charley and Darla through the back door of the house. They stepped into a vintage 1950s kitchen, with a Jersey diner theme. The chrome and aqua vinyl dinette was set with five places. Charley had envisioned pot roast served on a lacy tablecloth over dark wood, surrounded by floral dining room wallpaper. The black-and-white kitchen floor tiles made him a bit dizzy if he looked straight down.

Doris ushered them to their places at the table and began assembling their dinner. Talking all the time, she brought a bubbling casserole, a salad, and a basket of bread to the table.

"What kind of work are you doing for Dr. Harper?" she asked Darla.

While Darla told her about her duties at the veterinary clinic, Charley could hear Gunnar quieting the kids on the patio, circling them up, and leading a short prayer. The teenagers were quiet afterward, munching on their food.

Gunnar followed Celia into the kitchen and stopped on the step to turn to his young charges. "Anyone need anything? Remember the bathroom's through here. Don't forget, you guys have a duty to get rid of this food!"

Charley knew that he would like Gunnar, become fond of him if given the chance. A tinge of sadness that he hadn't known his father until now crowded his throat. When he had first learned about the boy his mother dated in high school, Charley thought he must be a certified son-of-a-bitch. His opinion mellowed when he met Doris, and now he saw a good man with no children of his own but with a love of children that became part of his ministry.

Charley risked being hurt if he gave up his anger entirely, but he had always been a pushover, he thought. So why not now? This must be what he'd been practicing for.

Charley thought Gunnar would be uncomfortable asking him all about his life, as in, "So what's it been like since I left your mom all pregnant?" So he opened with his own questions, the kind he used when getting to know new clients.

"Where were you living before you came back to Briargrove?"

"Down on the coast," Gunnar said, spooning a serving of Doris's casserole onto his plate. "Here, Mom, hand me your plate. . . . Uh, yeah, we were in Corpus for twenty years. I got tired of griping about the humidity and jumped at the chance when the position opened in Briargrove."

"I bet you like having him and Celia back in town," Charley said to Doris.

"Yes. We have to learn to get along," Doris said, buttering her roll. "It's been interesting, to say the least."

Darla giggled. Celia blushed. Gunnar looked at Charley and rolled his eyes.

"Oh, Doris, you make it sound like all we've done is fight," Celia interjected. Looking at Charley, she said, "Truth is, Charley, some people take longer than others to reach a point of under-standing. I think Doris and Gunnar understand each other better now."

"I get that. Completely." Charley thought about his new ap-preciation for his mother.

After lunch, Gunnar stepped back out to visit with his group of teens. As the kids left, Charley could hear him interacting. "Roy, let me know how you do on that entrance exam, okay? And Shelia, be nice to your teachers. They're not so bad."

So maybe Gunnar had been a shallow little jerk-wad in high school. If he was, he had changed. April reminded him often of how people change, by showing off her three-month AA chip. His pride in her bloomed. When he'd gone with her to the grocery store last week, she saw a baby in its carrier in a shopping cart and blocked the aisle when she stopped to make over it. She got all teary-eyed and sentimental, no less. The same day, while Charley helped her unload her groceries, she landed another surprise. She said, "I applied for a secretarial job at Clinton Oil Field Supply, and I have an interview." Her excitement and hope heartened his belief in her commitment to turn her life around.

Anyone who says people don't change doesn't know the right people, he thought.

* * *

On the way back to Sulfur Gap, Darla said, "That went well, don't you think?"

"Yep. Big relief to have it over with, though." He reached for her hand. "Thank you, darlin', for coming with me to meet my dad for the first time."

"You've been putting up with Bo Buchanan hovering like a Border Patrol chopper. Least I can do is stand by you while you get to know your own father. I think he's going to be easier to get used to than my dad. Gunnar's nowhere as crusty."

Charley thought, *Bingo!*

"What'll be next on the family agenda?" Darla asked.

"Doris has an appointment with me next week for a haircut, so I'll be seeing her. Celia said she needs a stylist, too."

"But what's next for you and Gunnar?"

"I don't know. I can offer to cut his hair, too. If it was hunting season, I'd ask him out to Wayne's to hunt quail. I guess I could see if he wants to hunt feral hogs. It's open season on them."

Charley had moved from the practical to the ridiculous. He

wasn't about to track and kill a hog, and he suspected that would not be Gunnar's sport of choice. Bo, on the other hand, probably owned several automatic rifles for just such pursuits and probably had plenty of friends to accompany him.

Darla chuckled. "I don't see Gunnar being a hunter. Especially feral hogs. But you never know. We could get a ride-along with J.J. if he knows where some are." Darla was on a first-name basis with the game warden these days, since he sometimes brought rescued wildlife to the vet clinic. Most recently, he had brought several ducks to be cleaned up after they had mistaken a slush pool beside an oil well for a good spot to land.

"I'm not much of a hunter myself. I could get him over to Hopper's for a few games of pool." Charley couldn't suppress a wicked smile at the thought of beating Gunnar at pool. The smile broadened at the thought of wiping the floor with Bo.

"Do Gunnar and Celia like to dance? There's that big Hawaiian-themed dance at Hopper's next Saturday, which, by the way, you are taking me to."

Charley groaned. It was Aloha Night again. Everyone was supposed to wear tropical attire. He hated being told what to wear to a dance.

"What's the matter?"

"I love the idea of holding you all night, on or off the dance floor, but I refuse to wear a Hawaiian-looking shirt."

"You could borrow something of Ed's. I have this little wrap-around. . . ."

"You wear your wraparound. And later, you can let me un-wrap it. But I'm not dressing up for a damn dance at Hopper's."

"You are one stubborn man," she said. "But at least you're not letting me bully you anymore."

"You can bully me all you want, darlin'."

"Okay. Invite Gunnar and Celia to the dance. I'll invite all my folks. And wear whatever you want."

"Yes, ma'am."

"Let's stop at the windmill and see how the renovation project is coming," Darla said.

Before they entered the clearing around the windmill, they could tell that major changes were underway. The small, rutty road that turned off the main ranch road had been graded level and graveled. Boulders from the creek bed were spaced along the sides, and the road widened to open toward the windmill. The big wheel turned, rotating at a good clip with the breeze. A freshly cemented concrete-block tank stood in the corner of the newly fenced area. The standpipe under the mill gurgled fresh water into it. Tables and chairs sat under the shade of the mesquite and live oak trees.

They made themselves at home, as Wayne would want them to.

"I think that now there's a fence, we should bring our sleeping bags out here some night," Charley said. "Or one sleeping bag for both of us. The fence will keep us from getting stepped on by a cow."

"What about snakes?" Darla said, swatting his hand as he tried to tickle her wherever there was an opportunity.

"Oh." Charley pulled his hand back. "I forgot about snakes." Then he shrugged. "I'll do it if you will."

Looking around at the flagstones and flower beds transforming the former pasture around the windmill, Darla said, "This will be a great place for the wedding. Maybe ours, too, if you can give me a couple of years to finish school and make some career decisions." She looked at him from the corner of her eye and leaned her shoulder against his arm.

"You'll marry me?" Charley almost choked on the words.

"I will, if you can wait," she said. "We can be tentatively engaged. How does that sound?"

"But what about Bo?"

"What about him?"

"He disapproves."

"You have to put him in perspective. I'm his only girl, and his firstborn, and on top of that, he tries to make up for not being a full-time dad."

"Guilty, huh?"

"Yes. Guilt makes people do weird things. Like when I was nine, he hired a live band for my birthday party. Mom found out and made him scrap that plan."

"Why so guilty? I thought the divorce was amicable."

"It was. Mom and Dad were always best friends—all through high school and college. Dad was in love with this girl he'd been secretly dating through high school and most of college. Mom was the only one who knew about it, and she helped out by sometimes being his cover date."

"Cover date?"

"She would go out with him and let his parents see them together. They thought that Mom and Dad were more than friends. But Bo was driving over to Midland to meet Addie."

"Why the sneaking around?"

"She was black."

"So?"

"His parents were against it. *Really* against it. My grandmother was too enamored with her own status in the D.A.R. I think that's really funny, because a lot of African Americans' lineage in North America goes back to before the American Revolution. Anyway, her parents were against it, too. So Dad and Addie decided not to tear their families apart."

Charley let out a low whistle. "Wow, that's family loyalty for you. Crazy."

Darla nodded. "Dad and Mom felt so bonded through it all, they decided that friendship and history would carry them forward. They got married during their last year at Tech and had me. Things were going fine, but the way Mom tells it, she could tell that Dad always missed Addie. Then they saw each other again at a homecoming game. A totally unexpected encounter. They tried, but they couldn't stop thinking about each other after that. Mom guessed why Dad was so depressed and suggested that he and Addie tell their parents to jump in the lake, live their own lives, and let her find someone to love that would love her back the way she deserved."

"Your mom is a spot-on kinda gal."

"I know! I've always loved the story about her telling Dad to be with Addie. And it wasn't like she was throwing him out. It was a unique kind of breakup."

"Ed seems like the right feller for her."

"He is. He's a very special man."

"So, were the families torn apart? Did Bo and Addie get disowned?"

"Nope. Dad went into a partnership in the tire business with Addie's dad, and they have B&B Tires in Big Spring, Lubbock, and Midland. B&B—Baker and Buchanan."

"I'm sure Bo's mother and dad didn't mind the business boom in the family."

Darla laughed. "Not a bit! It took a few years, but all the families get along better than you'd expect with all the in-laws and 'out-laws.'"

"So any brothers for you? You said you were his only girl."

"Yes, Dad and Addie have two boys—high school age. I'm proud of them, love them lots. You'll meet them soon enough."

"Well, I guess Bo Buchanan knows from personal experience that you can't stand in the way of true love."

"Exactly, Charley. He'll come around. He's already coming around. He can't help liking you. And soon he'll see that your life—and mine—are headed in a good direction."

He picked her up and spun around almost as fast as the windmill.

When he put her down, he held her and said, "I love you, Darla. I love every inch of you, inside and out."

"I love you, too, Charley."

25

Hawaiian Print

CHARLEY LOOKED IN THE MIRROR. The Hawaiian print shirt wasn't too bad—royal blue with small white flowers. Darla had found it in the Abilene mall.

"Wear it untucked, and wear your plainest boots," she instructed. No one had ever tried to dress him before, so he decided to go along . . . for now. He had to admit, it fluttered comfortably around his lean torso. He might even buy some more like it for work.

When he picked Darla up at her house, she bounced out in a little halter-top dress, color-coordinated with Charley's shirt. He groaned inwardly. Aren't we darling? He perked up when he noticed that the only thing holding the dress in place was a small knot at the back of her neck. He could have that undone in no time. She wore sandals, so he was glad they'd gotten their dancing so well in sync. He did not want to step on those precious toes.

At Hopper's, Charley parked at the edge of the lot, still in the habit of preparing for a quick getaway. Inside, they found Wayne staking out a large table. It was meet-and-greet night for Charley's growing family, an occasion Gunnar, Celia, and Doris had agreed to. Charley planned to put the "aloha" into Aloha Night.

Lou and the band were doing a sound check. She stepped off the bandstand to greet Charley and Darla.

"So have you decided on the date?" Darla asked.

"Yes, we're announcing it tonight. It's the twelfth of July. We still have to decide who's going to officiate. If we like Gunnar, we'll ask him."

"You'll like him," Charley said.

"What about weather? I guess we can count on it not raining, but heat and wind?" Darla seemed to be taking mental notes. Hot damn, Charley thought. She still wants to marry me.

"We'll have the pavilion finished, and there'll be mist machines to cool people down," Lou said. "If there's wind, we can lower an awning. . . . We've got it covered. Nothing will stop us but a tornado."

Charley was about to comment that Lou was tempting fate when Gunnar, Celia, and Doris stepped through the door. The trio looked around as their eyes adjusted to the light. Gunnar and Celia were dressed much like Charley and Darla, with Celia's dress far less apt than Darla's to produce a wardrobe malfunction. Doris wore a bright full-length dress. When he'd styled her hair earlier in the week, she told Charley, "Don't expect me to dance." But tonight, Charley thought that if Dick Raney saw her, they'd have to beat him off with a stick.

Charley strolled over and ushered them to the table for introductions.

"Hope you've decided to dance tonight," he said to Doris, offering her his arm. "I can have you gliding along that floor in nothing flat."

"Sounds like a lark," she said, and Charley detected not a hint of sarcasm.

"Wayne, Lou, this is my father, Gunnar Woodruff, and his wife, Celia." He felt a small hesitation on the word "father," but the word rolled off his tongue more easily than he had anticipated. "And this is my grandmother, Doris. Gunnar, Celia, Doris— these are my good friends, Wayne and Lou. Lou's my aunt, but we don't talk about it." Everyone laughed. All he and Lou had done the last couple of months was tell about how they were related.

Gunnar said, "You'll have to tell me the story soon."

"Will do," said Charley. Now he was looking back toward the door. April had agreed to come, and she was due any second. "Won't you feel uncomfortable around people drinking?" he had asked, concerned about her continuing sobriety. "I can drink club soda," she'd answered. "I like the idea of being the sober one. I won't start making a point of going to nightclub events, but it's not like I'll foam at the mouth if I smell liquor."

As if on cue, April walked in. Charley thought he would need to push his mouth shut, he was so surprised. He'd expected her to fish out one of her old muumuus for Aloha Night, but instead she wore flattering capris and a big, gauzy white shirt. A white silk hibiscus blossom was clipped into her short, asymmetrical haircut, and her silver hair glistened. If anyone had told him four months ago that this woman was his mother, he would have laughed in their face. And she wasn't through yet. If she stayed the course, she could be featured in the Miraculous Makeover section of a healthy living magazine.

"Gunnar, here's Mom," Charley said, grabbing both of their elbows.

"April! You're looking pretty tonight!" Gunnar said, offering his hand. They smiled at each other.

Doris held both of April's shoulders and stood back. "Oh, honey, I'm so glad to see you."

Celia took April's hand and pulled it toward her. "It's good to meet you," she said. April stiffened for a moment, but relaxed at Celia's sincere tone.

April had told Charley that Gunnar called the past week and asked her to meet him and Doris for coffee. April said, "I almost said no, because I knew they just wanted to apologize. I don't hold anything against them. But then I remembered that it's important, if possible, to meet with people to make direct amends. In AA they say it's not for the person who receives the amends but for the one who is making them. It helps them clear the path, sort of. I guess that works for anyone, whether they're in AA or not."

When all the introductions were made and everyone seated, it was time for Lou to join the band for their opening song. Before she left, she said, "Wish we were all meeting on another night so I could stay with you guys. I've cut back to playing only on Saturdays so Wayne and I can be together in the evenings."

Wayne gave her a quick kiss. "The nightclub scene in Sulfur Gap will have to put up with a substitute drummer," he said.

"Oh, it'll be fine. The Crew has lined up a rotation of guys from Austin and Fort Worth. I won't be missed."

"You will, too. No 'guy' can sing like you do," Charley said.

"Thanks, Chippie." Lou smiled at him. "It's good to be related to your press secretary. See y'all at the break, and have fun!"

Charley turned to Celia. "Mind if I borrow Gunnar for a minute?"

He guided Gunnar to the pool tables. Mitch sat in his usual corner.

"Mitch, I want you to meet my father."

Mitch showed a missing front tooth as he smiled and shook hands with Gunnar.

"Mitch taught me how to play pool. He spent a lot of time with me growing up."

"Then we'll have to play a few games, and you can tell me about young Charley," Gunnar said.

"Don't bet any money when you play him," Charley advised as they turned away.

"Oh, I wouldn't. I'm a rank amateur."

When they got back to their table, the Bartas had joined. They looked like they were getting ready to work in the yard, except for the skinny plastic leis they wore. That was the good thing about a Hawaiian theme. A broad spectrum of outfits was acceptable . . . at least in Sulfur Gap.

"This is Darla's mom, and also my second grade teacher." Charley introduced Janet to the Woodruffs.

April chimed in. "And this is my therapist," she said, gesturing to Ed.

"Mom, I don't think you're supposed to tell that." Charley was chagrined.

"I can if I want to," she said. "He's the one who can't say anything."

Ed pantomimed zipping his mouth shut with an exaggerated gesture. Charley realized his mother still embarrassed him, while everyone else was having a good time. He'd have to work on that.

Dorothy, Charlene, Loretta, and Bethany and Woody joined the growing group. Everyone was eager to explain how they knew Charley, with hints of stories they could share with Gunnar.

Jarod and Sue finally hustled in.

"Sorry we're late," Jarod said. "Sue was feeling a little iffy, stomach-wise."

"When are you due?" Darla asked.

"Not till December," she said.

"Good timing. You won't be big-pregnant in the heat of the summer."

"Oh, I took that into account. I bet if someone did a study, they'd find out that before the pill, Texas men didn't get any during the fall months, because if their wives got pregnant, the baby would come in late summer. Timing's important."

No one knew how to respond to Sue's comment but granted her some leeway since she was dealing with significant hormone levels. So it was a good thing that the band started tuning up and testing the mics.

At the same time, a new arrival made everyone turn to look toward the door. Bo and Addie drew the crowd's gaze. Charley thought how typical for Bo to make a grand entrance. Before he got far into the room, Darla met him with a tight hug. Addie received the same attention.

Bo and Addie were about the handsomest couple Charley had seen, except for him and Darla of course. Bo hadn't caved in to the instruction from Darla that tropical print was de rigueur, but Addie wore a rich orange and purple hankie-hemmed cocktail dress that made her look like she'd been in a *Star Trek* transporter with a bright-feathered parrot. The colors danced with her dark skin. Her smile was so gracious, Charley thought it was a good thing, since otherwise the other women would have a hard time not hating her for being so beautiful. Next to her, Bo was transformed, although nothing was really different about his hair, his beard, his dressy boots, and so on. Addie's effect on Bo was to smooth his rough edges and balance him delicately in a way that changed his vibe. As he shook hands with Bo and Addie, Charley realized, *Darla has four parents.* More in-laws. But Addie would be good.

She had probably saved Bo's soul. A saved man makes more allowances for others, he thought. Surveying all the good-looking people gathering around the long table he and Darla had staked out, he thought Hopper's should adopt the motto, "Where folks are always at their surface best." He chided himself for the cynicism, realizing that this was a special occasion for everyone. Why shouldn't they try to look their best? After all, he made a living helping folks look their best.

He turned to Darla.

The band drew the dancers onto the floor with their signature opening number, "Take Me Out to the Dance Hall."

Gunnar and Celia stepped into the flow of dancing couples,

close to Charley and Darla.

Wayne danced with April. Charley had forgotten that his mother danced. He looked around with a full heart. He knew almost every face in the crowd.

As the next song began, Charley's plan would unfold. He saw the dancers passing the word around to each other as the opening bars of "Could I Have This Dance?" began.

He led Darla in the slow waltz with Lou sounding like Anne Murray, singing the lines that asked for a lifelong dance, a partner for every night. At the first chorus, people began melting away, going to stand at the edges of the floor. Before she knew what was happening, Darla found herself alone in the middle of the dance floor with Charley.

"What's going on?" she said. He saw her quickly put together the song that the band played and his intent to publicly announce his commitment to her. She put her small hands to his face.

He whispered into her ear. "I want you to know I'm not going anywhere. I will be here. I'll wait forever for you to do whatever you need to do."

She shuddered from the effort not to cry, he saw, and finally gave up, tears streaming down her face. "I've waited for you all my life," she said.

Acknowledgements

I OWE A HUGE DEBT OF GRATITUDE to author Neva Brown, who read my first draft and provided advice to make it presentable.

I also owe a special thanks to my husband, Jim, who listened patiently when I'd say, "Tell me how this sounds," and made astute suggestions about cars and playing pool and is always accepting when the writing marathons begin. To my daughter, my grandson, and my friends Vanna and Janel, my gun consultants. And to my son, for advice on things a nice guy wouldn't say. To my friend Leigh Harbin, an early reader, who encouraged me before the story was finished.

To Kay Ellington and Barbara Brannon, authors of *The Paragraph Ranch*, whose educational workshop led me to working with them on the book production team. Extra thanks to Barbara for expert editing that saved me from many a pitfall.

To the San Angelo Writers' Club, for providing educational, networking, and social opportunities that inspired me to transition from writing short stories to crafting a novel. And to Readers P.S. Book Club for many discussions that helped me become more sensitive to the reader.

Deep gratitude to my friends who've encouraged me so much. Don't know what I'd do without you.

* * * * *

ABOUT THE AUTHOR

DANA GLOSSBRENNER, a retired English teacher and
school counselor, has lived in West Texas all of her life.
www.danagloss.com

ALSO BY DANA GLOSSBRENNER

Women Behind Stained Glass: West Texas Pioneers